I0743343

WE SEEK NO KINGS

THE STEEL CLAN SAGA, BOOK ONE

T. THORN COYLE

Published by PF Publishing,
An imprint of Triple Flame Inc
3439 SE Hawthorne #203
Portland, OR 97214

Printed and bound by IngramSpark.
Australia: Ingram Content Group AU Pty Ltd, Melbourne, Victoria. US: Lightning Source LLC, La Vergne, Tennessee / Allentown, Pennsylvania / Jackson, Tennessee, United States. UK: Lightning Source UK Ltd, Milton Keynes, United Kingdom. Europe: Lightning Source UK Ltd, with facilities in Germany, France, and Spain. The authorized representative in the European Economic Area is Lightning Source France, 1 Av. Johannes Gutenberg, 78310 Maurepas, France. compliance@lightningsource.fr

We seek no kings, no presidents, no rulers.

We seek no authority but the spark that dwells within.

We seek no bonds but friendship.

We seek no sovereigns but earth, water, and sky.

None shall rule over another.

We shall share what we have,

And ask for what we need.

We shall lead with open hearts and minds.

But shall you cross us?

Or attempt to enslave others?

With steel to hand we ride.

With steel to hand we strike.

No rulers. No masters.

The Knights of the Steel Clan will cut you down.

We seek no kings, no presidents, no rulers.

We seek no authority but the spark that dwells within.

We seek no bonds but friendship.

We seek no sovereigns but earth, water, and sky.

PROLOGUE

*W*ithout order and the rule of law, people would die.

With order and the rule of law, people would die.

People would die. Animals would die. Whole bioregions would die. Dead of greed, and guilt, and fear.

The sun scorched the land. The seas turned to stinking ice. Death stalked starvation. Disease followed war.

And then the rain of fiery clouds descended. Here. There. Not enough to kill the earth, but enough to sunder what was left of the human-made world.

Some called these fiery clouds The Reckoning. And The Reckoning did not lie.

It laid waste to good and bad, righteous and unrighteous alike.

The Reckoning burned fields and immolated cities, leaving twisted metal and concrete husks and corpses that had no flesh left on their bones to rot.

Shadows and wreckage.

Dead, dead, dead, dead, dead.

And it changed those it left behind.

The three-headed calves of prophecy were born, staggering on their hooves. Chickens with bones like gelatin. Serpents with three eyes and scales that shimmered in the dark.

Sterile humans, or those that bore only once, and painfully so.

The Great Gates Between the Worlds cracked, bringing the sideways realms closer to the now. And creatures walked the land that had not been seen in twenty thousand years. Legends. Fancies. Elves and trolls. Djinn, nightwalkers, nagas, and drakes.

The scent of magic once again perfumed the air.

The beings of the earth learned new ways to survive.

And thus, the future was born.

SEPTEMBER, YEAR 53

CHAPTER I
JENNY

Towering trees sped by in a green-and-black blur, whipping the citrus-and-pine Doug fir scent through the air, smacking Jenny's uncovered cheeks and whipping errant strands of fiery hair out from beneath the leather helmet firmly strapped beneath her chin. A red-winged blackbird flashed past her head.

The late September sun warmed the heavy pig hide on Jenny's back. The sumac-red coat was buckled close, to keep air from catching leather and creating a sail. Jenny's matching leather trousers were tight over the muscular thighs that cradled the bike.

The vibration brought Anandita's calm, beautiful face to mind. Not that Jenny had ever held the woman between her thighs. Yet. She hadn't even kissed those ripe, dark plum lips, unless her increasingly horny dreams counted.

But a Knight could always hope, right? Women were supposed to love sword-wielding brutes, but so far, Anandita had gently rebuffed Jenny's tentative advances enough times she'd had to back off or feel like a shit.

She already felt like a shit. But damn, Anandita was worth a little hope. Unless it turned out she actually wasn't into women that way. But Jenny had caught enough looks that said otherwise. Wistful looks. Heated looks. Glances that made Jenny hot beneath her leathers.

In your dreams, asshole.

Jenny grinned, then sputtered and spat as a bug hit her teeth. She'd forgotten to tie a kerchief around her face after the last rest break. That'd teach her.

She grinned again, closed-lipped this time. At forty-five klicks an hour, life was good. The old hog was just a little faster than her horse and twice as fun when there were roads to be found. Plus, bikes required less fuel to run than a horse.

Only trouble was, the PR tarmac was cracked—like most Pre-Reckoning artifacts—causing the hard rubber tires to judder and bounce, jarring all the way up Jenny's spine. The Steel Clan Knights had been riding hard for three hours now, heading back from a barely successful scrap run. They'd only gathered enough to fill two of the four bike trailers taking up the rear of the fifteen-hog convoy.

Barely successful was okay. Scrap was scrap, and always useful in the forge and machine shops. They'd only had to fight off one small band of tinker-scrappers. They'd busted a few heads and run them off, but nobody had died.

Jenny had a scab on one knuckle, and Berto had a cut over his right eye, but any run where no one got killed was a good one.

So, the scrap run had gone fine, but the real purpose of the trip was a scouting mission, and that? Well, there was nothing major to report yet. And while Jenny hoped it stayed that way so they could get their tired asses back to Go No More, the Knights had been charged by the council to find out what the fracked earth was messing with the area.

Because something was. And it wasn't the usual would-be warlords skirmishing for power due west of their valley. It wasn't trouble with the crops. It wasn't the seep of old nuclear waste into groundwater caused by an overabundance of rains on hard ground in the desert areas east of the mountains. It wasn't the aftermath of fracking that had cracked the earth and caused oil spillage on otherwise plantable or grazable land.

It wasn't, thank all the Gods and Goddesses and any nature spirits that were listening, a strange sickness sweeping across the land.

All of those things were possibilities still, even fifty years Post-Reckoning, but every mage said something else was brewing. Something magic. Jenny had to trust them on that one. Magic wasn't her thing.

The dragoons purred past an old, overgrown off-ramp that used to lead to what had likely been a thriving small town, now gone to green. An occasional rectangular structure could be seen poking through tangles of English ivy and half a dozen varieties of trees and clambering vines. Those towns had been picked over early on, and were now so dense with foliage it was barely worth hacking through for what was left. Let the animals and birds have at it. And the weird faery creatures that were native to this land.

The elves of Go No More sniffed something bad in the air, and the trolls concurred, but the township's two mages couldn't figure out what it was. Council member Rafiq and Abyad the djinn insisted it didn't smell like djinn magic—air or fire—and the river nagas weren't talking about whatever it was. Like all serpents —magical or not—the nagas didn't seem to like sharing intel. Anandita also mentioned the large, half-divine serpents had been staying further away than usual, even. Jenny couldn't parse whether that was worrisome or not.

So the Knights had ranged out to sniff the air themselves, the way Pig Boy's sounder sniffed out truffles after the first rains.

Bocan passed her and circled one huge, burgundy-leather clad arm in the air. His gloved fingers pointed to an ancient cutaway ahead. The pale blue halbtroll had good eyes beneath his tinted goggles. Must've come from his human mother, because trolls were notoriously fuzzy eyed by day. The cutaway was half buried in hemlock and Jenny barely saw it herself.

She circled her own arm to alert the rest of the dragoons, pointed, and then, fist closed, lowered her arm to signal a stop.

Fifteen hogs peeled off the battered road, rumbling to a stop in the vegetation-clogged, cracked area that had been a useful road itself, back in the PR once-upon-a-time. She pulled up behind Bocan's massive hog. He'd already switched off, which meant whatever it was needed more than a short conference. Jenny hit her own switch and the others followed suit. One by one, the noise of engines cut out, leaving behind the temporary silence of a forest whose creatures were still assessing possible threat.

Jenny pulled a soft hemp kerchief from her rear pocket and wiped the sweat and bugs from her face. Slowly, birdsong filtered back through the trees. Flickers and chickadees, sounded like, and in the distance, the scream of a hunting hawk.

Tegan approached, brown pigskin-covered helmet cradled in one whip-thin, strong-as-fuck arm. Where Jenny was big-breasted and broad-shouldered, and pale as the moon where she wasn't sunburned, Tegan was wiry, small-breasted, and tightly muscled, with skin as dark as the dense forest ahead. The slippery-gendered Tegan wore per hair short, segmented into squares topped by small, coiled knots, and per buckled leathers were a slightly browner sumac red than Jenny's. Tegan had already whipped off the kerchief per wore between helm and hair, and wiped per face with it. Per helm was painted with a badass pattern Jenny envied. When the Knights next had a quiet moment, she'd have to hunt up a township artist to paint her own.

Every member of the Knights—man, woman, or person—wore the same range of colors. Their leathers were variegated shades of sumac-dyed red, and the backs of their jackets were branded with the Steel

Clan's wheel and wings. But each rider decorated the leathers in different ways. Brass rings looped through epaulets on Tegan's shoulders, clinking softly together as the per stalked Jenny's way.

One of Tegan's three bladed kpingas was in per other hand, ready for throwing. A small scar sliced through per right eyebrow. The scar gave the Knight a permanent questioning air, which was funny, given that Tegan was an act-first, question-later per.

Tegan should have been a mage, but wanted nothing more than to be a Knight. Per ability to wield and shape magical energy was brutally strong. Stronger than Tegan's best throwing arm.

Jenny? While her six senses were all in pretty good working order, she had zero magic in this Post-Reckoning world where various forms of magic flowed in fits and starts.

All Jenny had was her intuition, and the tools and insignia that marked her as part of the Steel Clan. Magic be damned, all three were her inheritance and her pride.

Jenny's short sword remained firmly in its sheath on the gleaming, bug-spattered hog, though she grabbed the buckler hooked onto the hilt. The small shield worked equally well for smashing through thick vegetation, crushing an attacker's face, or protecting her tender bits from pointy things, whether animal, vegetable, or human.

She carried the buckler always, with few exceptions, and then mostly around Go No More. No buckler meant that Jenny was at home. On the road? She dropped it to eat or shit, and sometimes to fuck. If you were lucky.

All the Steel Clan riders were armed in one fashion or another. Each Knight had a favorite skirmishing or hunting tool strapped to their machines—ranging from short sword, to halberd, to axe, and machete—and every person in the township was trained in rudimentary polearm and bow. Children learned to use slingshots as soon as they could hold a steady arm, and trained in bow as young as six winters. Go No More wouldn't survive otherwise.

As idyllic as life tucked among the verdant mountains and snow-capped volcanoes could seem, the peoples of Go No More weren't the only beings in the area. There were men and beasts outside the township range, all struggling to survive. Winters were cold. Avalanches, bandits, wolves, fever, and condors were equally dangerous if timing was poor, or ill luck decided to descend.

And then yeah, there was magic. Not the ordinary small charms or spells. Not the magic most people had these days: special knacks, energy shaping, or simply the ability to be in the right place at the right time. No.

There was also old magic. Elven magic. Drake magic. Djinni magic. Magic that—up until the Reckoning—hadn't been seen in ten thousand years, except in legends. There were sudden flares of power that rocked the hills. Temporary portals that opened with no warning but a shimmering change in the air.

And further off, permanent portals leading to the old places. Places like Underhill.

More than one child had been lost to the temporary portals, at least they thought so, including Jenny's closest friend. Right around their change, it was, during the shift of body and mind that marked a child of an age for apprenticeship and testing. Maura had just up and disappeared.

Over a decade of years gone, and Jenny never forgot her. Right before Maura had disappeared, they'd shared a first kiss. Jenny could still imagine it. Imagine the way Maura's eyes had closed, right before her thin, pale lips had tentatively touched Jenny's own....

Jenny shook off the memory and scanned the woods behind the cutaway for the telltale shimmering of portal magic that even her magic-blocked eyes could generally see. There was nothing but the thick lace of hemlock spruce choking the spaces beneath the towering, ragged-angel shapes of the Douglas firs.

She caught a flash of russet underwing as a flicker swooped by. Its knocking started up fifty paces into the thick trees. The hunt for food was ever present. Jenny's own stomach rumbled in reply.

"Why'd we stop?" Tegan asked, then tilted up per chin to catch a stream of water from a deerskin bag.

Jenny looked up at Bocan. In the relative gloom at the forest's edge, he'd shoved his goggles onto the bald dome of his head. Two and a half meters tall, and solid as a rock with fat and muscle, his meaty blue fist was closed around the amulet every Knight wore somewhere on their person. His, like Jenny's, was strung on a thong around his trunk of a neck. He walked deeper into the woods, sniffing the air with a blunt nose, black eyes crinkled around the edges—with worry or thought, Jenny couldn't tell.

Jenny and Tegan both sniffed, too, then exchanged a look. Something was off, but who knew what? Jenny shrugged. All she smelled was the forest, warm vegetable oil from the bikes, and Knights who'd been in their leathers too long on the road. She gestured for the apprentice scout, Litha, to scope out the forest to the east. The girl was skinny, with shorn-off blond hair and square features. She was kind of intense.

Their main scout, Psych, was just ahead, where this old bit of road met the wild. Crouched between two hemlocks and a towering Douglas fir, the exposed skin of his hands, neck, and face were so filled with blue tattoos he might have been Bocan's brother, except for his scrawny size.

"Smells like bear shit," Psych said. "And something else I can't quite trace."

The scout smacked his tongue against his lips. "It tastes like some sort of magic, but I'm not sure."

"It is magic," Bocan rumbled. His voice sounded like his bike, deep bass and slightly gravelly, as if it needed a tune-up. "That's why I called a stop. Damn near smacked me in the back of the head."

Jenny touched her own amulet, but didn't feel a thing. "Shouldn't our amulets respond, then?"

Bocan gave her a funny look, and so did Tegan and, from two yards away, Psych.

"They are," Tegan finally said. "You can't feel that? I mean, I didn't notice it while the bikes were rumbling, but here on the edge of the forest?"

Tegan shrugged, as if what per felt was obvious.

Jenny ran her fingers over the knot of metal that was supposed to keep everyone in the Clan protected. The amulet was warm, but that was likely from her skin. She never understood how the damn things were supposed to work. Every once in a while she thought she felt something, but mostly, the metal was inert, like today. Mage and Jenny's sometime lover, Aphrodite, had said something about force fields and early warning systems, but to Jenny, the amulets were pretty hunks of metal, and not as useful as her sword or bike.

It was moments like these her lack of magic rankled. Why the fuck couldn't she feel anything? Way to lose the Clan's trust, right? She was such a fucking oaf.

The thoughts pinged through her head, like the sound of metal on a cooling engine.

Swallowing down her irritation, she asked the necessary question.

"What does the magic feel like?" she asked.

"Nasty," Tegan spat out. "The amulet's buzzing like a hornet's nest. Feels like tiny sharp needles rasping at my skin."

Jenny huffed out a short, irritated breath, then forced herself into a long inhalation. Dropping into the warrior's meditation she'd learned at her mother's knee, she focused on centering herself. Amulet still clasped inside her fingers, she slowed her breathing down. In through the nose. Pause. Out through the mouth. Pause. Her attention dropped like a stone, seeking out the stillness every warrior carried into battle and masters of every craft used before each fashioning.

Smelling the goodness of rich loam, ten layers' deep with needles, cones, leaves, and droppings, smelling the citrusy pine of the firs and the fresh spruce of the hemlock, Jenny reached out with her senses. She might not have magic, but she had training. Her awareness ranged forth like her bonded faery fox, Flex, who ran the woods of Go No More.

She felt forest and possibly an old, abandoned portal. She felt bear and wolf, flicker and raven.

Turning her consciousness back to the cast metal beneath her fingertips, she breathed in, and out again.

And felt nothing but hard metal.

CHAPTER 2
BOCAN

The muscles at the base of Bocan's neck were tight as a hundred-pound bow string, pulled taut and ready to loose an arrow at its prey. Gripped in his right hand, the magic amulet buzzed and bit at his fingers, sending whispers of alarm to his inner ears. It warned of danger, and bad things riding on the wind that rustled through branches, sending fir and hemlock needles cascading to his hide-clad shoulders.

This was bad magic, indeed, and it had the eternal springtime whiff of Underhill. Which was a fracked earth shame.

Since the New Era began, and the trolls and elves crawled out from beneath their thrice-damned rocks, life had been pretty good. At least, once the die off had ended, the earth had started to heal itself, and the human and animal survivors figured out new ways to live. The stories from the Reckoning itself were harrowing, and unparalleled in current times, thank all the Gods of Earth and Stone.

The horrors that had rocked the realms during the Reckoning had stilled, bringing the slow changes that led to the return of the vast forests and the opening of magical doors long thought closed forever. Humans, and all the other beings of the Joined Realms, learned to rebuild society, to make their place in the midst of a new order.

Bocan snorted, then spat a gobbet onto the ground. The gold-rimmed assholes still held court Underhill, bowing and simpering at the Queen and lording it over the ordinary rank and file.

As if, gold-rimmed or not, their asses didn't all shit the same.

He wished he could sic that old trickster Talapus on the royals but heard tell the coyote worked for no one but himself. Most of the local magical beings were that way. Anarchists, through and through.

"Those pig fuckers can crawl back in their holes to rot," Bocan muttered, then looked down at Jenny. She was a strapping woman, but still no match for his halbtroll height.

She frowned. "What the fuck are you talking about?"

He shrugged, but she wasn't paying him much attention. Her hand had dropped from the amulet around her neck and blunt-tipped fingers unconsciously stroked the embroidered patch stitched onto the left breast of her leathers. The winged wheel was the Steel

Clan insignia. It was a Pre-Reckoning artifact belonging to her great-grandmother Molly O'Brien, and if she kept worrying at it, it would soon be nothing more than fuzz.

She caught him looking and dropped her hand.

"Hail, the ancestors," she said, as if all she'd been doing in her stroking great-grandmother's patch was honoring the dead.

"Hail, the ancestors," he replied.

Yeah. Jenny was bothered. Same old story. Anything to do with magic filled her with a deep unease.

Jenny's inability to sense much magic didn't bother Bocan—everyone had their own skills—but he knew it bugged her good. Besides, magic was like any other technology. Sometimes it worked, and sometimes it didn't.

The old magics were potent and dangerous to humans. Brought with the beings who wielded them, they were suited only to those with magical forms.

The newer, human and animal magics? First of all, the magic of steel and hydroelectrics worked better and more consistently. They had their own rules and their own Gods and protectors. His da had taught him that. Most spells were weaker than Bocan's battle-axe, and like an axe, they were useful in one person's hand and useless in another's.

A magicked axe? Now that was another story. But Bocan didn't trust them, all the same.

As a halbtroll, Bocan knew that sometimes magic got in the way of your other senses. Some humans—

and creatures like himself—relied too much on their seventh senses, and everything else atrophied.

And that was dangerous. Because it meant you weren't paying attention. Someone who had no sense of smell needed to compensate with sight and touch and hearing, not give up the others entirely. All the senses worked together, that's what his ma taught him, and she was clever a human as they came.

Bocan's eyes focused further, into the depths of the dark, fragrant forest. Something was in there, beyond where Psych was crouched, looking for signs. Bocan shuffled toward the boy, careful to not get so close as to distract the lad from his work. Bocan walked, eyes focused on Psych, his other senses awake to the forest beyond. When he reached the edge of the copse, he stopped, then flicked his eyes up and down again, quick as a flash in the night.

A wolf. Silvery gray and brown, lean and tall at the shoulder.

It stared, gleaming-eyed, from the thick, mottled darkness of the forest. Bocan's nostrils flared. It smelled like ordinary wolf, not like magic, but Bocan wondered what it knew. No way to find out without spooking the creature, though, so Bocan turned his eyes back to the ground, trying to see what Psych saw, and feel what he felt.

His mind strayed back to Jenny. He could feel her standing impatiently behind him. A doer, that one, he knew standing still on this scrap of road on the edge of the woods while others worked grated on her. Tough.

If she was going to learn to be a better leader, she had to learn to cool her heels, not always come in swinging.

Jenny was sharp of mind, and a good enough leader already, though she'd tell you over a couple fingers of single malt that she wasn't a leader. That no one Knight should lead. But to Bocan's mind? Leadership in pack animals was a natural thing. Besides, she was child of the Founders of the township, and like it or not, that still mattered to folks.

Psych's hands hovered, tracing root and tree. His eyes were closed. Talking to the insects, most like, gathering intel from ants and gnats and bees.

Everyone knew to not interrupt when the scout had that rapt look on his knife-sharp, tattooed face.

Yeah, the Knights of the Steel Clan were technically leaderless, but just because everyone in the group had a job to do and a right to speak their opinion, didn't mean that experience and skill didn't win out sometimes. Some types of magic were more useful than others. Whistling could lift a heart, but skill with bandages and herbs could stop a person from bleeding out.

Trolls understood hierarchy. Humans fought against it or abused it. Nothing rested easy with humans. Bocan had seen that in his mother, now long gone. She was always dreaming up new schemes, trying new things...shaking up his stolid da's life, and Da had loved it.

These days, Bocan's father was back to living deep inside the caves, where things made sense, he said. After Ma vanished, he couldn't bear to live too close to the world of men. She was always so quick to laugh, and quick to anger. Quick to come up with new ideas. New weaving patterns. New things she wanted Da to make.

Being in the human world kept her loss too keenly close, Bocan knew, though Da never said it in so many words. Just said he needed to live more slowly again.

"Stones and mountains change slow, my son. True change takes time."

Da always said that, and yet, the quicksilver human and the slow moving, philosophical troll had fallen in love for a few short years, or two long decades, depending on who you asked, troll or human.

And here was Bocan, alive and making his own way, neither slow nor fast, but some steady thing in between. Trolls gave him shit and some humans treated him like a fucking, dim-witted pet, but the Knights knew his worth.

That was all that mattered, right? The earth beneath your boots and the respect of your clan.

"So, where's this magic coming from?" Jenny asked, her usually low voice gone reedy with concern.

"No place close," Psych replied. "But I can't catch the thread of it. Tegan?"

Tegan paced, ranging into and out of the trees, circling and twining like the wind itself. Per looked at the scout, but simply shook per head and, kpinga out, continued the peripatetic dance.

Bocan sniffed the air again. The magic was foul, and stunk of a place other than this forest. It was neither near nor far.

"Two hours' ride," he finally said.

"What direction?" Jenny asked.

"East."

Just past the foul scent of magic, he tasted the edges of snow. Cold. The rushing spray of a waterfall. The promise of familiar crags that felt like home. Except hidden within the velvet glove of coming winter was the choking scent of windfall apples, gone to rot. It scent of it clawed at the back of his throat, making him want to spit.

The feeling of it sat uneasy within him, buried deep inside the large cave of his heart. He cleared his tightening throat, pushing past the fear.

"We live and serve the township and each other," he said out loud, though with less fire than the ritual phrase deserved.

"We ride for Go No More," the dragoons replied.

The words were their mission and their calling. A reminder of who and what they were. An incantation of purpose.

But in the dappled light on the edge of an ancient road? The words hung as uneasy and uncertain as the feeling in the pit of Bocan's gut. Out here, with whatever was ahead of them, there was neither the lust of battle nor the promise of a meal and drink at home.

There was only the cold, iron spike of trepidation.

"Lead on," Jenny said.

Tegan retied per kerchief and smacked the patterned helmet back on, as Psych brushed off his hands and loped back to his own hog.

Bocan took one last look around the copse. He

wished for Serena, his bonded snowy owl. But she only hunted at night, within her home forest. Besides, she had a mind and an agenda of her own.

Perhaps he could convince her to go on a mission. Fly reconnaissance.

Bocan swung a leather-clad leg across his hog and stepped down hard on the metal bar at his right foot. The bike roared into life, quickly echoed by fourteen others, all tuned to their own song.

He hoped Serena could be convinced, because the Steel Clan was going to need help.

He felt it in his bones.

CHAPTER 3

ANANDITA

The township was quiet. The cottage windows were open to let out the heat of the wood-stove fire and circulate the air.

Anandita had been up and in her chair for hours now. Her butt was starting to complain, despite the relative comfort of the heavy canvas sling that made up the seat, topped by a cushion and soft, woven wool and hemp blanket designed to take direct pressure off her tailbone and other pressure spots. She usually wore her stubbies around home, but the hinge that attached the right footpad to the metal limb cap wasn't working quite right, and she hadn't been able to adjust the short prostheses properly herself. She'd dropped them with the machinists two days before and was already missing them.

Sturdy, with hard, fat tires and steel rims designed to fit her hands, Anandita's chair was as much a part of her as her arms. Her legs were crushed by a tree when she was in her early teens, damaging the nerves so badly amputation was the only recourse Doc Warren had. She'd lost both her legs just above the knee.

Working with Doc Warren had healed her body and increased her resolve to be a healer herself.

Anandita's workroom, small sitting room, and kitchen took up most of the modest cottage. She and her son, Hypatia, took their meals at the far end of the long work table, and two cozy chairs clustered in one corner near a window, facing the room and the metal woodstove. Her bedroom and Hypatia's sleeping cubby were behind a curtain near the back, along with a door leading to the small covered porch where a wash basin and privy were housed.

The household shrine was set beneath another window, and sunlight played over the painted clay statues of Lakshmi and Ganesha, a small vase of wild flowers, and the smooth clay of her chillum pipe and beads.

It was another gorgeous, crisp, early autumn day. Bees buzzed in the garden, and the woodstove fire crackled, sending out the fragrance of well-seasoned birch. Her apprentice's ladle clinked against the earthenware vessels, wielded by clever, pale brown hands.

Anandita and Tokki would spend tomorrow in the gardens and the woods, speaking with the yakshini who were the spirits of the plants and fungi, getting their permission to gather more stores for the dark months. She might call on Recoana for extra help. The troll knew her herbs. But today was decanting day.

Anandita was born into a healing family. Her nani had been a doctor of Western medicine—a surgeon—

up north in the PR days. Bebe studied the art and science of Ayurveda, and Papa tended plants, with his greatest loves being herbs for cooking and for healing.

Nani was long gone, and Bebe and Papa grew old, but still lived happily in the cottage next to Anandita's own. Two of her aunties lived on the other side of the township, one made dyes and the other worked making goat cheeses and yogurts.

Anandita's healing magic had manifested young, and she studied everything. From her parents she learned the ways of Ayurveda, and the ways of all the local plants, and with her magic, blended the systems into her own healing brew for the New Era.

The St. John's Wort had been steeping since midsummer. The long pine table was filled with jugs and small bottles, and drying herbs hung in clusters from the rafters above. Tokki, thick hair in a dark cloud around her finely featured face, strained the liquid into sterile glass jugs, while Anandita decanted the clear red liquid into smaller vessels, ready for those whose sleep was troubled or whose minds were not at ease.

She looked up to where pungent bunches of tulsi dried beside her papa's ashwaganda in the rafters. Ashwaganda had similar properties to St. John's, and would be next to distill. Anandita found that some bodies responded better to one herb than another, and her own healing magic worked with the spirits of the herbs differently.

What Tokki's magic would grow into remained to be seen. The girl was still skittish about using it. They would need to work on that.

The sharp scent of distilled grain alcohol mixed with the astringent flowers and the smoke from the woodstove where roasted barley tea brewed in a fat metal pot, releasing its nutty savor into the air. A covered stew pot sat next to it on the hob. It had served for lunch, and would serve for dinner, too, with rolls from Barry's bakery and honey from Mugwort's bees.

There was always work to do in Go No More, and Anandita sent up a prayer of gratitude. It was good to be busy, keeping the village healthy, prosperous, and whole.

But though her hands were busy, and her healing magic in good flow, Anandita's heart was not quiet. She needed something to take her out of the funk she'd been in for days. When the reports of bad magic gathering first came through, Anandita had made it through the council meeting, then took to her bed, feigning a mild autumn cold that her herbs miraculously cured in just two days.

Really, though, what she had been taking was last year's batch of ashwaganda. She should have gone to one of the others with healing magic in town, but sometimes, in that state? She didn't want to face anyone else. Hypatia was used to what he called her "low periods" and was responsible enough to make simple meals and keep her supplied with tea. The herbs and her son's ministrations had eased the anxiety and mild depression enough for her to get back to work.

That's what herbs and potions were good for. To treat ailments of body, heart, and mind.

But her herbs and healing magic were no match for the larger, older magics.

And her herbs could not bring back someone who was lost.

Anandita took a breath and refocused her attention on the task at hand. The liquid cascaded from the earthenware pitcher through a tiny metal funnel, and into the row of small jars that sat, squat and gleaming in the sun that streamed through the windows.

Across the table, Tokki worked with intensity, the pink tip of her tongue sticking out from her brown berry lips as she stood, carefully ladling the wort brew through the finely woven, red-stained cloth. Fourteen years old, with a body barely blossoming on her thin, vata frame and a sharp and curious mind, she was quick to laugh, but when there was work to be done, she attended to it with her full attention.

Anandita allowed herself a smile. Despite the focus on the teen's face, her feet tapped out a rhythm on the western hemlock floors. A dancer, she was, and no stopping her, no matter what. She was a good apprentice to Anandita, and learned quickly. Besides, she didn't mind climbing up and down the step stool for the things Anandita couldn't reach from her wheeled chair.

Tokki's heavy hemp trousers were tucked into calf-high boots and a long sleeved, green tunic was belted over the top. Work clothes, just like Anandita's, though Anandita's long tunic was dyed midnight blue.

Go No More was quiet with most of the Knights gone. That was a good thing. Though the Knights were a boisterous distraction, they were not the sort her heart needed right now.

Especially that Jenny. The gorgeous lummox had been half-courting Anandita for going on two years, but Anandita just didn't have time for it. She had a township to take care of, didn't she? She was in the middle of her three-year council rotation right now.

Add in the raising of a curious, rambunctious pre-teen and it was more than enough life for one woman. Wasn't it?

Besides, she'd known Jenny since the girl was, well, a girl.

And she'd never been with a woman before, not in that way.

Oh, Anandita had woman friends, and the friend of her heart was Inaya, one of the growers here in Go No More, but sex? Despite the way looking at Jenny sometimes made her feel, she wasn't certain she was wired that way. What would she do with a woman? Anandita blushed at the thought. It embarrassed her, the thought of fumbling around like a teen girl who knew nothing.

She'd only ever been with men, and frankly, hadn't been with anyone in quite some time. Not since Long had disappeared. Long was her first lover after she'd finally felt healed enough from the accident to try. Despite the free and easy nature of so many in the township, he'd been the only person Anandita was comfortable sharing her body with.

Jenny was a hard-drinking Knight who had fucked more women than Anandita could count. She didn't want to be just another one in a long line, or worse than that, an oddity. Some strange, maimed prize. Not that she was the only one in Go No More missing limbs, but still.

Reality was, thinking about making love to anyone just made her miss Long. She glanced up at the small carving above the cabin door. A firebird rising, wings spread.

Long had carved it in secret and given it to her at the spring equinox the year before he disappeared. She had Tokki take it down twice a year—autumn and vernal equinoxes—so she could re-oil the wood. Long celebrated the equinoxes in his own, simple ways. He adhered to no religion, but they were his favorite times of the year.

"A phoenix. That's what you remind me of," Long always said. "You're so bright sometimes I can hardly bear to look at you."

A dull pain lanced her heart. No longer sharp, but an aching all the same. She certainly didn't feel like a firebird. Not anymore.

Not since some unknown force had killed Long when he was out hunting in the woods. Traces of magic were found, but the only things left of Long were a splash of brown blood on the rocks and the penannular brooch that now held Anandita's own cloak wraps closed when the weather turned cold.

At least she had a child to remember him by. Someone to wear his smile, and speak in his voice. She was one of the lucky ones. Despite birth rates going up, there were many who could not produce offspring still.

So Anandita had her practice, and a rotation of young apprentices. And most importantly, she had her son, Hypatia—a name that made her aunties cluck. "Why not a Hindu name for a Hindu girl?"—but at age eleven, Anandita had found a book about the wise Greek scientist from ancient times and fallen in love with the thought of her. And then Hypatia had fooled them all by being not a girl, as they thought, but a strong, intelligent boy. He kept the name though, which pleased Anandita to no end.

And then there was the firebird above the door, and a simple, twisted piece of metal.

And memories. So many memories. Long, kissing the string of his bow before letting the arrow fly. Long, sun reflected on his dark shock of stick-straight hair, warming up his already golden skin. Long, face above her, leaning in for a kiss. The taste of his skin. The way his tongue made her cry out in the dark of their bedroom as he knelt before her. Long, bouncing a squealing Hypatia on his back, running through Anandita's flowers and herbs.

She had trusted him with her most intimate secrets, and now he was gone. For more than five winters. Time to move on, some would say. Go on a date with Jenny. Take comfort in the younger woman's well-muscled flesh.

Anandita knew she was at war within herself. Despite doing puja at the shrine tucked into her bedroom corner each morning and at the family shrine each evening, and despite the sun salutations and measured breathing designed to bring both peace and strength into her life, her heart and mind were still not quiet.

She still wanted too much, but what she wanted, she could never have again.

People from the township came to her for help, slipping through the heavy wooden door or knocking on the window frames. They expected steady guidance. Herbs and tinctures. Assessments of what ailed them. Words of comfort and wisdom. They looked to Anandita to provide healing and counsel. They expected her to know more than she did. More than she had known since her partner had vanished, taking a chunk from her heart.

She felt like a fraud. She should not even be working with the tincture until she got herself together. When it came to medicine, an unsteady mind was worse than an unsteady hand. But the work needed doing, still, and if she waited for the perfect conditions, well, there would be no stores of medicine to take Go No More through the coming seasons.

"Someone's coming." Tokki's voice cut through her woolgathering.

Sure enough, there was the sound of boots, running on the hard-packed earth path that wound between the garden beds.

Anandita stoppered a final bottle and Tokki set down her ladle and ran to open the wooden door as Anandita wheeled herself around the table.

It was Hypatia who came puffing to the door, the small Ganesh medallion he wore everywhere bouncing on his chest.

"Beta, what is wrong?" she asked.

"It's Jason. Doc Warren says he broke a bone. She needs a mending poultice."

"Tokki..." Anandita said, but the teen was already bustling in the cabinets, dragging out mugwort and comfrey.

Anandita turned to her son, whose light brown face was flushed from the run. "She's sure it's a break, and not a sprain?"

Hypatia shrugged. "Break is what she said."

Anandita wheeled her chair around. "Get the guggal and babool paste, too. The comfrey leaves will do for sprain, but if she wants to set a cast, the paste will be more stable and heal a fracture better." Thank goodness Papa had figured out ways to cultivate the heat-loving bushes here. His greenhouses were treasure troves.

Tokki's face held many questions. The apprentice wanted to know the reasons why. Anandita waved her hands. "Just put it all in a sack with extra bandages. Wrapped so the glass won't break."

Her voice was harsh, and the instruction unnecessary. Tokki knew what to do. But nonetheless, Anandita's words hurried the teen. The explanation of how to properly treat breaks and sprains would come later. After the crisis was through.

Hemp sack slung over one shoulder, wrapped jars clunking, Tokki was soon ready to go. Anandita slipped on her heavy hemp half-gloves, and wheeled her chair out into the bright, autumn sunshine, following her son toward Doc Warren's place. She would need to ask him why he'd been down in town, and not up at the waterworks with the engineers and machinists like he was supposed to be. The boy was curious and prone to following any number of people around, peppering their backs with questions, and trying various crafts and skills on for size.

Well, he still had time to decide where to apprentice. She would worry about today's wanderings later.

For now, the sun felt good on her face, and the bunching of her arm muscles as she wheeled the heavy, fat-tired chair across the township felt good, too. Exercise. Purpose. Something she didn't need to think about. Something basic, to mend and to heal.

Action. Perhaps Anandita, like the Knights, just needed action.

Her heart felt slightly lighter than it had in a long while. As her chair bumped down the packed earth pathway through the fragrant herb gardens, she offered up another quick prayer.

"Sons of heaven, swifter than mind, come to the clans, provide safety and healing. Slay the darkness of body and of mind."

"So mote it be," said Wiccan Tokki over her shoulder.

So may it be, thought Anandita. *So may it be.*

CHAPTER 4

JENNY

The small hairs on the back of Jenny's neck stood up, as if a breeze tickled the skin exposed by the part in her long braids. She grabbed her buckler, then slid her short sword from its bike sheath with a whisper of leather on steel.

What should have looked peaceful seemed menacing in the late September sun. Smoldering coal and the greasy tang of oil filtered to Jenny, but that wasn't what made her nostrils flare.

That was the scent of blood and flesh warming in the sun.

No breeze swirled through the small, tidy, wooden homes. This was a smaller holding, recently established, if Jenny's memory was correct. Inside the wooden palisade, a cluster of around twenty wee houses arced in a half moon, facing a garden plot and a clearing set with benches. A few slightly larger buildings were set at cross quarters—nothing near as large as what they had in Go No More—with a smithy off to the right. A few fruit trees were scattered through the town, and beyond space cleared for a fire break, the verdant forest loomed.

"Fuck a pig," she muttered, then gestured with her right arm.

The Knights fanned out, stepping carefully in their red-tinged leathers. All the riders were clearly spooked. No animal likes the smell of death.

The small holding felt empty. Desolate. Too still.

Except it wasn't. Snarls and growls came from one of the small timber homes and a flurry of black wings showed a murder of crows in a ravaged garden plot, feasting. Two crows squawked at one another, fighting over a particularly tasty morsel. Jenny's stomach lurched.

No animal liked the smell of death but those who cleaned its bones in order to survive.

Jenny noticed the dragoons hadn't moved very far. With a growl of impatience, she snapped her fingers and gestured five of the riders toward the town. Jerrod, a tall Black man, hair wrapped tightly in a red kerchief, nodded and strode off, the four other Knights following behind.

"Psych? You too, please."

Psych swallowed, but followed the other five. Jenny noted that he left his apprentice, Litha, standing safely with the ticking bikes and the rest of the dragoons. Good choice.

Tegan pointed west, toward a boulder three times

Bocan's size, where two impressively sized condors waited. One cocked a red, scaly head their way, while the other didn't bother. It preened in the sun, black wings stretched to their full length, showing the white tracery of the underwing. It looked just like the Steel Clan emblem, though Jenny knew that wing was based on a red-tailed hawk, if you had asked her mother, or a swan, if you believed the records.

Jenny thought that symbols changed according to who used them, and who needed them most. Her fingers found their way to the increasingly fuzzy patch sewn on the right breast of her leathers. She sought strength from her ancestors, particularly Great-Gran Molly, known as the baddest woman in the Willamette Valley once upon a time. Biker and grower, back in the times when both were still rare, which made Gran a drug runner, too. Molly sounded like one of the warlords, except legend had it that she treated her people well, giving folks a share in the business and the promise of a decent life outside the law.

With a flow of shit, one of the giant raptors white-washed its legs and the boulder beneath its feet. Nothing wrong with that. It would dry in the sun and flake off, killing any parasites that dared to ride along, clinging to the giant birds.

Legend also had it that in Great-Gran's time, condors were rare, barely making a comeback after being hunted to the brink of extinction. It was hard to believe, that. Who would do such a thing? Hunt an animal until it was almost gone?

That wrecked a world as fast as the fiery flashes said to have ended it all.

"Humans bring their own reckoning," Tegan said at her shoulder, echoing her thoughts. Tegan was a thought sensor, though per mostly tried to keep that quiet. Folks didn't like it when a person knew what was inside their heads. It spooked Jenny to no end, that power. Tegan just said it was a pain in the ass. The other magics Tegan held—like the energy shaping—per barely spoke of at all.

Funny, while Jenny had no magic, Tegan, who had more than most, didn't seem to want it.

Bocan sniffed the air again, staring at the condors as if he could speak to them. And maybe he could. The way he talked with Serena, the owl, was another source of envy. Jenny was barely able to mind touch Flex, the faery fox who had decided Jenny was worth a bond. The fox could send her vague images, and Jenny could do the same back, but that was about it. Sometimes Jenny thought the only reason the faery fox put up with her was because she supplied Flex with grilled meat from the spit on a regular basis.

Not that Flex wasn't a skilled hunter who could provide for her cubs and herself just fine.

But she was lazy.

"This is bad," Bocan rumbled.

Jenny dragged her thoughts back to the scene in front of them. She needed to be on point, not distracted by what she could and could not do.

Psych jogged back toward them, stopping a few arms lengths away.

"Everyone is dead," he said. Beneath the pale blue patterns and sunburn, his face looked pasty. He swallowed hard. Jenny spat on the hard earth.

"How?"

He shook his head. "It was hard to tell at first, because of the...you know. Wolves. Crows. But three of the houses had shut doors and windows. Jerrod showed me. We went in...." He swallowed hard again.

Jenny shook her head and threw him her waterskin. "Drink," she said. "And buck up."

Psych shot a stream into his mouth and coughed, then swiped at his face.

"At first glance, their bodies didn't look harmed at all. It was the spookiest fucking thing. Then I got closer to one...." He choked again, then paused, took a breath, and calmed himself. "It was a little girl with golden skin. On her forehead..."

Boy had to learn that when you rode with the Knights, sometimes death was inevitable. But that still didn't mean a body had to like it.

"On her forehead what?" Jenny interjected. While Jenny tried her best to practice patience, there came a time when a person just needed to *know*. Psych had a job to do and damn well better do it.

Jenny placed her hands on the scout's shoulders and fought to soften her voice. "Tell us, Psych. Speaking the words isn't going to make it any worse. And we need to know."

"There was a mark on her forehead. A sundered triangle made of three cracked leaves."

Bocan ran a huge blue hand over his face. "Gods of fracking earth and stone."

Psych looked down, unwilling to meet Jenny's eyes.

From the looks on her comrade's faces, they'd found the magic Bocan had felt, the thing they'd been out scouting for.

"Whatever did this. Is. It. Still. Here?" Jenny's head snapped to Bocan and Tegan. She cursed her fucking inability to feel.

Her comrades stilled, as if seeking answers in the stinking air, amidst the cawing of the feasting crows, but it was Psych who spoke.

"No. They are either long gone or..."

"Or. What?"

Bocan cleared his throat. "Magic like this? Is done from a distance."

Great. Just fracking great.

"And the others?" Jenny asked. Her heart beat in her chest as if she was running through the forest, dodging low-hanging branches, chased by a mother bear.

Slowly, she removed her hands from Psych's shoulders. "And the others, Psych?"

He raised his hazel eyes. They were rimmed in red and watery. Boy looked stricken.

"Just the same. Marked. Dead. Gone."

Jenny turned to Tegan, and then Bocan. The small dark human and the large, pale halbtroll both stood preternaturally still.

"What does this mean?" she asked them, before

turning back to Psych. "In all your scouting studies, have you ever seen such a mark?"

He nodded, then broke and ran for the trees. The sound of retching followed quickly after.

Her head snapped up to meet Bocan's black-eyed gaze. "What. Does. It. Mean?"

"It means we need to get back and report in to the council," Tegan said, already loping toward the homes, ready to spread the word to the few Steel Clan members still patrolling through the town.

"Bocan?"

He stood, silent, for the space of three, long breaths, staring at the condor pair.

The only reason Jenny didn't throttle him was that her hands wouldn't span his neck. She forced herself to stand still in her boots.

Finally, he blinked.

"Sigils—marks of magic—don't just appear, Jenny."

She threw a hand up in disgust. "I don't know shit about magical marks or sigils or whatever the fuck it is you're talking about."

He just stared. No response. A sudden fury filled Jenny. Maybe she could stab him with the short sword in her right hand. Geld the pig fucker. Instead, she started walking toward the houses in the back of the circle. The ones with the closed doors. Her fury wasn't for her comrade. It was anger at her fucking impotence.

The once neat and cheerful-looking village, with its white, clay-washed wood houses and dark, stained doors, was now just downright spooky. She felt the condors staring as they passed, and threw up three fingers in the sign of warding.

Who knew what those birds had seen? Or what might watch behind their eyes?

Bocan's boots thumped behind her, slightly out of cadence with her own footfalls. Crows fought. Wolves growled. The sense of tension increased inside her gut. She really didn't want to look at this shit, but she had to. How could she make a proper report back to the township council heads if she hadn't looked with her own eyes at whatever had made Psych puke?

They passed the convocation of flapping crows, shrieking, and rending flesh. The sound of it turned her stomach. The clatter of claws. The flap of wings. The sound of flesh being torn from bone.

A crow flew past her head, wings stirring Jenny's hair in its wake. Her brain tried to make sense of what she saw, what it carried in its soot-black beak. Something round and shining in its mouth. A human eye.

"Fuck a fucking fucked pig," she muttered.

"This whole situation is a fracked-up mess," Bocan agreed, bumping into her shoulder. She hadn't even realized she had stopped.

Bocan pointed at one of the closed doors ahead. The home was a pretty thing, with a small porch and pots of kitchen herbs set to either side of the dark door.

"Want me to go ahead?" he asked.

"No." Jenny swallowed down the acrid taste of bile and tried to focus on the scent of rosemary, basil, and thyme, instead of the scent of blood. Slowly, she headed toward that scent of herbs, focusing her whole being on that, and not on what lay beyond the door.

She'd tucked her gloves into her belt when they'd stopped. Now she wished she still had them on. She really didn't want to touch a damn thing, and walked up the three steps to the porch without using the rail. The iron doorknob though, that she had to grip. To turn. She had to push the door until it swung open on quiet, well-oiled hinges. She had to step across the threshold into the cheerful room. Her eyes had to scan the wooden chairs with woven cushions. The white curtains covering the windows. The polished wide plank floors. The autumn flowers in a brown-glazed vase on a wooden table.

The two bodies on the floor, wearing blue and green hemp work clothes. Trousers and tunics. Sturdy boots. The body on the right had sun-reddened white skin. Wide, staring brown eyes, with a shock of straw-colored hair fallen across the forehead. Mouth open, as if the woman still gasped for air.

The man beside her had golden-brown skin. His eyes, thankfully, were closed. His dark hair was short, forehead uncovered.

And in the center of the forehead? A thrumming, rushing sound filled Jenny's ears. Her own blood, pulsing loud inside her. She blinked, hard, trying to clear the gray spots that threatened at the edges of her eyes.

In the center of the bronzed forehead was what looked like a brand.

A sundered triangle. Three cracked leaves.

"Bocan?"

The halbtroll moved closer, towering over her like a mountain. Jenny took one step to the side, away from him. Away from the bodies. She needed space. She needed to breathe.

"Let's get out of here," Jenny said, shoving past Bocan, on a direct path to the door. To the porch. To air.

To the thrice-damned crows.

She hurried past them, hurried through the town. Not running, but eating up the packed-earth pathways as quickly as her boots would carry her.

"Jenny!" Bocan's voice forced her to a standstill, though her heart and mind ran on ahead.

Then she heard it. A rasping, mewling, whimpering cry that made her want to run and never come back.

She turned. Bocan was crouched in front of the dark, open door of what looked like a storage shed. She watched as he reached inside.

"Jenny!" His voice, sharp as two stones crashing together, sent her feet back into motion. She moved swiftly to his side just as he pulled out a trembling figure. What looked like a boy, dressed in a brown tunic and trews, feet shod in rough, ill-tanned leather. His dark brown hands shook, and he smelled of piss, his eyes rolling in terror.

"Sshhh. Ssshhhh. I've got you, boy." Bocan's voice gentled. Jenny helped him get the boy the rest of the way out of the shed, until he stood, hunched and quaking in front of them. The horrible noises had stopped, at least.

Jenny knelt in front of him. He was older than he'd looked at first. Maybe eleven autumns. Or twelve.

"What's your name?" she asked.

He whined and shook his head.

She stood again and looked at Bocan. "Do you think he's the only survivor?"

Bocan's black eyes scanned the town. "I hope to all the Gods of earth and stone that he is. But we need to make sure."

"Come on, boy. Let's get you away from here." They walked, a strange trio, back toward the entrance of the town. Bocan shielded the boy from the crows and wolves, but even without the sight of it, the sounds and smells were gruesome enough.

Jenny just hoped the boy was too far gone inside himself to notice.

And there were the rest of the dragoons. And Tegan. The cluster of bikes, shining in the sun.

As they approached, the dragoons moved too. The Knights filtered toward her and Bocan, hovering in shuffling, uneasy clumps, clearly waiting to confer.

"Search every shack and behind every stone! And the woods, too."

The Knights snapped to. Once it was clear they were following orders, Jenny ignored them, including Tegan, who walked to stand her side, face shielded from the autumn sun with per kpinga-free hand.

Blond-haired Litha came forward to take the boy. Bocan nodded at the boy and patted his shoulder.

"You go with Litha. She's safe."

Head down, the boy followed the scouting apprentice toward a patch of shade, where she offered him water from a skin. Jenny hoped she would offer him some cannabis tincture, too. Or even whiskey. Poor lad would need something to dull his pain until they could get him to a healer.

"Bocan?" Jenny said, finally ready to hear whatever it was he knew.

"There's only one person I know who uses that particular symbol." His gravelly voice was ruminative. Jenny could almost feel the slow turn of thoughts inside his skull.

"Who, Bocan? Spit out the fucking words before I stick you," Jenny growled.

"The remaining Queen of the West. Silverhair." Bocan shook his head.

"And?"

"I can't figure out why the triangle would be sundered and the leaves cracked."

"Unless that means something really fucking bad," Tegan replied.

Jenny's hands grew cold. She pulled her gloves from her belt and slid them on, flexing her fingers more firmly into the leather. Everyone knew about the reigning Queen of Underhill. She was half mad with grief at the loss of her King.

And something was wrong with her daughter, born only recently, in the past fifteen years or so. The first child of Elfland in a century, some said.

Jenny hadn't paid too much attention to the stories around the hearth, figuring it had nothing to do with her. She half-regretted that now.

She needed information to formulate strategy, and right now? She was shit out of any sort of plan.

The dragoons were back, and Jerrod approached. "No one else that we could find."

The boy was it. The only one left alive.

"Shall we torch the place, boss?" Jerrod finally asked. "Or open the doors and let nature have its way?"

"I'm not your boss," Jenny spat out. Jerrod had come from down Salem way when his daughter, Tokki, was a toddler. Calling folks "boss" was an old habit.

She shook away the irritation. "Give unto nature its due. Unless you think the spirits are still around?" She looked from Knight to Knight, questioning, because if that was the case, she had no fucking idea what to do.

Psych stepped forward, rubbing at his sick face with a damp kerchief. "They're fled all right. Long gone."

He shared a look with Bocan, who held his blue lips so tightly, they practically disappeared inside his mouth.

"What does that mean?" Jenny's voice was harsh as a crow's, throat tight with strain.

"It means they've been stolen," Bocan said. "So, nothing lingers here."

"We should burn the bodies," one of the apprentices said, making the sign of warding. The Wasco girl. Gladys Thomason. "It is respectful."

The apprentice was right, but Jenny knew they couldn't leave a fire like that unattended....

"Who's willing to stay back and tend the fire?"

Not one Knight raised a hand. She didn't blame them. She wanted the fuck out of that place, too.

"Let's roll," Jenny said. "Litha, you take the lad on your bike. And the rest of you? Say whatever prayers you need to once we're on the road. And may the ancestors have our fucking backs, and rest these poor people's souls, wherever they may be."

The scavengers would take care of the rest.

CHAPTER 5

TEGAN

Clean of road dirt, bike oil, and the stink of death, Tegan relaxed in the hot water of the communal bathhouse closest to the town center, near the stables and the bike garage. Per had helped build the place, and was always glad of it after a long day of training, or a long, jarring ride home on bike or horse.

Green and white kiln-fired tiles lined the walls and floors. Five open showers stood against one wall and three large raised, wood-fired soaking tubs dominated the central space. Pegs for towels were stuck on the wall near the curtained door that led to the anteroom where clothes and boots were kept.

The room was steamy, and almost unpleasantly warm.

Tegan's comrades were in various stages of scrubbing down in the showers or relaxing in the raised tubs. Bocan sat next to per, smooth blue head dotted with sweat and steam, his bulk displacing vast amounts of water. The Knights had learned to not fill the tubs all the way until they figured out which one Bocan would end up in.

Jenny climbed over the edge of the tub and eased on in, skin blindingly pale where the sun didn't touch it for a goodly part of the year. She hissed as the hot water sloshed at her muscled thighs and then up her sturdy torso as she slowly descended.

Once in, her breasts bobbed just beneath the surface, freed from the bindings that held them in place for battle.

Tegan was always grateful for per own compact, whip-thin frame whenever per saw the deep creases the bindings left in the other Knight's skin. As always, a stray thought of "Why not Jenny?" flicked through Tegan's mind before being dismissed as ridiculous. Jenny was almost big enough to be Tegan's type, but the small warrior still preferred large men, if at all possible. Tegan had tumbled a woman or two in per time, and other slippery gendered persons, too. But mostly, bulky men were how Tegan rolled.

Though Tegan hadn't rolled at all in way too long.

If Bocan didn't have his fool heart set on a woman who clearly wasn't interested, Tegan might have given the halbtroll a go, but as it was, per was stuck with per own hands for a while.

Tegan sighed, nestling deeper into the steaming water.

"Boy settled?" Jenny asked Bocan.

"Litha brought him to Doc Warren and then ran to consult with Anandita."

Jenny grunted in reply, then stretched her neck and sank deeper.

The Knights were quiet for a few moments, the only sounds the slap of water when someone shifted, or a soft groan of relief as the heat penetrated tight muscles. Per rolled tight shoulders and flexed fingers stiff from gripping handlebars and kpinga, both. There was never a day that didn't hurt. It was part of the price of the job.

And Tegan wouldn't have it any other way. Apprenticing with the Knights had been a dream come true. All three of Tegan's parents held different occupations in Go No More, and none of them belonged to the Steel Clan. Per mother Inaya was part of the Green Clan, and was on the committee in charge of the cannabis fields that were Go No More's major crop under master grower Hakim L'Ouverture. Mother number two, Inaya's partner, Winney, was a schoolteacher, and father, Angel, was a horse whisperer.

Tegan was good at strategy. At tracking signs. At throwing a kpinga straight and true, picturing the arc and velocity of the spinning blades before the wooden handle ever left the hand. Per had gotten the love of African weapons from Inaya, who had a single kpinga from a great ancestor who had reportedly been some sort of revolutionary badass during a tumultuous time in the late twentieth century CE, back when this land was part of the United States. That was way Pre-Reckoning, and as far from the New Era so as to feel like a completely different world.

At any rate, Inaya had never even learned to throw

the thing, but Tegan was fascinated and learned how to throw small weapons as soon as per little hands were able to hold a knife. Once puberty hit, Tegan knew exactly what clan per wanted to petition for admittance.

Finally, after much pestering, the Steel Clan Knights took on the skinny runt of a Black person, giving Tegan a place in the ranks after four years' hard training, polishing leather, and carrying blocks of wood around for no apparent reason.

Per'd been a full member for going on eight years now, and never happier.

Except when shit like that village today needed taking care of. Give Tegan a damn warlord to knock heads with any day. Give per a band of feral pigs or a rogue grizzly to deal with.

But soul stealing? Bad magic? It left an oily taste in Tegan's mouth that no amount of cider or beer would erase. Tegan's own magic roiled in response. Time was, Inaya and Winney thought Tegan would apprentice with the mages, and the mages had courted per, wanting per abilities to bend and distort magical space and time. Tegan gave that a hard no, preferring the feel of steel in hand to weird ass shit pouring through fingertips and lighting up eyes and skin.

Yeah, per magic was strong, but holding steel in hand made Tegan feel even stronger.

Jenny cleared her throat.

"Any ideas?"

"Shit, no," Tegan replied, running a wet hand over

per face. "Can't we let the mages and elves handle this shit?"

Bocan rumbled next to per, shaking the surface of the water. "I don't like it. The whole thing stinks."

"We know that," Jenny said. "What we don't know is what to do about it."

There was a clanking in the anteroom and a rustling as the curtain to the bathing room parted, letting in Case. A stocky, ruddy man with dark brown hair and eyes to match headed for the showers. Case and his son had moved to town a few years back, after fever took Case's partner. He petitioned for entry, saying he was good with a sword and needed a change from life dodging the warlords further south.

"You're late," Bocan said.

Case scowled and continued to scrub his thick body with a course brush. He rinsed, and rubbed soap through his shaggy hair, arms raised in an enticing vee.

Tegan tried to keep per eyes up, but failed miserably as Case's muscles bunched and stretched, and the soap and water cascaded down his chest, across rosy nipples and old scars.

Clearing per throat, Tegan scrubbed per hands over per face again. Yeah, per really needed to get laid. But Case was...complicated.

Shit. Everyone in the damn township was complicated. Maybe Bocan was right to travel further afield for sex.

"Jason fell off a horse today," Case said. "Broke his arm. I needed to make sure he was set up. Thank Lugh and Brigid for Anandita and Doc Warren. They had him fixed up fine and in bed with stew by the time I got to our home."

Right before they had to deal with another healing, this one of a possibly fractured mind. Tegan wondered if per would be called upon to offer service to the lad. Per didn't have healing talent, but the thought sensing sometimes came in handy when the healers were having trouble breaking through.

"Bad luck," Jenny said, then winced, as she realized what she'd just said. It didn't do to talk about luck—bad or otherwise—when unknown magic was afoot.

Case didn't seem to notice. He just sluiced off, shut down the water, and padded, heavy dick gently swinging, across the tiled floors to the tub.

Tegan was both disappointed and relieved when he was finally submerged.

"The mages want a report as soon as we're done here," he said. "They caught me on my way over. Wanted us right away. I told them to piss off. We'd come when we were ready. And some of the council wants to meet with you two after that, over dinner."

He pointed toward Jenny and then Tegan, flashing a grin at Tegan that made per glad water covered the important bits so he couldn't see per dark nipples tighten like green cannabis buds.

Or could he? Case swept a dusky lock of wet hair off his face and grinned again. Damn. The fact that he was as psychic as Tegan didn't fracking help. No one read each other without permission unless it was tactical, but a person couldn't help but pick up on strong emotions or a projecting mind.

Shoving embarrassment away, Tegan dragged per attention back to Jenny, who'd just said something Tegan had clearly missed. If it was important, she'd repeat it.

Jenny frowned, strands of deep copper hair sticking to her face. "I have no idea what to tell them. Psych?"

The scout shook his head. "Just that it was nasty. Unholy."

In the hot water, Tegan's flesh pebbled as if a someone had dumped a load of snow into the tub. Images from the village crawled through per mind. Per breathed out through per mouth, eyes closed, trying not to see.

"We tell them that their souls were gone." Tegan was surprised to hear per own voice echo across the bathing chamber. Tegan hadn't planned to say a damn thing. "And that it was bad."

Tegan hoisted perself out of the tub. The cozy bath-house had grown stifling with the palpable memory of disturbed and disturbing magic. Per needed more air than the swirling crush of bodies and steam inside the tub allowed.

"It's the worst thing I've ever seen. Or felt." Tegan crouched at the edge of the tub, warm tiles slick beneath per feet, and shook per head.

Jenny, Bocan, Case, and the rest of the Knights in the other tub looked at Tegan, then away.

No one said anything in reply.

But no one disagreed, either.

CHAPTER 6

KARAKTILLA

Karaktilla sat in the rear hall of her mountain aerie cavern. The cavern was a series of vast halls and cozy nooks, just large enough for a four-hundred-kilo drake to curl up with a weighted-down scroll and a bowl of tea. She had spent the better part of a century carving out rooms and shoring up ceilings, and now the place suited her just fine.

The drake wasn't the only being who loved the mountains and volcanoes that ringed the ancient cities and verdant fields and forests. Times were different now, of course. The human realms could see the realms of drakes and djinn, of nagas, spiders, kobolds, and elves. And the ghost elk, giant beavers, the magical corvids and coyotes whose realms had always lived two steps closer to the spaces humans dwelled? They flourished now, even better than before. Clear skies and clean soil and water were boons to their kind.

It used to be only a select few humans who could

perceive the liminal spaces where the so-called magical beings dwelled, but now there were damn few who could not.

The deep cavern was lit with glowing orbs, and shone with gems, copper, and silver. The far end was lined with hide scrolls of drake histories, and shelves of human-made books from the Time Before. Pre-Reckoning, the humans called it. Along the back wall, a more cheerful fire burned, its smoke vented through one of the natural fissures that had so delighted the drake when she was searching for a new home after the sky-cracking clouds of flame were dropped from human-made machines, shaking all the worlds. A large iron kettle over the fire brewed a fragrant herbal mix.

The tea smelled of spring and early summer, which is when the young troll Recoana had brought them for Karaktilla, in exchange for time with the drake's library. Karaktilla thought she got the better of that trade—not only did the troll bring herbs, but read to the drake as Karaktilla worked on other things. Much handier than using metal scroll weights and blunt pointers that turned book pages without the risk of shredding them with her sharp talons. But as long as the troll was happy, who was she to judge?

Karaktilla's brown and purple scales shimmered in the glow of orbs and the small fire, and her brown, purple-tinged wings were tucked firmly to her back. They wanted a good stretch, but for now, the drake had visioning to do. Flying would need to come later.

Karaktilla turned her attention to the rough orb of

a crystal ball set into a shallow basin hewn from gray basalt.

Filled with amber streaks and white occlusions, the crystal orb was her favorite tool. . Karaktilla had fashioned it with her own talons close to a century ago.

She watched the humans down in the hamlet they called Go No More. It was a lovely place, just outside her usual flight range, though she could make it if she pushed. Karaktilla was just lazy, said her closest neighbor and sometime sex mate, Daraktal. But what did he know? Karaktilla had deer to eat, stones to carve, and books to read. What more should she aspire to?

While flying, she had seen the warriors out riding their noisy, mechanical steeds, small dots in the distance. Rather than spook them by following too closely, she had come home to a salted joint of deer and her scrying ball.

They had found the blighted village, just as she had hoped they would. Now they were back at home, scuttled away in the tiny cluster of homes, awaiting dark.

She glided across the large, central carpet toward the fire, where the iron bubbled and steamed.

A long game of chess, this was, and one she and the dragons had been playing with the elven royalty for a century or more. Karaktilla hoped the humans prospered, but what would be would be, as it ever and always was.

Change always came, whether quick or slow. And wise dragons were always ready for change.

Karaktilla settled her haunches on the stone and lifted the kettle from the fire with one delicate talon. She poured the steaming, wild herb tea into a large, earthenware bowl. Her favorite. Mottled green and blue and dusky brown. The colors of earth and sky.

She sipped the bright taste of spring mountains, and gazed down the long cavern toward the small slice of blue sky and a sweep of white cloud, barely visible. Another autumn. Soon, the cold and snow would come.

The drakes had seen many rifts and changes. During Karaktilla's five hundred years, she alone had seen the worlds drift closer, then apart again, until the most recent cataclysm had caused the worlds to crash together again. Part of that was necessity. Whole swathes of all the realms were not inhabitable, and would not be, until time and microbes did their slow, inexorable work.

Drakes, elves, thunderbirds, piasa, trolls, djinn, peri, sea serpents, fey...they all counted time in æons. They all had tales of living side-by-side with humans and other creatures, and tales of all-out war.

The times when the worlds drew far apart were times of cultural richness for the other realms, and times of discovery. But the earth realms withered during these times, and since the humans came, and the first sundering occurred—some ten thousand years back in the histories—when the humans withered, the earth suffered. And when the earth planet suffered, all the realms began to fray.

The thing the humans never seemed to figure out, and that the more hubristic magical creatures didn't care about?

All the realms were interconnected. Their wyrd—or destiny—was intertwined.

Destroy one realm? Every single realm suffered.

And that elven fool up past the thundering waterfall didn't seem to care. Queen Silverhair put everything at risk.

Karaktilla sighed, and carried her tea back to the stone table and the crystal orb.

::*Ah! There you are again*:: she thought out loud, as her tongue and teeth clicked out a series of sounds that only drakes could understand. Between the milky occlusions, a large blue halbtroll stepped forth, followed by the others. And there she was, the red-haired one. The one who was marked by the ages, though she knew it not. The scrolls had foretold a warrior would come. First among equals, with a destiny entwined with the turning of the age.

The red-haired warrior needed Karaktilla's help, but did not know it, yet. The whole band of steel-bearing warriors needed to be tested for the times that were to come.

::*Things are not as bad as you imagine now,*:: she clicked into the ball. ::*But worse times are coming, and you must prepare.*::

She needed to take the warrior's measure, and to pass along a piece of information.

But how to draw the red-haired Knight toward her?

The woman had no magic, but she did have a strong sixth sense....

Karaktilla needed to ponder.

What would drive the red-haired warrior her way?

She turned away from the crystal orb, and set about making a plan.

CHAPTER 7
JENNY

The meeting of the Knights with the mages had been fraught, and the small dinner meeting with Tegan, Jenny, and the council heads was frustrating.

The sun was setting by the time that second meeting ended and they were free to join the rest of the Steel Clan. With Tegan at her side, Jenny walked past the gardens, inhaling the scent of night blooming jasmine. The town was laid out in concentric circles, with a large fir in the center, and benches set around it. Around that were communal vegetable gardens. Larger plots grew food around the edges of the cannabis fields, but some of the townsfolk enjoyed tending to their own beds. Besides, it was a good way for the children to learn cultivation.

It was a good place, Go No More. Jenny hoped to help keep it that way.

Her heart was troubled, but there was nothing to be done for it but head to the town hall. The rest of the council and whatever members of the township could make it were convening there, so the information could be shared throughout Go No More.

Small committees could make small decisions, but when danger threatened the whole township? The whole township was invited to the table. It was a cumbersome system, to be sure, but one the Founders had decided on to forestall the abuses that led to the Reckoning.

Most folks were happy to abide by the agreements. Those who weren't? Well, they were soon sent on their way.

Tegan and Jenny approached the big council house and meeting hall. Pre-Reckoning, the big, timber building was some sort of resort for folks who worked in the now-abandoned cities. What exactly that work had been, Jenny wasn't clear on, despite the history lessons every child in Go No More got. Bunch of abstraction, as far as she could tell.

The town was quiet. The horses huffed in the stables, settling down. All the children were inside, getting ready for bed. Most of the town was likely already at the town hall.

All of the Steel Clan riders had a tense meeting with the magicians that had frankly gone nowhere. Afterward, they'd agreed to Jenny and Tegan as spokespeople, leaving them to check in over dinner with the current council heads—Arcady, Rafiq, Anandita, and John, plus Jenny's mother, Danika, there to act as council scribe.

The other Knights had gone to their own homes,

with a plan to hook up at the large community meeting. She was sure they were all inside by now.

The building sure was pretty, though. Made from big old white oak beams with heavy steel bolts, it towered three stories high and had a gorgeous PR ridged steel roof. The same ridged steel covered portions of the front facade, and caught the purple and salmon reflection of the fading sun. Corrugated, the engineers called this form of metal. The stuff had held up so far, though the builders were working on how to best patch and replace it when the time came.

Despite complaints from the town history keepers, parts of the gracious porch had been patched in with slightly darker Doug fir planks. Jenny sided with the building cohort on this one. Fir was a softer wood than oak, and didn't last as long, but was easier to mill and plane, and grew in such abundance, it would be a shame to not use it.

The clear, PR glass windows glowed with soft electric light, courtesy of the hydro crew.

Their boots thumped across the broad porch, toward the heavy carved door set with thick, slightly wavy, New Era glass. Jenny held the door for Tegan, who strode on through.

The noise hit her as soon as she stepped in, followed by the scent of alcohol, cannabis smoke, and the fresh soap smell of people who had bathed off the work day's sweat. Yep. The township was quiet because half the town was crowded into the open floor of the public house.

The big stack-stoned fireplace was cold, and as a

consequence, the hearth was crammed with four people taking advantage of seating space. Behind the long bar that took up the entire back wall of the room, Jamie and Porrac had their hands full, slinging out cider, beer, and snacks.

Broad oak beams raised the roof to enough height for there to be a second level balcony with tables and chairs. Deeper in the second story were two smaller meeting rooms, offices, and some storage, along with a few bedrooms for single folks who didn't want to build their own homes. The third floor was where Jamie and Porrac lived.

Jenny scanned the balcony for an empty table, or even some of the Knights, and found nothing. The only empty table was the long one set aside for the current council heads, set on the small performing stage to Jenny's left.

"Let's get our drinks," Tegan said. "We can find the rest of our bastard comrades later."

Jenny nodded and kept her eyes on the elaborate pattern of square knots on the back of the Tegan's head as per threaded through standing clumps of townspeople toward the two-deep bar. Mostly humans, with a few slender, green-haired elves, some of the smaller fey-class beings, and a couple of deep blue trolls towering above the rest of the crowd. Jenny thought Bocan was big, but Recoana—full-time carver and part-time herbalist—and Feldspar the blacksmith were truly huge. The town's only djinn— the white-skinned, black-eyed Abyad—was absent, which was strange, though not as strange as a djinn deciding to dwell in Go No More. Djinn were notoriously solitary.

The farther into the cavernous space Jenny and Tegan got, the louder it became. The conversations were raucous and the bangs emitting from the other side of the swinging kitchen door signaled that Jamie and Porrac's current apprentices were keeping busy, too. Jenny smiled. If you wanted to apprentice with the brewery, distillery, or cidery, you had to take shifts at the meeting house pub. Jamie and Porrac had started out as brewers apprentices, fallen in love, and discovered that they both had a knack for people that meant running the pub operation for Go No More made sense.

As a result, pub service and food had both improved, for which the town thanked myriad Goddesses, Gods, and assorted spirits of place. The men's handfasting had been one township-wide celebration. Jenny was convinced it was Go No More's way of guilting Jamie and Porrac into remaining a couple for a very, very long time.

Tegan wedged per lithe body between two burly waterworks engineers wearing heavy hemp coveralls, gifting them both with a dazzling smile. Jenny shook her head. Tegan had a way with men, women, and other persons. Per could charm the aromantic and swooners equally. Which was weird, because with the Knights, Tegan was as rough and gruff as they came. But when per turned on the natural charisma, watch out.

Porrac's ruddy face split in a grin. "What can I get my hard-riding comrades today?"

"Two dry ciders and an extra big bowl of whatever the snack is, please!" Tegan said.

On meeting nights, it was understood by the townsfolk that they eat dinner before attending, because the town hall kitchen couldn't feed them all at once. So, snacks were it. Good thing the bison stew Arcady had served the two of them for dinner was filling.

Porrac turned and signaled to Jamie, who waved and ducked into the kitchen as Porrac poured a stream of pale gold liquid into two enormous, sturdy brown mugs. Jamie was back, dark hands full of two equally enormous wooden bowls, one of which he plopped down on the bar near the kitchen. The other, he brought their way.

"Here you are, comrades!"

Jenny inhaled the scent of crisply fried roots, salt, and rosemary. The bowl was filled with what looked like deep fried beet, carrot, and sweet potato. The combination changed according to what they had on hand, and the chips were Jenny's favorite snack.

"Thanks, Jamie. You know I love fried beets."

He grinned, crinkling the edges of his big, round eyes, gave Porrac a kiss on one of his red cheeks, and got back to work. Porrac had already turned to the next customers.

Mug of cider gripped in one hand and the large wooden bowl of fried roots in the other, Jenny looked through the crush on the main floor.

"Do you see them?"

"There." Tegan pointed with per free hand. Across

the room, Bocan's big blue arm waved and beckoned. In the lead this time, Jenny threaded her way through the tables, chairs, and standing folk, nodding and smiling, but not slowing down. If they stopped to talk, there would be questions, and not only would she never get any cider in her mouth, the meeting would never begin.

Finally, they reached Bocan, Psych, Jerrod, and Case. The four Knights had scored a standing table near the side beneath the overhanging balcony, which was good for now, even though Jenny knew she'd be called to the council table on the performing stage soon enough. Bocan, Jerrod, and Case had mugs in front of them, while the skinny scout puffed on a small joint.

She plopped the bowl down on the table next to a second, already mostly decimated bowl, then took a long swallow of crisp cider.

"Wud the council heads say?" Bocan asked around a mouthful of fried roots.

Jenny shrugged. "Just wanted a report back."

"Here they are now," Case replied, jerking his chin toward the big front door. Sure enough, the nine current members of the township council walked, or in Anandita's case, rolled, in.

Just seeing Anandita made Jenny's heart rate speed up. The healer was simply gorgeous. Dark eyes and plum lips set in the dusky oval of her face, ears adorned by small gold PR studs. Tonight, she wore a blue tunic that covered the ends of her thighs and had plaited that night-black hair into a thick braid that snaked over one shoulder. The silver strands starting to thread themselves through the black shone beneath the lights and a brightly woven shawl was draped around her to ward off the evening chill.

But the colors also lit up her face. If Jenny didn't know better, she swore the woman actually glowed, lit from inside somehow.

"You're gonna melt her chair wheels, you keep that up." Tegan nudged Jenny, who started, jostling the cider in her mug.

"Watch it!" She quickly set the mug down and wiped the escaped drops on her deep brown tunic. The tunic was clean and showed off the muscles in her shoulders, and she wore her second-best sumac-dyed leather trousers.

She scowled at Tegan. "I don't know what you're talking about."

Her friend just smirked, then looked her up and down. Jenny felt herself blush, and tried to cover by shoving some root chips into her mouth. The salt and rosemary was just right with the lightly fried roots. She crunched, swallowed, then took a drink of cider to wash it all down.

"Then why'd you clean your boots so well, huh? And aren't those your good leathers?"

"Second best," Jenny blurted before she could stop herself.

The Knights hooted and pounded the table, drawing the attention of the council, including Anandita, whose head snapped their way, a slight frown creasing her forehead.

"Shut up, you pig fuckers," Jenny muttered. This only caused more laughter, and more heads turned their way, questioning smiles on faces. She could see another couple of clumps of Knights elbowing each other throughout the room. Great. Just what she needed. More assholes in her face about her nonexistent love life.

They didn't get why Jenny just didn't bed one of the several people who were always offering.

And she had, once upon a time, with her own particular favorites among the mix. But the past six months or so? She realized Anandita was the one whose lips she wanted to taste. Whose sweet breath she wanted against her cheek. Whose...

Rafiq banged his gavel on the council table, calling the meeting to order. In his late fifties, Rafiq was a handsome man with a square face and dark eyes. His silver jewelry—PR family heirlooms—complimented the liberal swathes of silver in his almost-black hair. He'd been a toddler when Go No More was founded, and this had to be his third cycle on council. Jenny appreciated the perspective he brought.

"Thank you all for coming out this evening, and as always, thank Porrac and Jamie for their hospitality," he said. "Before we get down to business, let us honor the rightful keepers of this land, our neighbors the Wasco. We give thanks for the right they gave our ancestors and to us, to work this land."

It was part of the ancestor's agreements that Go No More was henotheistic and therefore home to a variety of religions. Everyone worshipped in their own way, and agreed in the existence of Gods, Goddesses, and spirits beyond the ones their families honored. Anyone who disagreed didn't last in the township. Though, in a world where the likes of Anansi and Coyote clearly existed side-by-side, and djinn and trolls walked next to human beings, how anyone could insist that their deity was the only one in existence, even non-magical Jenny couldn't understand.

The other thing the township agreed upon was that the first peoples of the land must be honored, no matter what.

The original settlers of Go No More had done their best to set up systems that protected the land, and would hopefully restore harmony between the people, the creatures of the land, and the land and water themselves. But the histories showed that had not always been so. To not protect the land and honor the first peoples was to forget that history. And to forget meant human culture would face another reckoning.

"Gladys?" Rafiq called up the young Wasco apprentice. The tribe had their own enclaves in the area, and Go No More traded with them. Cured leather for cannabis. Township and tribe also occasionally sent apprentices to cross-train in various trades. The Knights had an arrangement with the Wasco warriors, and as a result, Gladys Thomason was with Go No More for two years.

The young woman was around sixteen years of age, with black hair loose down her slender, lightly muscled back. She wore a dark brown tunic and brown leather pants over sturdy boots. She would not wear the Steel Clan red unless she petitioned her tribe and the Steel Clan for admission, which was unlikely, though she would be more than welcome to.

Gladys lifted her hands. A stream of Kiksht language flowed from her lips. Jenny could pick out one word in five as the apprentice blessed the land, the original peoples, the hidden peoples—some of them no longer hidden, but Jenny supposed the prayer was old—and the river and soil.

Switching to English, Gladys continued. "We ask for guidance, wisdom, and discernment. We ask help to better read the patterns, and to aid us in the task at hand."

Then she lowered her arms and bowed.

Everyone gathered in the hall bowed in return.

"We thank the ancestors, we thank the river, sky, and land," Rafiq said. "And I give thanks to Allah."

"We thank the ancestors, we thank the river, sky, and land," the people of the township replied, some of them thanking their own deities as well.

"Let us begin," Anandita said. "I call up Jenny and Tegan as representatives of the Steel Clan Knights, and ask the magicians Malloy and Wong to join us."

"All hands on fucking deck," Case muttered. "Talk true."

Jenny took one more swallow of cider, set her mug

down with a thunk, and wiped her mouth with the back of her hand.

"Let's go," she said.

Tegan nodded, and Jenny followed per to the low stage, where they would talk about the sort of magic that brought bile to the base of her throat.

CHAPTER 8

JENNY

Jenny and Tegan stood to one side of the council table, with Malloy and Wong flanking the other. The mages looked as grim as Jenny felt. Aphrodite Malloy's blond hair was a ratty mess, as if she'd been running her fingers through the short locks and tugging at them. She was a short, gorgeous woman, and Jenny had happily sunk into her lush rolls of fat on more than one occasion, her own hands buried in that wild hair. This evening, Aphrodite gave her a curt nod of greeting. No wink. No smile.

Jenny couldn't blame her. The stew Arcady had served at dinner sat uneasily in her stomach.

Standing next to Aphrodite, arms crossed over his slender chest, Charles Wong looked equally dour. He usually had a smile on his slender face, but tonight his face looked pinched with anger. Even if it wasn't, his black, semi-dress tunic edged with arcane embroidery in shades of yellow and green signaled that this meeting was a serious occasion.

Jenny didn't blame him for his anger. Even though he hadn't seen the dead villagers, the situation had to make him want to spit on shit, to have magic perverted that way. She knew that, along with his born talent, Charles had studied the arcane arts for at least fifteen years, and did the township a lot of good. Both magicians had, though Wong was the better of the two.

If a blockhead like Jenny could venture an opinion on the matter.

Fuck. Not only was an entire small town decimated by what-the-fuck, with the only survivor a traumatized boy, Jenny was going to have to speak. She just knew it. Because of her standing in the community, and the particulars of her fracking birth, people looked to her whether she wanted it or not.

If they only knew what a fuckup I really am. All I'm good for is swinging steel. That was an old voice, but strong. Her ma, Danika, said it was her dead father, who was disgusted with his long-awaited child's lack of magical ability in an age where magic ruled. Danika always snorted that swinging steel was as useful as anything, and that Jenny's dad was just bitter.

Mouth suddenly dry, Jenny wished she'd brought her cider up with her.

Wong caught her looking at him and raised one eyebrow in question. Jenny shrugged. Nothing to say that they hadn't already talked about earlier.

From the center of the table, Anandita cleared her throat. "You all know about the disturbances the magical beings have sensed. At our last meeting, they told us of bad magic. These past few days, our Knights have traveled, and brought back dangerous news, and a lone survivor."

Anandita turned her forest-dark eyes her way. Jenny swallowed.

"Jenny?"

Jenny stifled a sigh and shifted uneasily. Here they were. Talking about magic wasn't her strong suit, and she'd stumbled through it in both the meetings with the magicians and the council heads. But in front of a whole group? Jenny felt okay talking about dead bodies, but shit like stolen souls? Maybe...

She cleared her throat. "Frankly, we should bring Psych, Bocan, and Jerrod up, too."

"Just talk," Tegan muttered.

Right. She avoided wiping her hands on her tunic and *really* wished for that swallow of cider. Her right hand tapped absently at the hilt of her belt knife. Where to begin?

"Bocan felt the magic before any of us did, and led us to the village. It was..."

The images flashed through her mind.

"Brutal. The whole village was just gone."

Jenny heard a gasp from her left, and toward the side wall, she swore Feldspar growled.

"What do you mean, gone?" came a voice from the balcony.

"No. Souls." Tegan spat.

Per words were a knife made of ice that sliced through the overcrowded, overly warm room. There was a hush, and then an excited crush of voices.

Anandita banged the gavel on the table. Once. Twice. Thrice. The noise did not abate.

Jenny looked at Tegan, then at Anandita, who mouthed "Do something."

Jenny stuck two fingers in her mouth and gave a sharp whistle. That cut through the clamor. There were still some panicked whispers and mumbling, but the worst of it subsided.

Anandita banged the gavel once again.

"Aphrodite? Charles? Can you explain what this means?"

Charles cleared his throat.

"It's magic we barely understand."

"What good are you, then?" Another voice, from another part of the room. More grumbling.

Jenny whistled again, then raised both of her arms, palms out. And she just stood. Waiting. Let them look at the row of throwing knives strapped across her chest. Let them look at her muscles. The knife at her waist. The sword at her side. Let them look at her hair, half loose tonight, but with enough braids to keep it off her face.

Ready for battle.

"Knights, stand! Elves and trolls and djinn stand!" Her voice carried throughout the meeting hall.

There was a shifting. The scrape of chairs on wooden floors. The groan of benches as weight rose.

"Knights forward! Elves, trolls, and djinn forward! Please!"

And they came. The crowd angled and parted, as best as it could. Eighteen members of the Steel Clan.

Three elves, tall and slender, sage-green hair shining in the electric lights. Agate and Recoana followed, looking determined. And, amazingly, though she hadn't seen them before, the djinn Abyad strode forth, black dog padding alongside. As black as the dog's fur was, Abyad the djinn was pale. The bare muscles of his arms caught the light, dazzling Jenny's eyes. The djinn wore loose garments of black. Out of doors, the djinn completely swathed himself, whether to not blind the humans, for some religious reasons, or to protect from the sun, Jenny wasn't sure. Some djinn were of fire, but Abyad, it was said, controlled the wind. Perhaps the wind and sun didn't get along.

Jenny felt as taut as a bowstring but did not lower her arms. Not yet. When certainty gripped her, she followed its lead, no matter how strange or inconvenient. It hadn't steered her wrong yet, though it caused issues with the Knights sometimes, and embarrassment for her.

She just knew that to keep this meeting in order, the township needed to see the full force of the people most involved. Everyone still had a say, but it served to remind folks that experience mattered, too. And if the magicians and council heads couldn't keep order? Well, the Knights damn sure well would.

She stood, back muscles easily holding her arms in position. Her eyes clocked the progress of her crew. They knew to line up on the stage behind the council table, behind Jenny, Tegan, and the two magicians. She felt as they formed a shallow arc that extended out beyond the council row. Heard their breathing. Felt the solidity of sheer presence each of them brought. The elves flanked the magicians, and the trolls stood directly behind Jenny and Tegan, a towering and broad-shouldered wall. Abyad and the black dog took up one end.

Once the clamor quieted, Jenny lowered her arms.

She raked her gaze from one side of the packed space to the other, then scanned the balcony. There were no sounds of drinking. Talking. Shifting in chairs. No one coughed. Even the sounds from the kitchen had silenced. Jenny's eyes moved toward the bar. Sure enough, three apprentices in long aprons stood with Porrac and Jamie.

Finally, she lowered her arms.

"Thank you," Jenny said, speaking from her belly, voice pitched to carry through the whole space.

Jenny adjusted her stance, leather belts creaking. The room smelled of fried roots, beer, cider, cannabis, too many people...and the sour scent of fear. Jenny could practically taste it on the back of her tongue. She didn't like it.

Oh, fear was natural. Fear was fine. But when a large group was afraid? Stupid decisions got made. And the township could ill afford that.

"We are still putting the pieces together. The magical beings and the magicians need to pool information, and the Knights will go where needed to gather more. Hopefully, the survivor will heal enough to tell us something, too. But tonight's meeting is to share what we know, so wild rumors don't go raging through the township, or worse, the villages beyond the township."

She scanned the crowd again, picking out a face here and there to speak to directly. A trick, but one that worked. People needed to feel invested.

"We expect those of you here tonight to pass on what we know to those who could not attend. We ask that there is no speculation and no rumor shared. Speculation and rumor could mean more lives lost. Help us with this, comrades, please?"

No one spoke. Some crossed their arms over their chests, chins jutting out. They didn't like it. Jenny didn't care. Others, thankfully, nodded their agreement, and they seemed to be in the majority. The important thing was, no one stepped forward to block the process. That would have to do for now.

"Anandita?" Jenny turned her head. Anandita's dark eyes were trained on her, as if she knew exactly what Jenny was doing. She just hoped the other woman approved. "With the permission of the council and the apprentice herself, I would ask that Gladys speak again, to help us focus the next part of the meeting."

"Of course," Anandita answered.

She turned to Gladys, but the girl's eyes were trained off to the side. Jenny tracked her gaze to the tall, black-swathed djinn. Abyad inclined his head, then stepped forward and raised his arms, black sleeves falling to reveal blinding white skin.

The djinn's voice sounded like wind whipping across winter fields.

"What is done must be undone. The souls that walk come home again. The land and wind and rain will show the way. Think clearly. Speak what truth we can. Cultivate patience and discernment. Be brave in your hearts, even as we face the evil that flies across this land. Give up nothing of yourselves. Stay true to the task."

He spoke those final two sentences, black eyes boring into Jenny, but she heard nothing after that one harrowing word.

Evil. All the spit in Jenny's mouth dried up. She really wished Abyad hadn't used that word.

But, one hand on a knife, the other on the pommel of her sword, she felt the truth of it in her gut.

Whatever was at work here? Whatever had stolen the souls of those poor people?

Evil was exactly the right word.

CHAPTER 9
ANANDITA

Anandita crested the slight bump of the threshold and rolled out into the night. The meeting hall was too noisy. Too crowded, with too much emotion. She wheeled her chair, pushing through the heavy maple door, then let it thunk shut behind her.

After the cacophony inside, the broad wooden porch was relatively quiet. A fox barked from deep within the trees, and a horse nickered in response. Rolling toward the far end of the porch, she stopped next to a small table set just outside one of the rectangles of light thrown out by the big glass windows. The roar of conversation was muffled out here, praise God. The doubled layers of PR glass blocked a lot of sound.

Anandita exhaled and let some of her pent-up tension away float away on the light breeze. The wards surrounding the township buzzed lightly at the back of her mind. She usually didn't notice the network of magical protection, except when she was out at night, and enough other psychic noise faded to the background.

Not that tonight was a particularly quiet one.

People were right to be upset. She was upset, too. But damn if they didn't need to get a grip on themselves. She should talk with the rest of the council and the Knights, get some extra trainings thrown in. Let people work out their fear and anger with some exertion. Nothing like swinging a sword around after you'd already worked all day to quiet a body and mind. And those that couldn't work with swords? Well, knives or bows would do.

Anandita's throwing knives rested in a case strapped to her chair and a blade was always clipped to her belt. Speaking of, she needed more sessions with Tegan. She hadn't practiced throwing knives in a moon at least. It was easy to let training go by the wayside when there was always so much to get done. Especially this time of year, before winter set in.

Not that physical defense was going to help a damn against whatever evil had done this thing. Anandita sighed. Perhaps more ashwagandha tincture was in order until her emotions settled down. Some cannabis honey in her tea, as well. She'd left both with Doc Warren, for the lad.

They still hadn't gotten a name out of the child. Anandita hoped the herbs would help calm his body, soul, and mind.

Speaking of... She drew a small wood pipe from her

belt pouch and began to pack it with oily, fragrant herb. L'Ouverture's Finest, they called this particular bud. Sparking the metal flint match, she held the small fire to the pipe bowl as her lips drew on the other end until hot smoke filled her mouth.

"Praise God," she murmured, inhaled again, then looked back out into the dark night as the pleasant smoke wreathed around her head. It felt good to take a moment to relax.

Things had been going so well. Relatively. The cannabis was thriving in the green fields one klick outside of town. The golden brassica which fueled the Knight's bikes flourished next to fields of barley and wheat. Tokki was turning into a good apprentice, and was going to be a great help to the herbalism and Ayurveda practice and the township itself. Go No More had decent trade setup with several other autonomous townships and the local tribes. The cannabis salves and soaps Anandita made with a small consortium of other townsfolk were popular. The infused honey and goat's cheese were gaining more interest. Salmon had grown more plentiful in the rivers the past half dozen years. And the township's children were healthy, and the last decade had brought more of them than the New Era had seen so far. That was good. A sign that humans were growing strong again.

That they wouldn't have to fight so hard all the time.

Damn it. This should have been a time of relative quiet and abundance. Sure, there were the hotheads farther south who thought setting up some sort of neo-feudal warlord operation was actually going to work, but that was always going to be the case. Everything else was fine.

Except the disappearances.

But she didn't see what that nasty, sundered triangle had to do with the fact that Long had left to hunt and not come back.

Muffled shouting from inside the hall pierced her musings. The door opened, letting out a roar. Bocan and Tegan must be drinking too much and doing knife tricks again. Anandita grimaced. She hated that. It meant cuts to clean later. But she also knew it was their way of distracting people from the hideous news. The Knights were built-in entertainment when folks were too riled to listen to music and too pent up to head to their homes.

The door fell shut, blocking out the sound again. Two sets of boots walked across the boards.

"I've got to get back to Jason. Make sure he's resting okay." Case. Speaking to someone else. Boots thumped down the stairs.

"Good night, Case," Anandita said as the Knight walked by. "Let me know if you need more salve for the boy's arm tomorrow."

He waved a hand in reply, then strode off to the snug home he shared with his son. He raised the boy on his own, with the help of the township. Jason's mother, Swan, had been a volunteer, willing to give Case the child he wanted as long as she didn't have charge of raising it. Swan was the township's best bowyer and best shot. She was kept busy training the whole township along with keeping everyone supplied.

That said, Swan saw Jason a few evenings a week, and there was talk that he might apprentice with her, too.

Booted feet walked across the boards behind her. Anandita knew that particular footfall. And the scent of that shampoo. Grape root and sweet almond. One of Anandita's blends.

Jenny. Anandita turned her chair just as the warrior stepped in front of a window, the golden electric light setting her russet braids on fire. Her hair was the color of autumn leaves. Maple. Sumac. Loose ends curled past her broad, leather-clad shoulders.

"You okay?" Jenny asked.

Anandita didn't reply, drawing on her pipe again. She waited until the other woman dragged a chair over and sat with a huff, legs splayed, arms loose on her lap.

"Your comrades play fighting again?" She offered Jenny the pipe. The red-haired Knight waved it away. She rarely smoked, preferring whiskey or cider to cannabis.

Jenny gave a short laugh. "Got to keep folks entertained. Besides, after tonight, folks need a distraction."

Stars winked through the ragged peaks of trees. A waft of the skunky pine scent from the far-off cannabis fields rose and fell as the breeze shifted, mixing with her own smoke and the scent of Jenny's hair.

She could feel Jenny staring at the side of her face. She knew the other woman's eyes didn't stay put, either. Could practically feel the way they traced the outline of her breasts beneath her tunic.

Her nipples peaked. She crossed her arms, small pipe warm in her right hand, trying to hide her response. Tucked her shawl more firmly around herself.

"You didn't answer my question," Jenny said. "You okay?"

Anandita finally turned, looking into Jenny's whisky-colored eyes. "How can any of us be okay?"

Their eyes held for a moment, before Jenny broke away, gazing, not at the treetops and stars, but out across the dimly lit township. At the cozy homes. The general store. The smithy. The glassmakers. All the places they'd worked so hard to build.

The home the first settlers had gotten in a steward-ship deed from the Wasco, half a century ago.

If it was at risk now? That would be a damn shame.

"I don't know," Jenny replied. "That village was... uncanny. Horrible. Still makes the hairs stand up on my arms, and I can't even feel the worst of it. Psych got hit with it so hard he threw up. And that poor boy..."

Jenny's mouth twisted as if she wanted to spit. She swallowed instead.

Anandita inhaled one last round of smoke before setting her pipe aside on the small table next to her chair.

The healer reached out, grasping Jenny's forearm. The solid weave of muscle and tendon trembled beneath her hand, as if Jenny were an animal about to spring toward safety. Except it did not know where safety was to be found.

Jenny ran a single finger across Anandita's knuckles, looking at Anandita with sad, hopeful eyes.

Anandita removed her hand.

"You have magic, Jenny. It's just different from other people's. You sense plenty. It's why the Knights respect you."

And I do, too. Anandita didn't voice that, though. It wouldn't do to give Jenny any hope about the two of them. Because that wasn't going to happen.

"The Knights respect my sword arm," Jenny replied without much heat. She sounded tired. Half-defeated. "I'm just another piece of township muscle, and I don't know what good muscle is going to do against whatever this is."

The Knight waved her hand at that last, as if clearing cobwebs from the night air. Come to think of it, that's what the whole situation felt like. A mess of cobwebs, obscuring what was on the other side.

Anandita gave a short laugh, trying to lighten the situation. "Fighting is certainly one of your talents, Jenny, but if you think that's all it takes to gain respect around here? I'll call you a fool. Your mother taught you better."

Jenny shot her a grin, but Anandita could tell she didn't mean it, any more than Anandita had meant that laugh.

"What are we gonna do, Dita?" The planes of Jenny's face were half shrouded in darkness as she looked out across the township's central circle.

Anandita shook her head, then turned her own eyes back to the stars and the dark.

"Well, for one thing, we need to get people out onto the practice field. But after that? Only the Gods and Goddesses know, Jenny. I just hope they deign to offer us a clue."

And perhaps they didn't know either, but someone —or something—out there did.

CHAPTER 10
JENNY

The late September sun had warmed up the practice field. The shadows from the buildings on the edges of the open area shrank toward lunch break. But despite what Jenny's stomach was trying to tell her, that wouldn't be for a while yet. Her body just required so damn much fuel. She needed to start carrying dried fruit and nut bars around.

At the far end of the yard, tall Jerrod worked with a group of twenty township members wielding polearms.

Polearms, along with bow and arrow, and slings for the smaller children, formed the base of protection for the township. Only a few wanted or needed to train with sword and shield, and Bocan was working with them just ahead of where Jenny stalked, taking in the whole field.

Boots scuffed on dirt, raising puffs in the air as wooden practice swords thwapped against each other and clanged against bucklers and targe shields. There was the occasional grunt of effort and a sharp "Hey!" marking the moments when wood hit flesh.

"As you increase speed, make sure you don't get sloppy!" Bocan yelled. He stood in the center of the yard, a pale blue tower in the midst of the much smaller humans struggling through their paces.

Jenny walked around the edge of the practice field, sweeping her eyes across the half dozen sparring couples Bocan had charge of. Tegan was off to one side of the space, machete in one hand, kpinga in the other, working on multiple attacker scenarios with some of the more advanced people. Tegan's style was an unorthodox blend of the Tire Machét taught by Hakim L'Ouverture, and classic old European Florentine style. Tegan was master at using the kpinga not only as a thrown weapon, but as a shield, and with a flick of the wrist, could easily trap an opponent's blade in one of the three curved blades while closing in for a machete strike.

Abyad worked with per, pale arms flashing as the djinn demonstrated a rolling fall with what looked like a complicated-as-fuck spring upward to one knee, and then standing.

The djinn moved like a black and white whirlwind.

Jenny shook her head at the combination of grace and power involved in the move. Clearly, she needed to learn the technique, or whatever approximation of it a human could do. Looked damn useful. And this wasn't the first time Jenny wished the djinn was part of the Steel Clan. But they were too independent to join even a gang of anarchist Knights, and besides, were a master arrow maker. Abyad also crafted the most prized of the archer's thumb rings, carved from bison horn. If you were very lucky, the djinn would agree to do leather work as well. It depended on the season, how busy they were, and whether or not Abyad—and the black dog—liked you.

The djinn had made Jenny's jacket, as a matter of fact. And better work than that, Jenny couldn't ask for.

Anandita and Swan were over near the long row of straw and hemp targets, going over rapid release techniques with a group of five as Recoana trained some of the weaker or less steady-handed members in crossbow on three targets at the end of the row.

The archers went one at a time, to practice shooting while moving. The girl on deck reached in her quiver, set the arrow, and released. Over and over, with barely a stutter in between. She was good. Once her quiver was spent, she turned back to her teachers.

Anandita became animated, arms sweeping arcs through the air as she explained one of the finer points of shooting a composite bow.

She shot what some called Asiatic style. The style history books showed from far off lands of Turkey and India. It was perfect for horseback or wheelchair alike and could be taught to children as young as four or five winters.

Her face glowed a warm, golden brown in the sun. Jenny ripped her gaze away and back to Bocan's crew. They were the ones who needed the most help right now.

At Anandita's suggestion, the Knights were deepening the township's training in three different time slots throughout the day. Mid-morning for the livestock keepers and some of the artisans and crafters. After lunch for the planters and harvesters. Late afternoon for the rest of the crafters, plus parents and school-age children. Luckily, it wasn't the main harvest time yet. The township harvested barley in the spring and the cannabis harvest would begin in a week or two.

Not enough time to train a Knight, but enough time for folks to brush up, and more importantly, to regain rusty confidence.

"Switch partners!" Jenny shouted. Bocan nodded. They'd gotten enough out of their current partner, and had begun anticipating each other's strikes and counters. As Jenny walked into the center of the group, she stroked the amulet at her breastbone. It felt slightly warm, but she wasn't sure what that meant.

She strode up to Bocan, stopping one foot from the muscular wall of his leather-clad form.

"Feel anything?" She kept her voice low, and jerked her chin up, toward his amulet.

"It calmed down once we crossed the town wards yesterday. Why? *You* feel something?"

The muscle over his left eye socket raised.

Jenny shrugged. "Feels a little warm. Probably just from my skin."

He gave her a look, as if he wasn't buying it.

"You saying you're hot, redhead?" He'd chosen to play along for now, but Jenny knew he wasn't going to drop the subject that easily.

It didn't matter. The amulets were useless, as far as Jenny was concerned. If a thing couldn't give her accurate information, she didn't need it. Her instincts? They'd been tested, and usually checked out. Magic? Magic could go fuck a pig. There were people to train. She flipped Bocan a good natured, two-fingered vee, and turned back to the fighting field.

"All right!" Bocan yelled. "New pairs! Make sure when you're moving through, you follow through on each strike and parry. It should be natural. If it isn't, ask us what you're doing wrong! And take up space! We don't want you hitting someone on accident."

"That's right," Jenny quipped. "You only want to hit someone on purpose. Why?"

"They need to know they've been hit!" A few voices shouted back. Jenny grinned.

"One! Two! Three! Go!"

In ragged rows, the practice swords moved. It looked like a stuttering machine with several wooden arms. High strike to the right. Mid-parry to the left. Swing, step, and forward thrust. High left parry. And...

"Strike! Strike! Strike! Strike!" Bocan's voice cracked through the air. "No! Parry, you fracker!"

Jenny watched intently for a while before wading through the rows, making minor corrections to form. One couple, she stopped completely.

"You're not parrying from strength right now."

Alinda, the baker's assistant, was huffing. She took her rust-colored bandana off and tied it more securely around her frizzy brown curls. Sweat ran down the dark planes of her face and she just shook her head.

"Not sure what you're talking about there, Knight."

Jenny smacked her own belly. "You've got to move from your core. Your center of gravity. Otherwise, you're just going to keep doing nothing but panicked defense and getting smacked around for your trouble."

"Show me?"

Jenny knew Alinda had been shown twenty times, but nonwarriors needed to be reminded. Muscle memory was hard to build if you didn't do something every day.

Speaking of which...

"Halt!" She shouted the word across the yard. "Bocan! Permission to demonstrate?"

His mouth quirked at that. She didn't need permission, but it was polite to not trounce on someone else's class.

"Everyone! Practice this stance! Lefties, mirror image!"

She placed her feet left forward, right slightly back and pointing out. Bending her legs slightly, she smacked her thighs and then her belly. "Your strength comes from here and here. Not from your arms, your back, or your chest! You start at the top of the body, you get pushed over. Start at the feet. Then swing from the hips, belly muscles fully engaged. Follow through with the shoulders and arms."

She demonstrated, step by step, with the gathered dozen doing their best to follow. Bocan moved through the rows, correcting.

"Make sure your shield is doing its job. That's more important than your sword, even. The shield is protector, blocker, and weapon, all in one. Strike *through* the buckler. Cut down. Down. Up. Up."

Slow clanging punctuated each of Jenny's words as the trainees attempted the moves.

"I need you to practice in pairs every single day for the next month. At least fifteen minutes, twice a day! Okay?"

There was grumbling agreement to that. Folks never liked training in a thing that wasn't their specialty, and she didn't blame them. But the township knew it was necessary. Besides, even the Knights cross-trained in something. No one could specialize completely. In the middle of disaster, you never knew what you'd be called upon to do.

As part of her cross-training, Jenny had recently begun working with the blacksmiths a couple afternoons a week, learning how to make simple horse-shoes. She was almost at the point of graduating to nails. It was fucking hard work, but the challenge was good for her.

She picked up buckler and sword, and called Bocan over. Together, they demonstrated, slowing the movements down so the township members could clearly see what the Knights were doing with feet, legs, trunk, arms, and head as well as shield and sword.

"Build from the feet up! Pivot from the hips and your core on out!"

Besides, it was either learn smithing or go back to studying basic magic under Charles. He'd been bugging her about training again, insisting there were things she could learn despite her "somewhat blocked state."

But Jenny had tried. She'd tried and gotten nowhere. And she hated it.

"Halt!" This time it was Bocan who called a stop.

Jenny kept in fighting stance, but paused along with everyone else. Bocan was looking past her shoulder.

She turned. Anandita wheeled across the yard toward the fence and Tegan was ahead of her.

Charles and Aphrodite stood at the edge of the practice field, faces grim. Charles caught her eye and raised a beckoning hand to her and Bocan.

"Go through that form again," Jenny called out.

Practicing while distracted was good for everyone.

No perfect conditions. That's what her mentor always said.

No fucking perfect conditions. Ever.

CHAPTER 11

BOCAN

They were on the road again, on horseback this time, heading into the mountains, back country.

The mages had sent them here, heading toward Wy'East, also known as Dragon's Peak. They'd gotten some psychic push toward the area, or something. Bocan couldn't really parse it out. He knew troll magic, but whatever the humans did? Despite how hard Ma tried, some of that still escaped him, and likely always would. Recoana had told the magicians she didn't think they were heading the right direction. She had close contact with one of the drakes in the area, and insisted the great wyrms never bothered with the sort of magic they were seeking. Bocan was skeptical, but there were no other leads, so off the Knights went.

Who knew what they would find?

His Percheron, Bodie, walked steadily through the underbrush. The stallion was a steady walker, even laden with a halbtroll, fifty pounds of oats, food for

Bocan, and a bedroll. Luckily, Bodie was big even for a Percheron, and could handle the weight. Bocan patted Bodie's white neck.

"You're not much fast, but you're strong, aren't you, boy?" Strong and steady, like Bocan. Too bad Jimena didn't care about those qualities. All she cared about was sex. And if he ever breathed a word of complaint about that to the Knights, he would never live it down.

He'd take the sex, gladly. He hadn't seen Jimena in far too long.

Jenny and Tegan were ahead with Psych, the tattooed scout's head swinging, scanning trees and underbrush, and trying to avoid getting coshed by low tree branches. The rest of the Knights that had joined the mission spread out behind. They'd left a contingent in Go No More with Case in charge of training along with the bowyer, Swan. The rest were there to assist, and to make sure the township stayed safe in the absence of the rest of the Knights. Until things changed, there was just too much weird shit going on for the whole Steel Clan to be gone.

There was definitely consensus on that front. Only a butterfly head would think otherwise.

There were only deer trails here, and the lead horse's job was to push back the brush. Jenny and Tegan had machetes out, occasionally hacking at undergrowth. Jenny bashed at branches with her buckler, letting out the occasional curse when a branch whipped back and smacked her. Bodie followed the other mounts, taking care of the rest, muscling on through, breaking away the snapped branches and trampling vegetation beneath his solid, metal shod feet.

The magicians had come with news of another disappearance, this time from a village a few klicks away. Aphrodite also said their sense of the bad magic was increasing. The djinn and trolls had concurred.

The lad had finally been able to speak, but wasn't able to tell them much more. Simply that there'd been a great wind, a sudden smell of rotting apples, and then the marks started to appear. His ma told him to hide, and lock down his mind. So he did.

It had taken Tegan, Anandita, and Doc Warren two days to finally break through and convince the lad to speak.

And they were all rightfully worried about that sundered elven crest. What the fracking earth was Silverhair up to? Had she turned, or had something happened to her? Last he'd seen her, she'd been an ordinary golden-asshole, not an evil one. But that was before the King had died in some sort of freak accident with one of the distant portals.

Just because magical beings lived a long time, didn't mean they couldn't be killed.

Like his ma. Bocan still didn't know exactly what had happened to her. No one did. All he knew was that Da was lost in grief. Bocan missed Ma, but it had settled into an ordinary ache, only flaring up on anniversary dates. Like his birthday. Or on the rare occasions he thought about what it would be like to fall in love and settle down.

At any rate, the magicians didn't know what message the Queen was sending. The elves were working on it, with the help of the djinn.

Bocan sniffed the air for magic, but didn't catch much. Seemed like, if they were heading the correct direction, there would be more than just residue.

"Tegan!" he called ahead. Tegan turned per head and quirked a brow in question. The glossy brown mare beneath the small Knight huffed and paused to crop some grasses.

"You smell anything?"

Tegan tilted per head back and made an elaborate display of sniffing the air in his direction. Bocan grimaced. He should have known better.

"Just unwashed halbtroll dick," per replied. "Why? You catch something?"

He nudged the big horse forward, closing the gap. "Just seems we should be scenting more magic by now."

"Not getting anything yet. Want me to ask Psych?"

Bocan shook his head. Tegan shrugged, and turned back to the overgrown trail.

Two yellow breasted thatches whizzed by and Bocan caught a flash of red, followed by a knocking sound. Acorn woodpecker. Ma had loved birds. She had a PR book from her baba. Taught him as many names as she knew.

Sometimes he imagined she'd turned into a bird after she vanished, and checked on his progress from above.

He sniffed again, then sent his attention toward the

ground beneath Bodie's feet. Something was definitely off about the whole situation. If only Bocan could sense it better. He was best at communicating through rocks and stones. Once the dragoons settled down for the night, he would check in with the mountains and the cinder cones of the long-quiet volcanoes. See what they had to say.

Sure made him wish he could ask his da, though. If anyone would know about this situation, Da would.

But Da was deep in his own caves again, tinkering, one foot Underhill and one in this realm. Isolated. Too isolated for Bocan's taste, but Da insisted. The loss of his mate had hit him hard. Trolls were slow movers. Slow to anger. Slow to love. But once they did? It took them even longer to get over it.

Da likely never would.

Bocan yanked his thoughts back to the quest. To the forest. Flex, Jenny's bonded fox companion, ranged on ahead, spiral-patterned fur flashing orange, white, and black through the thick growth. A faery fox was a good friend to have. Jenny was lucky. The lynx that stalked Tegan half the time was nowhere to be seen.

Not everyone in the township had a non-human companion, but at least a third or so did. It was something that hadn't happened too often PR, according to the stories. But after? For some reason, when the magical beings moved closer, some of the animals did, too.

His bonded owl, Serena, rarely left her home territory, and this trip was no exception, though he could have used her reconnaissance right now.

Meanwhile, Jenny was bugging the snot out of him. She was skittish as a colt for no reason. He looked over at her. Red braids glinted in the shafts of gold that filtered through the trees. Grim look on her face. Well, all of them had that now, didn't they? But ever since the scouting mission, she hadn't been pulling her weight. Not like usual. Her discomfort during the big town hall meeting was apparent, and during the smaller meetings after, she'd been holding back. Something was brewing, and he wanted to know what the fracking earth it was.

He nudged the Percheron toward the lead horse with his thighs. Jenny scanned the trees and chewed a piece of venison jerky.

"You gonna tell me what's wrong, or just be an ass about it?"

Jenny jerked. "What the fuck are you talking about? I'm scanning for physical danger or anomalies, just like I'm supposed to be."

"I'm talking about you, Mopey Face. What'd Charles say to you, anyway?"

The mage had taken Jenny aside after speaking to the rest of the group. There was a lot of hand-waving on Charles's part, and a lot of crossed arms and clenched jaw on Jenny's. Jenny had stalked away, then motioned for the rest of the Knights to follow.

But she'd said nothing during the meeting that led to them saddling up and hitting the hills. And that nothing was turning into a problem.

"None of your business," Jenny grumbled.

"It is. Because you're being a pain in the ass to

everyone, and I want to know why." He pulled in closer and lowered his voice. "You need to pull your head out. The Knights are getting worried."

"We run by consensus. Why don't you take the lead if you're so all-fired worried about it?" Her lips were practically white. Anger and frustration rolled off her in waves so thick, Bocan could practically feel them battering against him.

"Because, consensus or not, you're the one they trust. The one we trust. And part of why we trust you is you don't want the seat of power. You think anyone else is better suited?"

Her shoulder jerked up and down in an annoyed shrug. "You fuckers have been listening to Jerrod's Salem goat shit, haven't you? Leaderless. That's what we all agreed."

He barked a laugh at that, which earned him another scowl. "Well, Go No More is leaderless, right? But we still have council heads that rotate through. All leaderless means is we have no kings or presidents. Like our creed says. No one who can be corrupted by absolute power. It doesn't mean we don't look to folks with talent and wisdom for guidance. I know your mother taught you that."

"And what talent and wisdom, exactly, do I have?"

Bocan snorted this time. "Fine. Wallow in your own pig-fucking self pity. But just know that the Steel Clan needs you. And if you don't step up, we're all fracked."

Ass.

He squeezed his thighs together and spurred Bodie

on ahead with a light thump from his boot heels. Jenny should have been right. It shouldn't matter that she was checking out for a while. It was part of what made the Knights strong. That they could trade off, according to skill, temperament, and energy.

But a spike of pain worried at his gut. It was his deepest intuition, telling him that in this case? It was Jenny they needed most of all.

He just hoped they weren't following her foul mood into a fracking disaster.

He'd check with Tegan when they camped. One of them was going to have to take lead, and soon. Or Jenny's bullshit would do just that. Because anyone who ever trained at anything knew one sure thing: not making a decision was a decision all the same.

And drifting carried a person all sorts of places without their will.

CHAPTER 12
JENNY

It was a pleasant day for a ride and Jenny's roan horse, Dandelion, seemed happy to be out, stretching her legs. A nuthatch crab-walked down a hemlock spruce, small head bobbing and turning, listening for something tasty wriggling beneath the bark. Bridles clinked and horses *whuffed* behind her. Tegan hacked out brush just ahead and Psych rode quietly as usual, leaving Jenny alone with her thoughts, smashing back encroaching vegetation with her buckler.

Jenny swallowed the last of the hard jerky, having chewed out all the venison flavor ten minutes past.

Even though he pissed her off, Bocan was right. She was trapped in a loop inside her heart and head. While they were back in Go No More, training, Jenny had been fine. Combat was something she knew she could do, and she was a decent teacher. Her body knew the forms and her mind could explain it clearly enough. Short sword in her right hand, buckler gripped in her left, Jenny was fully herself. It was as if she had been born to move that way. Some said it made her a good lover, too. Now, if only those people could convince Anandita...

Sometimes the best fighters were shit teachers, but Jenny was good at observing when others began to seize up inside, where physical habits or inner fears interfered with how a person held a knife or sword, how they played defense or attack.

She needed someone to look at her soul and see the same. But there was no one. No one she'd found, anyway. Maybe she was just too defective to be fixed. Maybe they'd just given up on her, accepting that she didn't have magic like the rest of them, and never would.

And maybe she needed to accept that, herself, instead of fighting it all the Gods-damned time.

She probably should talk to Ma about it all. Jenny had seen Danika hovering around the edges, very deliberately not interfering. No one in the O'Brien family was very subtle. Jenny's inheritance was to be bold, brash, and take no shit. She wondered where she got her tendency to worry from. Likely her dad's side.

"Fuck," she muttered. *Probably* should talk to Ma and *wanting* to talk to Ma were two fracking different things. *Buck up, Buttercup,* her mind replied.

A flurry of images hit her head. It was Flex, shoving through her reverie with a sense of urgency. Something about the boulder up ahead.

The fox's mind message snapped Jenny out of her spiraling thoughts. She jerked up in her saddle, then raised an arm, fist closed in the signal for a halt that she backed up with her voice. Clinking and scuffling, the dragoons stopped on the path behind.

"Halt!" She pitched her voice to carry to the riders up ahead.

Tegan reigned up, sliding the machete into its saddle sheath seconds before per hand smoothly reached for a kpinga. It was almost one motion. A deadly dance.

"What's up?" Tegan asked, turning per horse toward Jenny. Per narrow face grew hard. Serious. But though the warrior was clearly ready to fight, per didn't reach for the helmet strapped to the saddle. Off the bikes, none of the Knights much liked to wear helms, but they were still handy when steel got ready to fly.

Dandelion skittered away from Tegan's mount, making room. The horse liked her space, which they needed to work on. It wasn't the best behavior for a mount that was pretty much always going to travel in a group. Jenny patted her neck. Dandelion bobbed her head, then bent to crop some grasses.

"Flex found something."

Psych had already swung off his mount and loped ahead to where the faery fox sniffed around the base of a moss-covered boulder.

Flex was tall at the shoulder, but the boulder towered over the patterned fur back of the fox. In shades of gray, brown, and mossy green, its broad base rose smoothly from the forest floor. Gangly Psych was a head or so shorter than the rounded peak of the majestic stone. He circled the boulder, one hand lightly tracing the moss, the other held out ahead of him, seeking information with what he called his "scout senses."

She looked back over her shoulder toward the big blue halbtroll. The disgruntled look had left his face, leaving his broad brow furrowed with concern.

"Bocan?"

His head snapped her way. She quirked an eyebrow. With a quick nod, he closed his eyes. Jenny knew he was communicating with the boulder, just the way she'd asked-without-asking.

Because you're the current leader of the Steel Clan, a voice in the back of her mind whispered.

Because every fucking Knight knows their fucking job, she spat back at herself, training her eyes toward Flex and Psych again. The scout waved a skinny arm, beckoning the rest of the riders forward.

She and Tegan walked their mounts forward. "What is it?"

"It's some bad."

Tegan and Jenny both swung off their horses and stepped carefully through the tangle of green. Flex stared at Jenny with big, black eyes, then blinked.

Psych's tattooed index finger pointed to a spot on the boulder down low to the ground. The area was clear of moss, and deep scratches marred the surface, edges worn with age.

It was an emblem. Three leaves and a sundered triangle.

"Well, shit," Tegan said, then turned to Psych. "How long do you think it's been there?"

He reached toward the boulder, but curled his fingers into a fist before touching it. Jenny knew he'd been about to trace the carving and thought the better of it.

"By the wear on it, looks old. Fifteen years? Ten?"

New Era, then.

Tegan gave a low whistle and Bocan crunched forward as the other Knights talked among themselves or sat tall on their mounts, waiting. That was the thing about being a Knight: there was a lot of waiting to be done between bouts of patrolling, going on scrap runs, and bashing heads.

"Stone has traces of magic." Bocan scratched his bald dome. "And not its own. Not rock."

Tegan rolled per eyes, impatient with the litany. "What kind of magic?"

"Elf. Which I'd expect. But not the kind we're used to. Tastes...rotten. Like fruit left out to spoil. Think we should head back? Bring Peridot and Damson up to check it out?"

Jenny felt uneasy, as if there was more still ahead. She sniffed the air, but neither smelled nor tasted the rotting fruit smell the survivor and Bocan spoke of. She looked at Flex, and sent a questioning thought her way. The fox just yawned. Bastard was no help at all.

"Jenny?" Psych said. "What do you want to do?"

She turned to Bocan. "You're sure we should turn back? We were charged to gather information, and this doesn't seem like much."

The sumac-red leather creaked and stretched as he shrugged. "Don't see what good pushing on will do. Need more intel from the mages, I think. I keep sniffing for magic or something, and don't get much more than what I said. This seems like a wasted scouting trip, to me."

"Tegan? Psych?"

They both shrugged and nodded.

Jenny raised her voice to carry further. "Anyone else have an opinion? Forge ahead, or head back to get the elves?"

"Head back," said a couple of voices. Jenny didn't blame them. This sort of scouting was worse than boring, with no guarantee of finding anything at all. The Knights would rather be home in their beds or patrolling the edges of their property, making sure the warlords were staying put. That was shit they understood.

Bocan nodded and turned his horse. The other Knights followed suit, and began picking their way back down. Toward home.

Jenny mounted her horse, but found she could not move. It felt as if she was rooted to Dandelion's saddle, nose facing up the mountain. Dandelion huffed and jerked her head, clearly annoyed to not be following the others.

Tegan gave her a look, but remained silent. Waiting.

What a fracking situation this was. The one person without magic was the only one of the cohort who felt they should forge on.

That bugged the shit out of Jenny, but she shoved down the pinging warning in her gut. She would not gainsay consensus. Not when she couldn't explain why.

"Coming?" Psych asked.

Jenny wouldn't go against her comrades, who had decided to bring the news of the old mark home and get some magical back up from the elves, but she also could not force her hands to turn Dandelion back around.

She might not have magic, but the intuition in her gut spoke loud and true.

Everything inside her said to forge on.

She looked into Psych's pale, questioning eyes. "No. I'm not."

CHAPTER 13

QUEEN SILVERHAIR

Nothing would give her succor. Nothing would ease the pounding beneath her breast.

Queen Silverhair paced the smooth, hewn-stone floors, her pine-needle-green silks swirling about slender ankles. Sumptuous silver hair flowed in elaborate plaits down her back; Dark Elf–forged jewelry sparkled at her ears and chimed around her wrists.

She knew all of this, because each time she passed the grand mirror in the corner of the room, she glanced at her reflection.

She could not help but look and who else could, really? Elven royalty was never anything but beautiful.

Silverhair swung back toward the sniveling coward hunched in the tapestry-covered chair that she circled and paced around. Her servants had set the chair in the very center of the room, fully exposed. No pleasant vista of apple and cherry trees to gaze upon through the sparkling windows. No cozy corner near the fire for the man who was supposed to be her pet alchemist. Her scientist. Her magician.

No.

The elf—with his pale green hair, narrow nose, and goldenrod-stained fingertips— would be placed where he belonged, in the center of an open field, awaiting the falcon's strike.

"My daughter is no better. And yet, you refuse to do what is necessary?"

She heard the rasp of hair upon Carondel's chin as his quavering hand scraped across it, again. She heard the swallow of a dry tongue in a dry mouth, attempting to squeeze moisture down a bone-dry throat.

She whirled again, braids and silks flying, and snapped a strong, delicate finger toward his face.

He flinched.

She smiled.

"Kill the next human that passes through the portal, if necessary."

"But Majesty...that...that did not work!"

The harvest of the town had worked at first, the power of the concentrated souls drawing Elzabetta's wayward souls back into alignment. For the first time in far too long, the Queen had dared to hope. Dared to hope that her daughter would be returned to her in her full, beautiful glory. Dared to hope that her daughter would take up her rightful place upon the Silver Throne.

Dared to hope that things would return to the way. They. Fucking. Were.

Before the fucking humans had ruined everything. Poisoned every. Single. Thing. Sent the realms into disarray. Fractured the nine worlds with their stupidity, greed, and billowing, stinking bursts of fire.

This was worse than the First Sundering, when the magical worlds had first retreated from the humans. At least then, the Elven realms had been safe from human interference. But this last? The Reckoning? That had wreaked havoc on them all.

And now her daughter was slowly dying, soul leeching away toward the Great Nothing.

"Just do it."

Humans would pay for what they had done to her daughter.

They would pay for what they had done to the worlds.

She swept out of the room, leaving the magician behind.

Entering her bedroom chamber, Silverhair placed her beautiful face into her pale and delicate hands.

She wept for all that she was losing. All that she had lost.

CHAPTER 14
ANANDITA

It was late afternoon, and well into round three of the day's training exercises. Anandita had worked during round two, leaving things to Swan, but she was back at the edge of the field now, working with five archers as Swan attended to her own business.

This crew wasn't bad. Some of them might even be able to take out a deer for dinner if pressed. And in a lineup of twenty or thirty others, they could climb the gates and defend the town.

She hoped.

She also hoped it wouldn't come to that. While the self-styled warlords mostly kept themselves further south, you never knew when trouble would come knocking. And depending on the season, and how the growth cycles had been, the township might also have mountain lions, wolves, or hogs to deal with.

"Chin steady, Stacy! And regulate your breathing." The blond weaver gave a short nod to show she'd heard Anandita, but kept serious eyes on the target. The young woman settled into herself, exhaled, and, with a twang, released. The arrow sped through the autumn air, thunking into one of the middle rings of the painted hemp canvas. She repeated the action, one arrow every three seconds, until her quiver was spent.

"Good!" Anandita said. "You'll be down to an arrow per second soon enough, if you keep that up!" The young woman's pockmarked face shone with satisfaction at the praise. "Jairo, you're next."

A young, very talented man just out of his apprenticeship with his parents, Jairo was a third-generation potter. His great grandparents had brought their craft north from Guatemala some time long before the Reckoning.

He was sweet on Tokki, and the two were of an age to do something about it. Speaking of...Anandita hoped Tokki was doing all right without her. She'd left her apprentice to labeling bottles, figuring her penmanship needed some work. It was an easy task, but you never knew if something would come up.

Tokki would know to come fetch Anandita if it was serious. She returned her attention to Jairo, whose thick black hair shone in the sun. He was a well-built, stocky young man. Where slender Stacy needed to increase her steadiness and strength, Jairo needed work on flexibility.

She heard a shout behind her, along with the smack of boots, running on hard-packed earth. Anandita called a halt to the the archers and spun her chair around.

Two of the engineers walked quickly down the hill, following Hypatia. Anandita's son seemed to be turning into the message runner of Go No More. Poor thing must always be in the right place at the right time to be saddled with that duty. First the glassworks disaster a few months before, and now this.

Hypatia scuffed up dust as he ran, followed by grizzled old Gears limping next to Yolanda. Both engineers had hemp aprons over their work clothes and boots, with heavy leather gloves tucked into the ties at their waists. They waved kerchiefs in front of their faces to clear dust from the air as they walked.

At least their appearance explained why Hypatia was playing messenger again. He'd been hoping to apprentice with the engineers or the fine machinists and often spent time after morning school fetching and carrying for them. That's what you got when you named your only child after a famous scientist and scholar from times that were ancient even Pre-Reckoning. He decided to become an engineer. Or a glassmaker. Or a carpenter. He was currently supposed to study with the engineers, but...

At his birth, Anandita had thought she'd birthed a girl who might follow in her footsteps as an herbalist. Neither wish had ended up being true, and Anandita was just fine with how Hypatia was turning out.

He was a good, strong, intelligent boy. She couldn't wish for more, really. But she didn't like seeing the concerned look on his slightly grubby face.

An emergency at the waterworks was bad. Too many operations in the township depended on hydro-electricity, including her experimental greenhouses, not to mention lights at night, pumps, and field irrigation.

Hypatia ran directly her way, panting.

"Mom! Call the council together! Trouble at the waterworks. Looks like sabotage."

Shit.

"Thank you, beta."

Before she could give him further instruction, her son was already headed off. The engineers walked toward her now, clearly intent on lodging a report with the first council member they saw.

Anandita turned to Jairo, who carefully pulled the arrows from the hay bale targets, dark hair shining in the sun, and was piling them up neatly, while Stacy checked the fletchings and tips.

"Jairo, can you gather the rest of the council? And..." Anandita tapped her lips. "Ask them to convene at the meeting house in half an hour?"

That should give her enough time for this initial briefing.

"Stacy? Will you ask Case and the other Knights to stop training and come over here?" She'd seen Case glancing over, and was actually surprised he hadn't called a stop yet. Must've been waiting to see what was up.

Anandita breathed a sigh of relief that only half of the Knights had headed out on the reconnaissance mission after the magicians had come by this morning.

She hoped the remaining Knights would be enough to deal with whatever news the two scowling engineers were bringing. And she couldn't help but wish strapping, brooding Jenny was around to help deal with it.

"What happened?" Anandita asked when they were within easy speaking range.

"Sabotage." Yolanda's expression was grim, which meant whatever had been done was major. She and Gears were both grimy; clear that they'd been at work with the mechanics trying to fix the problem.

Anandita grew very still inside, every scrap of her herbalist's and healer's training kicking in.

"Who?"

Yolanda shrugged. "Can't imagine it was anyone around here. I mean, why would they?"

Even though life in an anarchist commune wasn't all bread and Oregon roses, she was right.

"There were two sets of horse tracks in the mud around the waterworks." Gears interjected. "Gotta assume it's out-of-towners."

Which could mean anyone within riding distance. There was occasional trouble with the warlords down near Salem. Maybe they'd decided to escalate. Or who knew? Maybe the enclave out at Cannon Beach had decided they didn't like the latest trade deal.

"Well damn. Could be anyone. Go clean up. Meet me at the council house as soon as you can."

They nodded, then strode off, backs stiff with anger, stride a little tired.

Anandita didn't blame them. She felt angry and tired herself.

Stacy came up beside her.

"You know," Anandita said, "We live our lives, try to keep the township going the way the founders wanted it. We try to honor the First Nations. And to live with equality and justice among ourselves. But some earth-frackers always want something different, don't they? Some people just need to have power over others or they don't feel right."

Stacy didn't reply. Both women just stared at the receding backs of the engineers for awhile. Finally, Stacy cleared her throat.

"Shall I take the practice bows and arrows back to the armory? Since we're done today?"

Anandita looked up at Stacy, blinking. The young woman's hair was a golden nimbus, reflecting the sun.

"Thank you. Yes. I've got to check in with Tokki."

And then there was a long council meeting ahead. She hoped Porrac and Jamie had something good cooking at the public house, with some chicken or fish for protein. Anandita and Hypatia were mostly vegetarian, but not strict about it and she had a feeling she wouldn't be home in time for dinner.

None of the council heads would.

Her healing magic pricked at her fingertips, seeking something to do. She breathed deeply, turning her awareness inward. Her magic flared, hot and wild, ready to move before death came.

Because more death was coming.

Whether this sabotage was connected or not, she couldn't tell. She hoped it was just another random act, part of living near to people who didn't hold the values that kept Go No More strong.

Yes. She hoped it was just that. And not a larger conspiracy to wreck everything they worked so hard for.

"Peace is hard won," she said, opening her eyes. "Every damn time."

She turned her chair toward Tokki and her cottage, shoving at the wheels, wishing with all her might that she could keep Hypatia, Tokki, and all the other youth of Go No More safe.

But such was life. A battle for breath. A battle for sustenance. Creature against creature. The battles of too much rain or too little sun.

All she could do was try to make life better for all those who crossed her path.

CHAPTER 15
KARAKTILLA

Purple haunches resting on a brightly colored rug, Karaktilla gazed into the crystal sphere, bowl of tea cold and forgotten to one side.

As the drake watched the changing shapes and shadows, Karaktilla recalled the centuries when the human world itself had been a shadow through the mists. When most humans thought the world of drakes was one of legends. Fancies. Delusion.

Oh, some humans had seen them. Ridden on the mighty, scaled backs of the drakes, or faced them in highly unequal combat.

And then there were the times in history when the mists had parted, and the worlds of full magic and human had merged. These times never lasted long.

Karaktilla felt that this time was different. That this time, the gates had altered, if not forever, then at least for a very, very long time.

And Karaktilla needed the humans to understand what was at stake in this time. That things were not all

peaceful valleys, the planting of crops, and the enjoyment of the autumn warmth before the snows came.
The shifting of the worlds meant something more.

And what Silverhair was up to?

It was not any good that Karaktilla could see.

JENNY

Tegan rolled per shoulders. "You think we should head on? No one felt any magic like in the village, despite the mages thinking something's out here. That's why we consensed to turn back. Seriously, if anyone felt that kind of bad magic, symbol or not, we'd be heading north again. Psych?"

Psych shook his head, tattooed face thoughtful. "Nothing. Not for klicks. And Bocan didn't feel anything either, which I trust even more than my senses."

Irritation tightened Jenny's mouth. She tugged on a braid and looked into the thick green tangle of forest. Damn her lack of magic. A jay screeched overhead. "This isn't about the Knights. This is about me."

She looked her comrades dead in the eyes. "I need to go ahead."

Magic or not, her gut rarely lied.

The faery fox barked. Having already started down

the hill, the other Knights stopped. Jenny saw Bocan dismount and start moving up the hill on foot.

"What the fracking earth is going on, you pig fuckers?" he rumbled, once within easy earshot.

"Jenny's having second thoughts."

Bocan huffed as Jenny held up a hand.

"No. I'm not." She tugged the braid harder, trying to get her thoughts in some sort of order. "I can't....the Knights still need to head back to Go No More. Take the message back. Besides, Tegan's right, none of you felt the magic here, so surely this isn't the correct decision. Right?"

Her comrades just stared. Waiting. She felt their annoyance, but was grateful that Knights were also trained to respect gut feelings. And Jenny's gut was telling her what exactly?

She closed her eyes. Slowed her breathing down. Dropped into her still center. The place she fought from. The place she listened from. Doing the thing that every single apprentice learned their first six months in.

::What are you telling me?:: Jenny didn't really have the hang of mind speech, either, but she practiced "thinking out loud," as her mother, Danika, called it. A series of images flashed through her mind. Dense forest. A waterfall. A series of caves. And Flex, looking back over black and red swirled shoulder, waiting for her to follow.

Jenny opened her eyes to see the faery fox skirting the horses, trotting through a stand of ferns. Heading her direction. The fox flashed something toward

Jenny's mind that she could only read as a sense of "it's about time."

"I need to head on. Flex and I need to head on. But I think the rest of you need to return to the township. That feels important, too."

"No way are we letting you head off on your own, you fool." Tegan's mouth pinched in annoyance. Per right hand clenched, as though the Knight was itching to grab one of per elaborate throwing blades.

"No. Jenny's right, we all can't go. So how do we split up?" Bocan asked.

Jenny's shoulders sagged in relief. This was going to be easier than she had feared. No one spoke.

Someone shouted from further down the hill. "What the fuck's going on? Are we conferring again? I thought we had consensus!"

Bocan turned and waved an arm.

"You all have to decide," Jenny said. "All I know is what I have to do."

"Tegan and I should go with Jenny," Psych finally said. "Bocan, you're a strong voice with the Knights, right? And Case is still down there. They trust you both, even the new ones. You should go."

"I hate to...." the halbtroll began.

"No," Tegan interjected. "Psych is right. I should go. But Psych, are you sure? You're the one who found the symbol. You and the fox. Shouldn't you be the one to relay the information?"

Psych screwed up his blue-tattooed face, clearly warring inside. "Shit. Maybe you're right. But I don't want to leave you without a scout, and Litha isn't here.

That feels bad. And like, bad intuition and bad magic bad, plus, you're asking me to not do my job! Can't someone else tell them about the fracking elf symbol? Bocan?"

The halbtroll crossed his arms over his chest, leather creaking as it strained across his shoulders. If his muscles didn't stop growing, he would need to be fitted for a new jacket again.

Bocan nodded. "I can. The Knights won't like it, but they won't like you being without proper backup, either. Why don't you all head off and I'll let them know what has been decided."

"But..." Jenny felt grateful that there might be a reprieve from yet another mountainside meeting, but it also felt irresponsible to let someone else take on the unpleasant duty.

Bocan held up a hand, palm out. "Stop. I have no patience to litigate this decision when we all know what the outcome will be. The Knights will be with you. We all trust your gut, Jenny."

The unspoken words hanging in the balsam-scented air were clear. The Knights trusted Jenny, whether or not she trusted herself.

He looked back up the mountain. "Besides, I feel the drakes have something to tell us, no matter what others may think. According to what Recoana says, we're likely close. Perhaps your gut leads you there."

"But there's no magic..."

Bocan shook his smooth head.

"Magic is as inexact as any other science. Sometimes we get messages that are not clear. We need to read other signs, in other ways. Besides, I think you are correct. It's you that needs to go on. This isn't about the bad magic—or not only that." His blue lips pursed, as if tasting something. "This has something to do with you. With your magic."

"But I don't have..."

He trained his black eyes on her, as if he could drill his meaning into Jenny's skull. Whatever it was, she wasn't getting it, but she stopped her protestation all the same.

"Fine. We'll go."

White-tipped tail flashing through green and brown vegetation, Flex padded up the mountainside ahead, too impatient to wait on the humans anymore.

Clearly, it had been decided.

Jenny held out a hand to Bocan, who gripped her arm with his own. His hand stretched all the way to her elbow, while hers only reached mid-forearm. But it was a warrior's grip nonetheless.

"Thanks, pig fucker," she said.

"You're welcome, asshole," he replied. "Ride for Go No More."

Jenny raised a fist in response, clicked at Dandelion, and turned the horse around. Tegan and Psych did the same.

It was up the mountain, and who in the fracked earth knew what they were heading toward?

CHAPTER 17
QUEEN SILVERHAIR

The whole realm was falling apart and her daughter hated her. Her daughter, whom Silverhair had risked everything for, could barely stand to be in her presence.

Her daughter. All that she had left of him.

Tollias. The beautiful. The noble. The brave. The only one who ever made her laugh.

Human stupidity had caused his death, as surely as if one of them had held an iron knife to his long, pale throat and spilled his silver blood onto the waiting earth.

They would pay, and pay again.

CHAPTER 18
TEGAN

Tegan's horse, Eshe, was not happy, and frankly, neither was Tegan. Per would always have her comrade's back, but Tegan would have rather been at home, smoking a spliff with per parents. A Knight's work was mostly on the road, but that didn't mean a person didn't long for home.

Rain fell at a steady pace, sending muddy rivulets down the mountainside. Per leathers were warm enough, at least, and per'd donned the waxed, wool-lined canvas hood that extended down in triangular points to cover the shoulders. The hoods were part of the standard kit, permanently in the Knight's packs. Psych and Jenny both had their hoods on, too, dyed to match their sumac leathers, though the rain had turned everything a brownish cordovan.

The horses' hooves churned at the soft ground and the faery fox ran up ahead. The higher they went, the colder the air got. The forest itself was quiet, both the physical plants and creatures, and the spirit of the place. It was also getting late enough that they needed a place to camp, but the last time they stopped, they'd decided to push on, hoping to find a solid outcropping, or at least a big boulder to block the wind. If nothing appeared, Tegan would insist on a halt, despite whatever was tugging at Jenny's gut. They could head into the thick trees and sling up the oiled hemp tarp in one of Psych's saddlebags.

Per still didn't sense any of the magic they'd felt in the forsaken village, which was a relief. There was something unfamiliar dancing around the edges of per awareness though. Maybe that's what Flex the fox was following. And Jenny, too, though she insisted she had no magic.

The Knight's sixth sense was so strong, Tegan didn't understand why it even mattered. But they all had their shit to shovel, didn't they?

The rain increased, whipping the branches overhead. Wind tugged at per hood and sent a spray of water directly into Tegan's face. Nice. Tegan was fucking ready to be out of this weather, and in the moment, regretted not forcing Jenny back home with the rest of the Knights.

Eshe's dark brown head was down. The horse walked stolidly, one hoof in front of the other. Dispirited, she'd given up on giving Tegan the stink eye an hour ago. There was a flash in the distance, and thunder rumbled. Well, damn. Electrical storms were in these parts, and this time of year? Beneath the layers of wet leather, hemp, and wool, Tegan felt a spot of warmth. The amulet. Per sniffed the air. Threaded through the scents of Douglas fir, kicked-up earth, and hemlock spruce was something dry and musky.

And it felt like magic. Finally. It was a magic Tegan hadn't encountered before. It felt...not menacing, but interested, which was strange, considering it was clearly manipulating this storm.

Tegan nudged Eshe toward Jenny's mount and shouted over the clamor of the storm, "We have to stop! Something isn't right!"

"What?" Jenny's white face was pinched with the cold. "You want to stop?"

Tegan shook per head. "This storm. Something isn't right!"

Psych and his mount stopped just ahead, turning in his saddle, peering from beneath his hood through the dark gray torrent. Jenny and Tegan encouraged the miserable horses his way.

The scout looked petrified, and not just from cold.

"Magic," he said.

Jenny cursed.

"What do you feel?" Tegan asked.

He closed his eyes. Droplets ran down the whorls of blue tattoos covering his slender face. "Old. Smells like a nest of snakes. Feels huge. And determined. Damn. I really wish Bocan was here."

"Does it feel dangerous?" Jenny asked. Dandelion picked up her hooves. Nervous. Must be sensing Jenny's tension. The Knight was never one to show fear, but animals picked up what most humans would not.

Psych shrugged. His leathers had turned almost as dark as the forest.

Almost as dark as the sky had turned. They had to get out of this fracking storm.

"We should head for the trees!" Tegan shouted just as a flash of lightning struck the top of an ancient fir.

Boom! The sky cracked overhead, the earth shook, the horses whinnied and shied. Ears ringing from the thunder, Tegan clamped per thighs around Eshe's sides and pulled firmly on the reins. Reaching out one gloved hand, Tegan stroked the roan horse's neck, trying to gentle her. Maybe heading for the trees was a really bad idea.

"Cave!" Psych shouted.

"Where?" Jenny bellowed back.

Another lightning flash, this one further east, and Tegan saw it. A dark opening fifty paces into the thicket of trees. The lightning-struck tree was another fifty paces beyond. Too close for comfort.

At least the pounding rain was finally on their side. At the top of the tree, sparking flames sputtered, struggling to get enough air to fully catch. Tegan could only hope the storm would extinguish the fire completely. But there was an equal chance that embers would smolder deep inside the blasted trunk, and burn all night. If they stayed in that cave, they ran the risk of being in the middle of a raging forest fire by morning.

If the cursed storm ever passed.

"I don't like it!" Jenny shouted.

Tegan didn't like it either. But now was not the time to argue the finer points of shelter.

What was the safest option? A rock cave, too close to a possibly burning tree? Or a tarp strung up in a forest, open to the wild weather, not knowing if another wave of storms would bring more lightning their way? The amulet burned like a spark against Tegan's chest. Was the magic in the storm? Or was it coming from somewhere else?

"What do you think?"

Jenny looked at Tegan, fear flashed in her eyes like lightning, there and gone.

Tegan waited, ears ringing, buffeted by wind and rain, holding steady on Eshe's sturdy back, trying to convey to the horse that she was safe. Or as safe as any creature could be given the circumstances. They needed to move, but to move in the wrong direction would be deadly.

"Psych is right. Cave."

Psych sagged with relief. Tegan turned Eshe as Jenny and Dandelion took the lead.

Behind them, lightning flashed again, lighting up the sky, illuminating the towering trees. They waved and reached like marching giants, branch smacking branch, needles flying though the air. As thunder rumbled, a heavy branch cracked overhead. Tegan nudged Eshe with the heels of per boots, moving the horse through the dense brush, just as the branch crashed through the canopy, hurtling to the ground.

Machete in gloved hand, Tegan followed per comrades, and hoped like fuck they were all going to be okay. The longer they were out in this storm, the more Tegan became convinced it was unnatural.

Per just hoped the big old nest-of-snakes magic wasn't in the cave.

And driving them there.

CHAPTER 19
BOCAN

Though not yet visible, the eastern gates of the township were less than a klick ahead. The road they were on curved sweetly through the vast cannabis fields, green and fragrant in the aftermath of the sudden storm they'd left behind them. Harvest time would be coming soon. The founders of Go No More had chosen a good place to stop when they'd fled the Portland disaster area just fifty years gone.

The Wasco had been suspicious at first, not that anyone could blame them, but had allowed the settlers a temporary stay. After three years, they'd signed a deed to the township for the use of the land, and settled on agreements for trade.

The open land was fertile, and protected by the dormant volcano just northeast, and a smaller, craggy peak just southwest. Directly south was the Clackamas River, which provided plenty of water, along with the township's electrical power. These days, the fishing was good, too, though that hadn't always been the case even two decades ago. Bocan wasn't sure if the half-divine nagas helped clean the water, or if the massive serpents lived in the Clackamas because the water was clean.

Bocan gave Bodie his head, and the Percheron picked up the pace. The other horses did, too, recognizing the oily, cannabis-tinged scent of home.

The rain had started when they were halfway down the mountain, but the small squad felt only the edges of it, hearing the roll of thunder and seeing dim flashes from farther up.

Which meant the other three Knights had caught the driving end of what sounded like a stone-breaking storm. Bocan hoped they were making out okay. If they weren't, there wasn't a fracked earth thing the Knights could do about it. Not right now. Tracking people in a violent storm when you weren't even certain they were in danger was something every Knight was trained to not do.

Not unless someone's sixth sense told them to, and so far, no one looked like they were in any hurry to turn around. Bocan's worries weren't coupled with any extra sense of danger, so he did his best to squash them and just enjoy the ride.

One of the cannabis workers paused and waved. Bocan recognized Tegan's mother, Inaya. He raised an arm and grinned. She scanned the riders, a slight frown creasing her dark face. Probably wondering where in the nine worlds her child was. Well, he'd check in with her later, and with Tegan's co-parents, too.

Inaya was one of the main forces behind the growing operation. Under the direction of Hakim L'Ouverture, her team was key to the success of the whole township. Not only did they grow enough hemp to make sturdy rope and canvas and clothing-grade fabric, under Inaya and Hakim's guidance, they grew the best buds for cannabinoid-based medicines. Once the Green Clan started working with Anandita and with Barry's bee-keeping team, the whole town grew even more prosperous. Everyone within trading distance either wanted Go No More's products, or wanted to consult on their operations.

Everyone except the warlords who only wanted to steal or gum up the works. The Knights had been in more than one skirmish with those pig fuckers. They were a dangerous distraction, wanting nothing more than to own the whole Willamette Valley down south. If they ever turned their full attention further north, the Steel Clan would have its hands full.

Autonomous townships were an insult to people like that, who believed that some folks belonged on top and others under heel.

"May an avalanche crush their homes," Bocan muttered. As beautiful as the day was, and as happy as Bodie was to be heading home, he simply couldn't shake his unsettled mood.

From a slight rise in the road, he saw the first township buildings soon enough, just beyond the tall wooden palisade that was both a demarcation of town borders and a fortification against raiders, animal and human alike.

The horses entered the township four abreast, clopping past the crescent moon clusters of small family homes with garden beds fanning out between them and the fir at town center.

A slight breeze brought the scents of rosemary and lavender, along with a hint of burning wood smell from the glassworks and the smithy. The soft clink of metal hitting metal rang across the circle, along with the thump and whir of the weavers' looms. Busy day in Go No More.

They were heading past the ring of garden plots when a call went up.

"The Knights!"

It was a lone child's voice at first, quickly joined by others. A dozen children streamed from the schoolhouse opposite the main circle from the meeting house. Bocan and the others grinned at first. It was always good to be home.

But then he caught the gaze of dark-haired Winney, dressed in a green tunic and dark brown pants, standing in the doorway. The schoolteacher was even paler than usual, and, wiping chalk-covered fingers on a kerchief, walked quickly toward him.

"Where's Tegan?" she asked. Winney was Tegan's co-mother and had a right to be concerned. "And why are you back so early? Where's Jenny?"

Bocan waved the other riders on and dismounted. The horses clopped past toward the stables, chased by the children. Winney would have a chore getting them back to lessons now.

Winney wrapped her arms around her own torso, bracing for news.

"Peace, Winney. Tegan was fine when we left per. Jenny and Psych, too. Jenny just felt a tug onward while the rest of the dragoons had information we wanted to get back to town."

She let out a sigh of relief and released her hold on herself, some of the color coming back, ghost-white skin regaining some of its peach.

"Well, things are not good here. The rest of your clan will be glad you've returned."

"What has happened?"

Winney shook her head. "Trouble at the water-works. I'd best let the engineers explain themselves. Or talk with Case. He'll be sore that Psych isn't with you, though, I can tell you that much."

"Why?" He stared down at the human woman.

"Because, they'll want their best trackers on the job."

"Warlords?"

"Who else would it be? But so far, they've got no proof."

"Fuck a pig," Bocan said, looking out across the town center. "Why don't those assholes mind themselves?"

"If you read history—human or magical—you'd know the answer, comrade."

He turned back to the teacher, who looked at him, expectation in her eyes.

"You gonna tell me? Or make me look it up like one of the children?"

"Because, no matter how good life is, some assholes always think they deserve more than their fair share."

Winney, as always, spoke the simple truth.

CHAPTER 20
ANANDITA

Anandita and Tokki were in the herb garden in front of the cottage and workshop. The apprentice was on her knees in the middle of one of the quarters of the big circle of garden. Anandita sat in her chair, basket in her lap, the scents of coriander, lemongrass, brahmi, tulsi, thyme, and lavender wreathing her head.

The scents should have helped to calm her, but they were having a hard time doing their job.

It didn't matter. She and Tokki needed more herbs for another round of distillation, and had to get other herbs and flowers drying before the hard rains of winter came. Or worse, a freeze and snow. What helped the plants grow so well here could also ruin things, as the barley growers knew all too well. Waterlogged barley rotting in the fields wasn't even much good for whiskey if left too long.

Anandita rarely drank alcohol, but sometimes a

small amount helped her think. She sure could have sipped at a whiskey right about now.

But the plants would not wait, so despite everything else on her plate, Anandita worked. The council meetings had been long, and they still didn't know what the right course of action was. She wished half the dragoons hadn't hared off now, despite what the magicians had seen.

At least the yakshini seemed happy. The herbs and flowers bobbed their heads in the sunshine, glossy and vibrant with life. Happy plants housed happy spirits.

"Why didn't they see something useful, like the fact that our waterworks were going to be sabotaged?" The herbs she sorted and cleaned had no answer. Not that she expected one.

"Did you need something?" Tokki raised her head. The teen's dark, fuzzy curls framed her brown face, which was shaded by a hemp hat but Anandita didn't need to see her expression to know her apprentice thought she was strange.

"No. Just thinking out loud."

Tokki shrugged and bent back to work.

A magical threat was serious, she knew that, but it was not the immediate threat that a broken waterworks offered. They needed a functional mill. They could do without electricity for a while, it was true, but too many of their light industries had come to rely on that, too.

"Ancestors help us," she muttered, sorting the herbs Tokki brought her and tying them into bundles. Luckily, her fingers knew what to do, so her mind could wander to the problem at hand. Maybe that was a thing she could do. Do puja at her shrine to the founders of Go No More. The ones who knew where to stop on the trail and prepare the ground for what was yet to come. The ones who knew how to survive when they were half dead from fear and walking until their shoes wore out. The ones that believed they would survive, even when so many others were dead, buried in the rubble of gasping cities, poisoned by tainted water, or killed in the battle for scarce stores of food.

They hadn't needed more than the Clackamas River, a place to scratch in the earth, and some felled trees to build shelter.

Anandita was grateful to the engineers, but technically, Go No More didn't really need the waterworks in order to survive. They were stronger for it, sure, and it made it easier to grow the large fields which provided goods to eat, weave, smoke and trade. The loss of the waterworks meant they would need to scale back, but it didn't spell the end of anything.

This was a blow the town could eventually recover from, no matter what the ones who wrecked the pumps and the machines intended. Go No More was an autonomous township, and the clans within it were autonomous, too. This meant they were nimble and could adjust should circumstances make it necessary.

Regardless, this needed to be dealt with. And to make sure nothing worse happened, they needed more safeguards in their little utopia. Because when bad magic and bad action arrived together?

It foretold something worse coming.

Anandita just hoped that, just as she and Tokki worked toward the coming winter, the township had time to prepare.

Tokki stood and turned toward the center of the town. "Horses."

Sure enough, horses and riders were heading through the town. Anandita had grown so lost in her thoughts she hadn't heard their approach. She scanned the Knights. There was no bright banner of red hair.

No Jenny.

Strangely, her heart sank a little. Then she realized there was no Tegan, Psych, or Bocan, either.

"Tokki, would you go down and see what's up? That's still not the remainder of the clan."

Tokki dropped her pruning shears and gloves, dusted some of the dark earth from the knees of her canvas pants, and ran off after the horses, dark hair puffed out like a dandelion clock around her head.

Anandita shaded her eyes with one hand, watching the beasts straining to get back to the stable yard where there would be water and food for them in short order. Already, two of the Steel Clan apprentices were running out to help with the horses as the Knights dismounted.

Case stalked over to confer. There was movement to Anandita's left. Heading past the meeting hall was blue-skinned Bocan on his Percheron. The draft horse looked as happy to be back in Go No More as the other, smaller horses, but the halbtroll looked angry and concerned.

Tokki reached the stables just as Bocan

dismounted. The apprentice wove her way toward Case, which was good. Smart girl. She knew that Case had been left in nominal charge, and that he would check in with Bocan.

Anandita realized that her hands were gripping and releasing themselves in her lap, and her shoulders were like rocks. She couldn't wait for Tokki to come back anymore. Couldn't sit passively, waiting on a report. Anandita needed action. Needed to feel as if she was doing something to help the township, instead of biding her time, waiting for something worse to come. Something they couldn't know how to prepare for.

Taking the basket from her lap, she set it down beside her chair, wiped off her hands, and slipped on the fingerless gloves that helped her manage the chair wheels without messing up her hands.

She rolled down the central pathway of her gardens, wheels brushing mint and rosemary as she went.

If Bocan had information, better that the council knew it as soon as possible. Better that Anandita knew, so she could figure out what needed to happen next.

And the sabotage of the waterworks, the bad magic, and whatever had kept Jenny and Tegan split from the rest of the Knights? She just hoped they weren't all intertwined.

Because on their own, each situation left Anandita's stomach cold.

CHAPTER 21
JENNY

The cave fit them and their horses well enough to ride out the worst of the storm. Flex had immediately curled up to take a nap. Traveling this far afield, the faery fox often rode pillion on the small leather mat behind Jenny's saddle. She hadn't this time, though Jenny had no idea why.

The thunder and lightning rolled further and further away, and when Psych stood to pee at the cave entrance half an hour before, he'd declared the fire in the tree to be out.

Jenny just hoped that remained true. She leaned against Dandelion's saddle next to the three horses, who sat, legs folded, breath condensing on the dark gray of the cave walls. Soft hemp cloth in hand, she absently cleaned her short sword, staring out at the forest and the steadily falling rain. You never knew what would happen with banked embers, but with the continued rain, things would likely be okay. If lightning had struck during the height of summer, there could have been real trouble.

"Remind me to get some goats up here to clear the undergrowth this summer," she said.

Tegan grunted around a mouthful of jerky.

"Does it smell strange in here?" Psych asked. After they'd done their best to dry off the horses and get them settled, the young Knight had proceeded to do what he did best. Scout. He'd poked around the cave as Jenny and Tegan had dried off the leather saddles and themselves as best they could. Looking for what, Jenny couldn't imagine. But she'd learned to trust that he had good instincts and knew his job.

"Of course it smells strange," Tegan said, having finally swallowed the tough venison down. "First of all, there's whatever magic is in the area. That probably stinks. Second, it's a fracking cave. What did you expect? A bed of roses?"

He waved an impatient hand. "You know what I mean. It should smell of rock, earth, and damp. Maybe wolf or bear. But it doesn't. It smells like…"

"Reptile," Jenny said. She sniffed the air again, and sure enough, there was that strange, dried-paper scent she sometimes got during paper-making season, or when she visited the schoolhouse, to look at some of the old PR histories Winney kept stored in a series of locked, glass-fronted shelves.

"No shit?" Tegan was on per feet now, pacing the cave behind Psych, clearly trying to see or sense whatever it was he had picked up on. "Nagas?"

"Not this far from running water, unless there's an underground stream I haven't found," Psych replied.

As if something had heard them, a slow rumble filled the cave, vibrating the stone beneath Jenny's ass. She leapt to her feet, dropping the cloth, as if she could attack the earthquake, or the thunder, or whatever the fracking earth was causing the solid structure to tremble. The horses snorted and started, clambering to their feet.

Softly, Jenny picked up her buckler, and Flex came to stand next to her. The fox's eyes were watchful, black nose working and whiskers quivering.

"What the fuck?" Tegan said.

And then Jenny heard it. They all did. The sound of something big moving toward them. The weird, papery scent increased. Jenny clenched her muscles, willing herself to not piss her leathers. She set her sword down just long enough to strap on her buckler, then picked it up again. That done, she slowed her breathing down and moved easily into defense posture, short sword at the ready.

She stared into the darkness at the back of the cave. Psych had declared it free of animals and other danger, and she believed him. So how the fuck something was moving toward them now, out of that dark hole, she couldn't fathom.

Tegan had a kpinga in one hand, and two others ready. Per left hand held a machete, and per dark eyes glinted dangerously.

Jenny felt Psych behind her. He was breathing hard.

"Psych?" She kept her voice low, though with as

much noise as was coming down the cavern, it was likely that whatever it was couldn't hear her. "You okay?"

A pause. "Yeah. Fine."

"Got your weapons?"

"Yes." That last word sounded steadier. Good. He was getting himself under control.

"What do you think it is?" Tegan asked, eyes trained into the darkness. "And I thought you said this place was empty!"

"I...I must've missed a tunnel. A bend in the darkness. I don't know!" Psych's breath was coming hard again, voice rising in panic.

"Psych. Calm the fuck down. Slow your breathing," Jenny said. "Find your center."

She heard him struggle to comply, breath rasping in his chest, but didn't have time to do more, because whatever it was was coming toward them, and the horses started to freak. She heard the clatter of hooves on stone, and a wild snorting and whinnying.

"Fuck! Psych! Get the horses! Take them just outside! Tether them to something!"

How could she have been so stupid? She should've had him do that right away. The last thing they needed were horses bolting out into the storm, getting lost in the forest. At least their bridles were still on. Should make it easier for Psych. She heard him struggling behind her, trying to calm the horses down, but didn't have time to spare a look.

The papery smell filled the cave, and had taken on an undertone of the worst of Anandita's healing herbs.

Valerian. Ashwaganda. Mugwort. All those bitter, nasty things the healer only trotted out when something was really wrong. Jenny swallowed down bile, and fought to keep from gagging.

The whole cave shook, then stopped.

Her knees almost buckled from the sudden stillness.

"Damn," Tegan swore.

Sound whispered from the darkness. Skin lightly rubbing skin. Fingers ruffling through pages. The fine hairs stood up on the back of Jenny's neck.

Out of the pool of darkness, a terrifyingly huge, triangular face appeared. It shimmered in the dim light, flashing from purple to brown to purple again, as if it was two colors at once, and couldn't decide which to show. There was just enough light in the cave to make out black eyes shuttering with a pale, nictating film, then opening wide again. Staring directly at her.

Jenny's leather trousers grew strangely warm. Damn it. She'd pissed herself.

Weird clacking and clicking noises filled the cave, and then words, as clear as day, filled Jenny's head.

::*You came.*::

Jenny had always thought Bocan's voice sounded like gravel tumbling down a hill. Well, this sounded like boulders scraping against earth. Inside her skull.

Then the meaning of the words penetrated.

"We...what?"

A long, sinuous neck—thick as the trunk of a three-year-old spruce—came into view, pushing that giant, terrifying wedge—a compilation of scales, horns, eyes, and teeth—toward the cave ceiling and bringing it forward, too close for Jenny's comfort. She fought the urge to duck.

What use was a short sword against a massive, scaled creature such as this?

::You came.:: Its breath was hot as a blacksmith's forge. Its mouth a giant wedge of sharp teeth, its meaty, black, arrow-shaped tongue flicking against the yellowed, clicking peaks. *::I called you, and you came. Did not Recoana send you here?::*

"What the actual fuck?" Tegan said.

The rumbling, scraping boulder sound filled the cavern, emanating from deep inside the purple chest.

The drake was laughing.

CHAPTER 22
BOCAN

It was beautiful up at the waterworks. The Clackamas sent up a fine mist of spray where it tumbled over rocks. Green ferns grew close to the ground, along with some sort of berry plants Bocan was sure he had eaten in a jam tart before, but could not name.

But he wasn't up here to admire the scenery in what should have been a relatively peaceful spot.

The engineers, machinists, and mechanics yelled instructions at apprentices who ferried tools and other equipment from person to person and loped across the hard-packed earth from the huge open door of the timber-framed workshop to the great metal machines at the river's edge.

The machines should have been rumbling and humming in counterpoint to the river's song. They were silent today. The only metal sounds were the clank of the wrench and the curses of the people working.

It wasn't good. Was not good at all. This close to harvest, a problem with the waterworks could mean the fields were not being properly irrigated. He doubted the recent rainfall was enough. For one thing, given reports from the townsfolk, Go No More had only gotten a couple hours of light rain. The plants preferred a steady drip.

"Should we push up the harvest?" Bocan asked.

Inaya shrugged, mouth pinched tight. She whipped a length of undyed hemp from the rear pocket of her canvas pants and tied her heavy locks back. Hair secure, the grower crouched down for a closer look at the shattered metal Gears was cursing over and then discarding in a pile.

The engineer's graying red beard and pale skin were both streaked with lubricant. Bocan was glad to not be that close to the whiff of slightly rancid hemp oil.

"I don't want to do that," Inaya finally replied, rising from her crouch. "Hakim wants to give the plants another week at least, and I agree. They should be okay without extra water for that length of time. We're already doing a second harvest of the buds, and should have enough that sacrificing the rest of the crop for hemp won't be too much hardship."

Bocan scratched his dome, glad the experts knew their jobs. He turned to Case and jerked his head. The short, ruddy-skinned Knight nodded, and turned toward the path that would take them back into town.

"Any idea who did this?" Bocan asked as they followed the path beneath the towering trees. Sun peeked through the branches. A jay screeched from an overhead branch.

Case looked grim, and Bocan could not blame him. The sabotage had happened on his watch, so to speak. The Knights patrolled in shifts, but sometimes got lazy and didn't switch things up enough. A regular patrol was ineffective and they all knew it.

But in times of prosperity and peace, it was easy to forget why they patrolled in the first place. Just because Go No More was a friendly place didn't mean the world outside was the same.

And the forests held more danger than boars and bears.

"There were hoofprints, which means riders, but that doesn't tell us much. They led to and from the west."

"Salem?"

"That's the obvious direction, but we've got no proof, and we likely won't have. Not unless some asshole is bragging about it over their beer."

And the warlords of Salem weren't stupid. Otherwise they wouldn't have lasted as long as they had.

Case took a swallow from his waterskin and continued. "Doesn't mean we couldn't go crush their skulls, just because. Those pig fuckers are always up to something, and I don't like how they treat their people."

Bocan laughed, but there was no joy in it.

He didn't like the way they treated their people either, and one of those people was Jimena. A small, tough woman with sparks in her brown eyes and a temper like a forest fire. If she were less dedicated to her craft, he would have tried to lure the mind and soul healer away by now. But she insisted the people around Salem needed her.

And if she were less dedicated, he wouldn't find her as attractive as he did. He sighed.

"Too bad the Steel Clan has a code of ethics."

"Yeah." Chase laughed. "And too bad if we didn't, the township would kick us the hell out, no matter how useful we are."

Except they weren't useful now, were they? The two Knights walked in silence for a few moments.

"We've got to vary the patrols again. How'd the training go while we were gone?"

Case kicked a small stone down the hill. "Pretty well. Some people grumbled about being taken from their work, but they know it's gotta happen. If the town council agrees on it, and the Clan councils buy in? Not much people can do. That's how the township works."

It was a good system, overall, and the people supported it. But being asked to take time off to practice what was considered to be someone else's job? That had to rankle. Oh, they all cross-trained to some extent. They had to, for the township's continued survival. But this sort of intensive battle training cost more time than that.

"Hey," Bocan said. "How about taking the horse and smithy apprentices out on some local scouting expeditions? It won't really be taking them from their work, just showing them different aspects of the job, eh?"

Case looked up at him, slowing down, then stopping. They were almost at the top edge of town, just above Anandita's garden. A hummingbird danced a pattern in the air above the fragrant herbs, then dove with a pop before zooming up again.

"That might work. Let's talk with Angel and Feldspar. It's worth a try, at least. But I've gotta tell you the truth here, Bocan."

The halbtroll just waited, gazing out over the town. He loved the way the September sun reflected off the fir-shingled roofs. He loved seeing the flourishing gardens, and the people, free to simply live. To go about their business.

He only wished his Da was still here to see it all, too. But he understood the grief that drove the older troll back into the caves.

"I think we're not gonna find these pig fuckers. I think we're just gonna keep going, the way we have been, and double down on patrols for awhile. Maybe get the smiths and all to help, like you just said."

"And we need to make sure the township supports that. This sabotage is serious business. The townsfolk know it. If we didn't have so many systems in place and didn't know how to act autonomously, everything could be at risk."

That was the beauty of systems that didn't work top down. They were nimble. They could always adapt. The founders had made sure of that, and all these years later, every time someone wanted to simplify things, or let one person be in charge for too long, they were corrected. Immediately.

It was one reason Bocan stayed. Da's stories had been filled with disgust at the very thought of Underhill hierarchy. It always grated on the trolls, but they went along because that was how things were.

Well, out here, Da reminded him, that was not how things had to be. There wasn't royalty. The elves could learn something from the magical beings native to this land, who, sure, fought and skirmished at times, according to the stories, but didn't lord it over anyone.

Bocan agreed. This way was better. Like the Steel Clan code said, "Seek no kings."

He hoped they didn't have to follow the rest of the code, and strike some pig fuckers down. As much of a Knight as he was, he far preferred peace and prosperity to war.

CHAPTER 23

JENNY

J enny and Tegan exchanged looks. What in the fracked and devastated earth? Tegan shifted on per feet, and Jenny realized she had, too. Still in defensive posture, buckler up and short sword ready, but...no longer sure that anything at all was going to attack.

A laughing drake was not what she was expecting.

Finally, the rumbling stopped.

The dragon opened that terrifying mouth again. Hot, pungent breath caressed her cheeks and ruffled the edges of her braids. If Jenny hadn't already pissed herself, she would have done it again. Fucking fuck.

But there was no roaring. No flames. Did this drake even spew fire? Or was that simply another tale?

The drake spoke, at least that's what Jenny thought the rumbling, clicking, clattering noises were. These were quickly followed by more words inside her head.

::Tell the other human to come in from the storm. He

will find iron rings embedded in the cave walls near the entrance. The horses can be tethered there.::

"I'll go," Tegan said, before Jenny had the chance to. Great. Now Jenny was alone with the enormous beast. Flex sneaked up beside her, sniffed at Jenny, and then actually slunk on her belly across the stone, heading for one of the large, silver-taloned feet.

Halfway there, Flex stopped and raised her head. The drake looked down, cocking one eye toward the faery fox. Jenny could tell they were communicating, just as Flex and Jenny did.

And then Flex scooted around the drake's giant body, trotted with fur brushing up against one craggy wall, and disappeared.

::You will come. Be guests of my home.::

The drake withdrew that fluid, tree-trunk neck into the darkness.

Jenny looked at Tegan, then at Psych who had returned again.

Both Knights shrugged, so Jenny strode forward, into the darkness, following the papery scent and rustling, heaving sound, entering the depths the cavern. A blue light glowed to her left. The passageway that Psych had missed. She turned, then figured out the source of the glow.

As the bulk of the drake moved down the carved-out hallway, luminescent blue globes lit up, reflecting on the shimmering, rough-hewn ceiling and walls.

"Did you know about this shit?" Tegan whispered near Jenny's ear.

"No." And Jenny had no more words to say about it.

Not now. Not yet. Though she cursed Recoana for not telling them more. And then Flex was back, trotting at her side, sniffing the slightly damp air and the weird, dried-paper smell of drake. She wondered what the giant lizard had said to the fox, and vice versa.

The long hallway widened to an immense cavern, five times larger than the one they had sheltered in. Jenny couldn't hear the storm in here. Couldn't smell the rain. There was the sound and scent of contained fire, crackling and snapping, that perfumed the air with the scent of birch and spruce.

There was a strange hush here, despite the sounds of sparks popping as flame ate through seasoned wood. It was the hush of thousands of tons of rock and earth surrounding a hollowed-out space. Jenny could feel it, just as she felt the vastness of the space even before the drake's monstrous, beautiful form moved in far enough to really see.

And what a vision it was. Shimmering gemstones glinted from the walls. There was the fire, set back in a giant stone hearth carved out of the cave. An iron kettle was suspended above the flames from an iron pot hook secured to a side wall of the hearth.

Cushions lay in heaps like faded jewels around the space, and the center of the smooth stone floor was covered with a magnificent rug patterned with flowers in purples, reds, and greens. A second rug was placed a yard or so from the fire, with plenty of cushions and deer hides to make a cozy spot.

"Look." Psych spoke the word so softly, Jenny barely heard it. She turned. The scout had stopped, facing the wall opposite the fire that had captured her attention. He stood, leathers dripping on the floor, staring at the most impressive collection of books that Jenny had ever seen. Scroll upon scroll and bound volume upon bound volume filled cubbies and shelves carved from stone and fashioned from hewn planks of fir. Anandita and Winney would give their eyeteeth to visit this place. So would Jenny's ma.

Jenny turned to the drake, who was doing something with the kettle at the fire with what looked like one talon from its enormous right forefoot.

"You're a scholar," she said.

::*Of sorts,*:: it clicked and rumbled, as that clever, wicked-sharp talon delicately tilted the iron kettle over five earthenware cups set on a wooden tray, though two of vessels looked more like bowls.

"But how do you...? You know. With your...?"

Jenny gestured toward the scimitar of the drake's talon, then felt heat rising up her face. Fool. Insulting someone in their own home was against all protocol. And insulting a drake? Plain stupidity.

::*I have tools to help. Weights and blunt pointers. Page turners. But that's not important now. Come. Sit. Have some tea.*::

Tegan approached first, kpinga still in hand. Per and Jenny both knew that was rude, too, but Jenny did not blame the other Knight. She just hoped the drake didn't notice, or if it did, that it would not take offense.

"You need no weapons here, Knight. If I meant you harm, you would already be dead. No. Set your weapons down, or keep them as you please. Take off your outer clothing and hang it by the fire."

It gestured toward the side of the hearth where more iron hooks were embedded into stone.

The drake was correct. One claw could pierce her leathers in a second, before she could jam her sword between its scales. She rested her buckler against the stone before shrugging out of her heavy leather coat and hanging it on one of the sturdy hooks. Short sword back in hand, Jenny went to stand by the fire to dry her pants out before sitting down.

Tegan and Psych paused for a moment, then followed suit, keeping one weapon each, mostly because it was too much trouble to take off their cross-body and waist belts and scabbards for a visit that would last an unknown length of time. All three of them stood near the fire until the Drake gestured toward the cushions in a clear request to sit. Jenny wanted a few more minutes in front of the hearth, but Tegan and Psych crossed the rug and picked out cushions before folding themselves down.

Flex was already curled on a cushion, which meant she trusted the drake enough to let down her guard. At least for now.

::Take the cups, please,:: the drake rumbled. *::And relax your bodies and minds. I have waited to speak to you for quite some time, and would rather we be comfortable while we do so.::*

Jenny was dry enough, and hoisted the heavy wooden tray the cups sat upon, passing first one to Psych, then Tegan. By this time, the drake had settled its bulk on its own pile of cushions. She set a masterfully glazed bowl at its side.

That left one cup and one more bowl.

A flickering image filled her mind. It was Flex, long pink tongue lapping at the pale green tea.

She nodded, gave the faery fox the second bowl, and then sat with her own brown and green glazed cup on a fat blue cushion on the edge of the rug. She set the wooden tray in the center of the rug and placed her short sword on the rug at her side.

The tea was good. It tasted of spring. Of green herbs and sunshine.

::Recoana gathers this tea. It is my favorite.::

"How...?" Tegan began asking, but the drake waved a taloned forefoot and the Knight grew silent once again, taking a sip of tea.

::There will be time later to speak of such things, but right now, I would like to answer questions from you, Knight.::

A giant, purple-rimmed eye stared at Jenny.

By holy Brigid's name, she would not piss herself again. She swallowed some of the nutty, grassy tea. It burned her tongue, almost too hot to drink. "What questions do you have?" asked Jenny, sidestepping the fact that the drake had said it—she?— would answer *Jenny's* questions. And questions, Jenny had aplenty: *Why me?* And *How did you know we were coming?* And *Did you cause the thunder and lightning storm to drive us to your damn cave?*

But she held her tongue and waited, part of her not

really wanting to know. The drake would tell her in its own time.

::I have been watching you.::

Jenny almost spit out a mouthful of tea, swallowed hard, and began to choke. She set the cup on the carpet and pounded at her chest, finally choking out one word. "How?"

::My scrying ball. I have taken an interest in you Knights, but you in particular caught my eye. I asked the young troll about you.::

Jenny just stared. She knew the rules of chess and war. The more she showed her bewilderment and asked her stupid, stumbling questions, the more it gave advantage to the drake. So she picked up the cup again, and took a careful sip of fragrant tea. Tegan and Psych did the same.

She sent a vague, questioning thought toward Flex, but got nothing more than an opaque look before the fox went back to lapping at her own tea.

::You are an intriguing human, Jenny Knight.::

"You know my name, but we do not yet know yours."

The drake bowed the huge, triangular wedge of its head, acknowledging her words.

::Too true. I have forgotten the basic tenets of hospitality, it seems. I offered refreshment and a warm place to sit, but since I know you so well, I have forgotten that you know nothing of me.::

The drake looked past Jenny's shoulder, toward a far wall. Jenny turned, and saw a table with a hollow in the center. She'd been so captivated by the library, she had missed it. Rising from the hollow was a crystalline sphere as large as Bocan's skull. She looked from the sphere back to the drake.

The great beast seemed to be communicating with the orb somehow. Or gazing at something in its milky depths.

::My name is Karaktilla,:: the drake finally said. *::And I have been waiting to talk to you for years.::*

CHAPTER 24

ANANDITA

Anandita looked toward the brightness coming in the tall glass windows of the town hall, wishing she was in the garden with Tokki.

The council was gathered in the big main room of the town hall and public house. They usually met in a room on the second level, but when Anandita rotated onto the body, they had moved the meetings downstairs. It sometimes made it difficult to schedule around other town functions, but the township was committed to every qualified person taking a turn to run the town. And if one of those people was in a wheeled chair or had knees bad enough they could not get upstairs?

Well, the council and the town adjusted. It was only right.

So once again, the thirteen-person body sat around a rectangle of a table, with Anandita at one end, Arcady to her right, and Rafiq to her left. Another endless meeting. The rest of the council and the current spokespeople for the town's clans ranged down the long expanse of polished maple. They all wore working-day clothing in muted shades of blue, green, or brown. Tunics and pants, or skirts on a few.

Everyone had a mug of tea, water, or mild cider to hand. Danika, Jenny's tall, rangy mother, sat in a central position, paper, pens, and ink in front of her. Her dirty blond hair was slicked back into a braid. Her eyes reminded Anandita of Jenny's own. It was her grandmother that was the legendary biker and cannabis grower of Pre-Reckoning times, and her mother, now dead, was one of the township's Founders.

Danika was co-head of the Growers Association with Hakim and Inaya. Currently, it was her task to act as council scribe, though she represented the Green Clan's interests as well and likely wished she was out in the fields, or in one of the green houses, figuring out how to get through this current lack-of-proper-irrigation issue.

Every single council member was aware that until this decision was reached, they would stay here, away from the work that Go No More relied upon. But sometimes, that was just the way things were.

"The remaining Knights belong here for now. At least until we assess the threat." Danika continued the thread of conversation, drawing Anandita's attention back. They'd been going around for forty minutes now and getting nowhere.

"No!" Arcady slammed a meaty hand on the long table, right next to Anandita's mug of tea. The pale green tea sloshed, threatening to overflow. She reached out a hand to steady the blue-glazed vessel and gave the engineer what she hoped was a quelling look. He held her gaze, dark brown eyes almost black with fury and frustration. Usually a source of steadiness on the town council, the Black engineer with his carefully picked out hair and sturdy, dark green canvas clothing was agitated today, and Anandita couldn't blame him.

But that didn't mean she agreed with his request.

No one replied to Arcady's outburst, though, because they all sympathized. If it had been their project that was sabotaged? They would want the responsible parties tracked down, too.

Anandita took a sip of nettle tea and sighed, then spoke gently.

"You want us to go haring off, chasing phantoms? What do you expect the Steel Clan to do? Their best tracker isn't here." Because he was off with Jenny and Tegan. And Anandita really wished all three Knights were here for this cockup.

Especially Jenny.

But she shoved that thought away. Her missing the big Knight was of no consequence.

Danika leaned across the table, pale face tight with frustration. "And besides, we all agreed the Knights are needed to run the extra training sessions and *protect this Gods-blessed township!*" she said.

Down the table, John, a white goat farmer dressed in tan coveralls cleared his throat. He ran a hand over his scraggly, graying brown hair.

"Danika and Anandita are right, Arcady. I hate to

say it, because I would be as upset as you are. Hell, the animals need that water. And there are baby chicks that need heat lamps."

Arcady started to interrupt, but Danika raised a hand to forestall another outburst. "And yes, we all know that our main crop could be in danger. But reality is, it isn't. We're close enough to harvest that, pain in the ass though this is, we'll be just fine."

John continued the thread. "And the baby chicks have already been moved into my barn, with plenty of insulation. The heat from the goats should keep them warm until you and your team figure things out again, Arcady. We all trust the mechanics and the engineers."

They had to, didn't they?

Rafiq raised a hand to signal he wished to speak. John grew quiet. Even Arcady settled back in his chair with a *humph*.

"I agree with Danika, Anandita, and John, *and* with you, Arcady. The sabotage is bad and needs to be addressed, but we simply cannot afford to send the Knights off without more information. Not with this bad magic the mages are warning us against. The stories the Steel Clan brought back about that village? And the mark in the forest? It spells out bad times coming, and we know it."

"But what if the sabotage and the magic are connected?" Arcady burst out.

"Better hope to all your Gods or Goddesses they are not," Abyad replied in a steady voice. The djinn was swathed in black, as usual, and his bushy dark eyebrows were drawn in a serious line across their unlined forehead. Anandita had no clue how old the being was, though she imagined at least a couple of centuries had gone by since their inception. "Because if they are, we are in for worse times than we can imagine."

Rafiq nodded in agreement, which only made her feel worse.

With all her heart, she did not want worse times. No one did.

But she couldn't help but wonder if she'd worked Tokki so hard, and asked Recoana to gather extra herbs in the troll's forest wanderings just because it was prudent, or because somehow she knew that Go No More was going to need extra stores.

Because there would be more wounds and injury to tend, whether from magic or from sword.

She sipped at the cooling nettle tea, wishing her stomach would settle back down. At least one thought was clear.

"Until we have a plan, we should stay put," she said.

"Do we have consensus on this?" asked Rafiq.

"With an amendment," Arcady grumbled. "That if we don't have a solid plan within seven days, a contingent of Knights heads toward Salem."

Anandita shook her head, but this was the way things worked, right?

"I consent," she said.

Eleven other voices echoed her, around the table.

The Knights would stay for now.

CHAPTER 25
TEGAN

The series of caves was impressive, Tegan had to admit. And the fire was great, the tea was tasty...but per didn't like the situation. If it weren't for the fact that the faery fox was curled up happily, Tegan would be back out of this mountain and out into the forest, storm be damned. Especially once it turned out that the drake had manipulated them here. Watching them from afar like some creep. Spying through that giant hunk of crystal rock.

From what the drake said, Tegan suspected the creature had caused the storm. Or at least increased its fury. Lighting and thunder at the autumnal equinox? That was so rare as to feel impossible.

Oh, the weather around the volcanoes could be strange, it was true, but this? Damn lizard caused this storm, though per couldn't begin to tell how. But the beasts and beings per grandparents thought were only myths all had their own magics, ones that humans would likely never understand.

Jenny looked half freaked out, and Tegan did not blame her. The big Knight had already pissed herself, and would get shit for it later. Not now though, not while the situation was still so...uncanny. Uncanny in a way that made a warrior like Tegan want to cut and run. Even with the books and tea and all the rest, the drake was still terrifying. Formidable.

Besides, if per was being honest, it was practically magic that Tegan had held per own water. Maybe Tegan would just let the subject of Jenny's incontinence drop.

As the drake spoke to Jenny, Tegan only half listened, pretending to attend. Really though, per was scanning the huge body, looking for weak spots.

There were not many. Two under the armpits. Probably a couple near the groin, if you could get that close. The eyes. Nostrils. So far, that seemed to be about it. All of them tricky, none of them easy to hit with a thrown kpinga.

::You'll be hard pressed to kill me, warrior.::

The falling-rock voice inside per skull jerked Tegan back into the cavern. Aware of per surroundings. Fuck. Per had stopped paying attention the further per got into the scan. Basic. Rookie. Move.

Pay attention, fledgling, per mother Inaya would have said.

Tegan forced perself to hold the drake's gaze. It was one of the hardest things per ever had to do. Tegan knew exactly how a doe must feel, frozen in front of a mountain lion.

::Drink some more tea,:: the drake said. It seemed

calm. Which meant it knew it was in charge. *::I wish to work with you, not against you.::*

"But why?" The words were out before Tegan could call them back.

The drake clicked, rumbled, and clattered.

::Because Silverhair does things no being has a right to. Things that bring danger to us all. She holds to the old ways of royalty and uses others' lives for her own gain. It is far past time for the old ways to change. The Reckoning, as you humans call it, was a blessing to us all. A chance to begin again.::

"Why would you want to?" Jenny asked. "I would have thought the old ways suited you. You'd be top of the hierarchy, wouldn't you?"

The drake's eyes darkened. Tegan held per place on the cushion. Psych was just as still. Flex and Jenny seemed to be the only ones able to move freely.

But no one spoke. The hushed cavern with its cozy spot in front of the huge fireplace, and its high, curved ceiling was suddenly oppressive. It felt as if the stone were shrinking, moving closer and closer, ready to crush their fragile human bodies in a torrent of stone.

The fire popped, sending out a spark that landed on the rug before smoldering out into a black smudge.

"The symbol...." Psych finally whispered.

Karaktilla turned that terrifying triangle wedge of her head his way. *::Yes. The triangle and leaves that were once whole and healthy have split. The king is dead. The Queen does magic so evil it should not be spoken of. This affects all the realms.::*

"How?" Tegan asked, barely noticing the squeak in

per voice and the slight tremor in the hand holding the smooth, warm cup of tea.

The drake shook its terrible, wedge-shaped head. *::We know not. At least not yet. But rest assured we shall do what we can to set things aright again.::*

Amazing. That a creature so old would care.

The dark eye fixed on Tegan, and slowly, the nictating film winked down, and up again.

Tegan took the challenge, and held per gaze steady, too.

Though there was nothing inside per that did not still wish to run.

CHAPTER 26
JENNY

Karaktilla finally convinced Tegan and Psych to take some rest, and Jenny agreed. There was no use in them sleeping out on the bare stone of the entry chamber with the horses, and there was no way they were heading back out into the dark and rain. By the time they'd gone to check on the horses the rain had slacked off to a more ordinary shower, but it had been heading toward full dark, and the horses would have turned an ankle in the gloom.

The drake fed them a good meal of roast mutton and spiced wine. The warm fire and full bellies seemed enough to convince the two Knights to curl up on the rug and cushions after having checked to make certain that the horses had everything they needed.

Jenny, an earthenware cup of fragrant wine in hand, sat near the shimmering dragon, entranced by its purple and brown scales. She inhaled the scents of cinnamon and clove, both rare treats. Karaktilla must have a greenhouse in this warren. Such things didn't grow well outside, not in this climate. The tension coiling her stomach muscles unfurled. This was a nice place. A good place. A place that felt safe, warm, and comfortable. She could see why the troll Recoana made the trek here.

What she couldn't figure out was what the drake wanted. What had set such an urgency tugging at her gut, drawing her to this place. And she had other questions too. Questions of a personal nature. Things that she alluded to sometimes when she, Tegan, and Bocan were deep in their cups. But their only answer was drunken impatience and hand-waving. Telling her that she was foolish. That there was no need to worry.

That her lack of magic didn't matter. Even though they all had magic of their own.

"Why did you draw us here?" She kept her voice soft, though it didn't seem that either of her comrades were in danger of waking. It had been a long day. Jenny's eyes were feeling sandy, but she needed answers while she had the chance. And she preferred to get them in what privacy there was to come by.

The Drake rambled and shifted, then picked up its bowl in one somehow delicate forefoot though how an appendage larger than Jenny's head could be considered delicate, she didn't know. But it was. The dragon sipped the wine. Its nictating eyes stared at her, periodically shuttering themselves against her gaze. Jenny finally turned away, and stared into the dancing of the fire.

::You are special. Marked.:: The drake began. Jenny snorted.

"Are you kidding me? You didn't call me all the way here and send a lightning storm to make sure we'd end up at the entrance to"—she gestured toward the fire, the domed ceiling, and the library filled with scrolls—"whatever you call this place, to feed me that crap."

The drake's gaze was unwavering. Considering.

::*Why such a response?*:: the beast finally asked.

"Do you expect me to believe I'm some pig-fucking chosen one, like the tales read to me in nursery? I'm just a warrior. Among other warriors. I'm a woman in a time filled with magic, with no magic of my own."

Jenny's mouth filled with bitter bile, and she hastily swallowed some more of the wine, choking as the spiced concoction hit the back of her throat. Tegan shifted in per sleep but didn't rouse. And Psych snored softly, sleeping on his side, his back turned towards Jenny and the drake.

::*Mark my words, human, you are special. You have your own magic. Every being does. The fact that yours is different from the others matters not.*::

"You're speaking in riddles. What the fracking earth are you on about? And why did you draw us here? If you can't answer that question, you've wasted our time."

Now it was the dragon's turn to stare into the flames, before emitting a terrifying sound that must have been clearing that long throat.

::*I have watched your clan of warriors, traversing the land. Searching and not finding. Hunting and not seeing. I wanted to help.*::

"Why?"

The fire hissed and crackled. Jenny's body was tired, but she wanted this conversation done. She set down the wine and wished her waterskin was close to hand. Adjusting her spine, she breathed in one long, wakeful breath, forcing her being to attend to the scaled creature across from her. It was beautiful. And Jenny wished circumstance was different, but peril stalked the land and she had no time for the comfort the drake offered.

Karaktilla turned its black eyes back her way. ::*My answer is complex, but I will try to simplify. Along with watching you warriors, I and the other drakes have kept an eye on the parties Underhill.*::

"The elves."

The drake nodded her big wedge of a skull, then tucked the sinuous neck more deeply into the scale-covered, meaty scaffolding that were its broad shoulders.

::*The parties Underhill have always gone their own way, and we drakes, the djinn, and others have gone our own. But since the Change that caused the realms to crack and open once again, since the fires and deaths...the elves have grown concerning. A sickness grows in Elfland. A sickness that may seek to destroy us all.*::

"What the frack are you talking about?" The words flew from Jenny's mouth, even as her body shuddered with the memory of that empty-feeling village. Her eyes stared down at the patterned rug, as her head filled with the images of condors, crows, and wolves, all feasting as was their right. Feasting on the spoils of a war the Knights could not see.

Feasting on bodies which—if Tegan and Psych were to be believed—had no trace of a soul.

The drake did not speak. She felt it waiting. She finally raised her head again, and looked at those impossibly large eyes.

::I am speaking of that which you think. Of souls lost. Of the sundering of magic that once ran strong and clean. I am speaking of defilement. Of danger. And the possibility of war.::

"And me?" The question hung in the air, a palpable thing. Jenny's pulse raced with sudden fear.

::And you are key to it all, though I do not yet know why.::

"You called us here to tell me that? To tell us there is war coming, but not how to prepare? To tell me I have some role to play but not what it might be? What the fucking use is this?"

Her chest heaved. Her breath burned as if she was sparring.

The next words came softly into Jenny's mind, with a minimum of clicking from the drake's terrible mouth.

::You need to know what the drakes know. You need to know what to look for. And is not knowing the direction danger is coming from better than hunting shadows?::

Jenny forced her breath to slow. Forced her stomach, which was clawing its way up her throat, to settle down into its rightful place again.

"Tell me more, then. Give me some information that might be of use."

::We fear that Queen Silverhair's mind has broken. Her daughter is sick and.....:: There was sorrow in the words

and, for the first time, it was the drake who seemed uncomfortable, who shifted on her cushions as if wishing the conversation could go away.

"And?"

::And we believe the Queen is stealing human souls to keep the girl alive. The king's death broke her, the weakened magic of Elfland has sickened her daughter, and the Queen, in seeking to repair the damage, risks breaking us all.::

CHAPTER 27

JENNY

They rode hard all morning, and by midday, were stabling their mounts.

Jenny handed Dandelion over to one of Angel's apprentices, peeled off her leather gloves, and gave the roan horse a pat on the nose.

"Sorry, girl. We've got to get this information to the council."

Usually Jenny and the other Knights dealt with their own mounts after a ride. They tuned their own motorcycles and rubbed down their own horses. That was what they'd all been taught, passed through Jenny's family from her great-grandmother on down.

She wished she could have met Great-Gran. She sounded no-nonsense, and had lived in a world where magic wasn't used and the realms were still worlds apart. When she had ridden her bike into battle, it was with other rival growers, or a clan called The Feds, who held some sort of power over the people that Jenny didn't pretend to understand. It sounded like a pig-shit situation, though.

Bocan had already sent a runner to the council, to tell them there was news. Jenny longed for the bath-house, but first things first. She just hoped Jamie and Porrac had some soup or stew ready.

Tegan, Psych, and Jenny all walked next to Bocan, trying to match his ground-eating stride from the stables to the town hall.

Jenny's eyes scanned the township from force of habit, but she was only faintly aware of the sounds and smells from the stables, the smithy, and the glass-works. She barely registered the concerned looks as their small group stormed by shops and homes, speeding past gardens and the children on break from lessons, playing in the large circle in the center of the town.

Her mind was still back in that vast mountain cave.

Jenny had slept fitfully, and the drake roused the Knights a scant few hours after she had closed her eyes, proffering a hot beverage. A stimulant grown only far south, in warmer climes. Kahvay, she called it. It tasted slightly bitter, like roasted nuts left too long in the coals, but it opened Jenny's eyes and brought a strange, frenetic energy to her limbs.

All she cared about was that it, and the fuel provided by cold mutton and bread, would get her home.

After the revelation about Silverhair, the drake had tried to feed Jenny that story about a red-haired warrior being foretold in some scroll. She had thrown the remnants of her wine cup into the fire at that, and said she was going to sleep.

The drake's words troubled her soul, but she just wanted to get home. Because if war was at their doorstep, the drake was right: the whole township needed to prepare. The mages would figure that magic and prophecy shit out. Jenny and the Knights knew their duty, which was to physically protect the town.

Whether she had a destiny beyond that, she knew her primary job was acting as a Knight.

The sound of heavy boots on broad wood planks brought her back to the present. They were climbing the steps that led to the large double doors of the town hall.

Bocan heaved open the door, holding it as first Jenny, then Psych and Tegan, entered the big hall. Jenny breathed in the scent of stew from the kitchen, which made her stomach growl, plus the ever-present smells of cider, whiskey, and beer, and the ghostly tang of cannabis smoke mixed with fire and ash from the cold hearth.

Half of the council was already seated around the long maple table. There was Arcady and John. And her mother, Danika, whom Jenny greeted with a kiss to her pale cheek. No Anandita yet.

And then Jenny remembered. During one of her bouts of sleep in the drake's cave, she had dreamed of the healer. She dreamt of dark hair and darker eyes, and the soft heft of breasts that pressed against her own. But with Anandita's sweet breath on her face, right before her plum-colored lips touched hers, Jenny had awakened.

She was really going to have to do something about this. She either needed to find someone else to fuck—lush Aphrodite was almost always game, and it had been awhile—or she needed to get over herself, stop dancing around in half-assed courtship like a shy teen, and ask the woman outright....

Behind her, the door opened. She turned and there, wheeling across the threshold wearing a green tunic, was the healer herself, followed by Peridot. Jenny wondered why the elf had been called in, but supposed it made sense. If all of this had to do with Underhill, the elves would have insight.

"Jamie says the stew will be ready in five minutes." Tegan's voice broke through Jenny's consciousness. She wrenched her eyes from Anandita's lips, suddenly aware that she stunk of horse and sleeping in caves. Jenny turned to the smaller Knight and nodded.

"Thanks."

And then Jamie and Porrac were slinging bowls of stew and plates of bread onto the long bar, the rest of the council members were arriving, scraping chairs out from the table, and Jenny found her own seat.

As Rafiq opened the meeting, she, Tegan, and Psych shoveled stew into their mouths.

All too soon, it was Jenny's turn to speak. Again.

She swallowed some clear water, swished it around her teeth, and swallowed.

"Bocan told us about the trouble at the water-works. And I know you all got the report about the old mark on the stone. But I'm afraid there's something worse."

How did she even talk about this? Where could she even begin?

She felt her mother's eyes on her and remembered what she always said, early in Jenny's training: *If something scares or confuses you, take a breath, and cut straight through to the heart.*

"We met with a drake. Name of Karaktilla. She says Queen Silverhair...that there's something wrong with her. And the Queen's daughter is fading."

"And what does that have to do with us?" That was John. The dairy man wasn't usually impatient, but Jenny supposed that everyone was on edge by now.

"The sundered triangle and leaves *are* her crest, but damaged. And the village we encountered?"

She raked her eyes around the table. Every single person was focused on her, and she could feel Jamie and Porrac grow still behind the bar.

"Tegan and Psych were right. Those people had no souls."

Arcady's fist clenched on the table, but he said nothing. No one did.

"Silverhair is stealing them somehow."

The table erupted at that, everyone but Anandita, Danika, and Rafiq talking over each other. Finally, Rafiq pounded on the table, calling the meeting back to order.

Rafiq looked her way. "And did the drake tell you why? Or how?"

The stew felt like a lump of stone in Jenny's belly. She shook her head.

"She didn't exactly tell us how. Just that it was some sort of Underhill magic. But she knew why. Or thinks she does."

Jenny heaved in another breath, wishing she could run from the room. Wishing for one moment that she was not a Knight, sworn to protect these people from whatever dangers they might face. Because this was not a fucking danger she had trained for.

And then Peridot's voice broke through her thoughts, and spoke the words she had not been able to.

"She's trying to save her daughter by feeding her human souls."

Her head whipped toward the thin, pale elven face. He looked half sick, and on the verge of weeping.

"You knew this?" Her own voice rasped like a raven's call, and her fingers twitched over the pommel of her sword. "You knew this and did not tell us?"

The air of the meeting hall was thick, roiling with anger and with questions unspoken.

Peridot held up one graceful hand, rings winking silver, catching the light. "I suspected, but wanted to be sure. I was about to head Underhill when the waterworks was sabotaged."

"You can't communicate in some other way?" Danika's face was hard as granite, her brow thunderous. But Jenny's mother kept her voice even. Calm. Controlled.

Peridot licked his lips, then shook his head. "No.

It's too easy to weave half-truths from a distance. To get truth from an elf? You have to be able to look them in the eyes or smell their skin. One or the other. Without that? Well."

He paused, and tilted his head down as if looking for the words in his cider cup. His pale green hair left his face in half shadow. The elf swallowed and looked up again, gracing each council member with his gaze, until he turned to Danika once again.

"We elves have the gift of speech. From our lips, even a truth can become a pretty lie."

Arcady's face was dark with anger. "How do we know you aren't lying now? What changes? How would we know?"

Good question. Jenny waited for the answer.

"You wouldn't. But another elf would."

Jenny stood then, and stalked toward where the elf sat, his spine erect, hair falling like spring rain down his back. She didn't stop until she stood just behind and to his left. She felt him flinch, but he didn't turn to look her way.

Jenny carefully placed her right hand on his shoulder, then leaned close, until she could smell the moss and jasmine scent upon his neck. She placed her lips next to the delicate arch of his ear.

"If you are lying...if you fuck this up for us...I will shove my sword up your ass and keep pushing until it exits your lily-white throat."

He was preternaturally still. Barely breathing. But she heard that hard swallow that meant he felt the truth in what she said.

She clapped his shoulder and stood again.

"The drake feels that this is a call to war, and I agree. Peridot, we will need every fracking scrap of information you can give us. And then we need to make a plan."

The council members shifted in their seats, and several spoke at once. Jenny looked at her ma and Rafiq. Both gave her the nod.

"But first," she said, voice carrying to the two of them, over the babble of conversation, "We've got to shower. We'll meet back here when we're done."

She jerked her head at the other Knights, who rose and turned their boots back toward the door. Anandita gave her a look she didn't understand, so she simply inclined her head toward the healer and strode across the wood floor, following her comrades out, looking forward to a shower. The soak her muscles longed for would have to wait.

But along with all the questions bouncing through her head, her thoughts kept returning to the same one, worrying at it like a child worried at a loose tooth.

If there was even one small chance that drake was right, why the fuck had Brigid, or destiny—or a complete fucked-up act of chance—placed this in her lap?

CHAPTER 28

TEGAN

Heavy vegetable grease coated Tegan's hands. The Knight grabbed one of the soft hemp rags from the workbench and wiped off per fingers and palms before picking up a water skin. Nothing tasted better than Go No More water, fresh from the Clackamas and filtered through rocks and sand. Not cider. Not whiskey. Not beer. Tegan enjoyed all those three, but Clackamas River water was what per always craved when the Knights were far from home.

After a late night arguing with the council, mages, and a handful of Go No More's magical beings, it felt good to work with per hands. The clank of tools and the scent of oil was comforting, as was the companionship of comrades. Bocan sat on a sturdy box in front of his enormous hog, wrench in hand, frowning at something. Psych was busy polishing chrome and cleaning off anything that could possibly turn to rust as Jenny wrenched at her own bike engine.

"If you need any new parts from the machinists, let me know," Psych said. "And anything worn out, thrown in the box here."

Jenny and Bocan grunted at the scout, and Tegan shot him a smile.

In the field behind the garage, the horses trotted, playing in the fresh post-rain air.

Sometimes Tegan wished that this was all there was to life. Working on bikes with friends, happy horses frolicking in a green pasture, and a prosperous township. On the other hand, if per wasn't having sex, there was nothing better than the feel of a kpinga grip nestled tight against palm. With all the shit going on right now, this other part of Tegan wished for battle. Wished for an opponent per could see, taste, and touch.

Oh, the magic was strong, and now that Tegan was aware of what it was, per could sense it, crawling like fire ants across per skin. But Tegan was sworn to fight, not to work magic. And despite per natural talents, magic was not where per was trained. And without training, skill was left up to the ancestors, chance, and God.

Tegan had chosen. Tegan had sworn to fight and protect with hand, and blade, and fist.

Per patted the polished pigskin bike saddle, much as per patted a horse's nose, and walked towards the open door, breathing in the grass- and chamomile-scented air. The horses chased each other back and forth across the field. Maybe they weren't playing. Maybe they were restless too. But despite Tegan's wish for steel in hand, there was a feeling in the back of per skull like the tick of a cooling engine. *Tap tap tap.* It kept bringing her back to the magic. The pig-fucking, earth-fracking magic. And then Tegan knew.

It was as clear as the blue sky. Tegan could see it. Taste it. Smell it. Feel it in per bones.

Per turned to the three Knights working in the sun-washed bike garage.

"We need to close the portals."

"What?" Jenny said, still wrenching away.

But Bocan set his tools down carefully. The halb-troll stood and turned, stretching to full height, solid as a stone.

"Tell us," he said.

Well, fuck. Now a person had to actually explain.

CHAPTER 29
BOCAN

ocan felt the small Knight's words rattling the cages of his bones. They shook the mountain of his consciousness.

They disturbed him.

And he knew, deep in the pit of his belly, that Tegan was correct.

He stared out at per dark silhouette, backlit by the autumn sun that spilled across the paddock. Past per shoulder, he saw the horses pause in their playing, as if they sensed something had changed. A figure entered the field. Angel. Talking with the beasts. Bocan's Percheron Bodie lifted his head and stared toward the garage before trotting after the master horse handler and out of view.

Tegan walked toward him, past the work benches and wall racks filled with tools. Past the rows of bikes, waiting for their next foray out onto the open road.

"We need to close the portals," per repeated. "Contain the magic. It's the only thing I can think of that just might stop the Queen." The Knight was close enough now that Bocan could make out per expression. Eyes wide with understanding, mouth set in a straight, serious line. The muscles in per whipcord-thin shoulders bunched, prepared to strike.

"I need some cider for this conversation." Jenny's voice came from behind them, followed by the clank of tools on packed-earth floor. "Or a whiskey."

When Bocan turned, the red-haired Knight, the woman who was his comrade and best friend, and who was a stupid, donkey-stubborn fool, was wiping her hands on a rag and heading to the trap door in the corner of the garage floor. Crouching down to hoist the wooden door, she rooted around in what the Knights called "the booze cellar." He heard the clank of pottery and glass before she turned her head, eyebrows raised in inquiry.

"Cider," he said.

Next to him, Tegan shook per head. "I'm lighting up a spliff."

"I'll share with Tegan," Psych replied.

Jenny pulled out a brown liter jug and got two mismatched, castoff mugs from the closed cupboard up above.

"What do you mean?"

The press of magic rose from Tegan and he just wanted per to get the words out in the open air.

Jenny raised a hand, one finger pointing upward in the signal to pause. "Outside or in?"

"Out," Tegan said, heading for the benches on the front of the garage.

They were soon settled, Tegan and Jenny sharing a bench set against the wood garage wall, Bocan and Psych on a larger, reinforced bench, set at an L angle to the other. All four Knights looked out toward the large, central circle of green where a single Douglas fir towered.

The cider was crisp and tart, made from last autumn's harvest. But it didn't ease the tension he still felt crawling off of Tegan's skin.

"Sorry," Jenny said. "I just...after the drake and everything? This is a bit much. Go ahead."

Bocan knew the words cost her, and she wouldn't have said it were she not with her two closest friends. There were things she wasn't sharing, and he wondered exactly what happened up on the mountain to have left Jenny so pensive.

Tegan pulled a half-smoked joint from a pocket, followed by a steel match and flint.

"If the Elven Queen is stealing people's souls somehow, trying to figure out how to stop it magically just doesn't make sense," Tegan said, striking a spark.

Now, that was interesting. "Why not?" Bocan replied. He was intent on the conversation, but his senses were alert to the town, as well. The clash of practice swords. The clang from the smithy. The smells from the glassworks. The lush scent of burning herb swirling through the afternoon air.

And the children, voices faint, singing some learning rhyme from the classroom across the green.

None of it took away the sense of bad magic still crawling on his skin.

He sipped more cider and spoke. "I hate to say this, but right now? The mages don't know shit. They're grasping at straws here, saying they need more research. More time. Saying they'll try this spell or that attack. And meanwhile, the council is stalling and…"

"Meanwhile, we don't know when the next village will be decimated by the Queen." Tegan nodded at his words. They were all silent for a moment.

Jenny broke the silence.

"So, what's your idea again?"

Tegan leaned forward, arms on per leather-clad thighs, mug held loosely in fingers that could kill a man in seconds just as easily as they could smack dice onto a table. And the killing was a surer bet.

"Instead of using magic to attack the Queen, or ward off whatever the fuck alchemy can actually *steal people's fucking souls*, why don't we use our magic to seal the portals between the realms again? I mean, not all of the portals, but the one closest to us. Whatever magic she's doing has to be traveling through that gate, right?"

Bocan shook his head, trying to clear a path through the thoughts that crashed through his skull. He downed his cider and reached past Psych, holding the empty mug toward Jenny, shaking it slightly, until she unstoppered the jug and refilled it. He downed that, too, and held the mug out for more.

Jenny sucked her teeth and handed him the jug. "Fill your own mug, you pig fucker."

Once the light gold liquid bubbled up to the top of his mug, he stoppered the jug and set it beside him on the bench. Next to him, Psych looked slightly ill, and inhaled deeply, holding the smoke for a long time before exhaling a cloud of fragrant smoke.

Bocan swallowed a quarter of the fresh mug, then looked back at Jenny. Hunched over, forearms resting on her thick thighs just above her knees, her posture mirroring Tegan's. But where Tegan looked ready to spring up at any moment and sprint across the town, Jenny stared out across the township, worry and misery etching furrows into her pale face

"I don't see how that will help," Jenny said. "Won't closing the portals cause a bunch of other problems? And do you think the elves and trolls and djinn and everyone else will agree to that?"

Jenny raised her eyes toward Bocan. "Won't that leave the Underhill beings trapped out here?"

He shrugged. Not that she didn't have a point. "Those who left Underhill after the Reckoning left because they couldn't stand to live beneath the rule of the elves. They wanted the freedom to live as they are, and to give themselves and whatever offspring they had a chance to become who they truly are. I would not be here otherwise. My da and ma would never have met, or fallen in love."

And even now, with Ma gone, Da still hadn't chosen to go back living with the trolls. While there were Free Trolls further off in the mountain range, Da's family was part of an Underhill clan. Living with humans was too painful, but living under elven rule was worse.

"As for the other magic ones?" He shrugged again.

"They make their own way, just like us. Everyone chooses, and if what Tegan says has a chance of working, we need to put it to the council, and the rest of the Knights, and all the magical beings we can find. Because if Silverhair is this far gone, the danger will only increase."

"How do you know that?" Jenny asked.

"Because, being the son of a troll, I've heard a lifetime's worth of stories about how deadly the heel of aristocracy can be. And a ruler whose magic has turned? That's the worst thing I can imagine. It has the potential to undo everything your families attempted when they traveled from the collapsing cities and settled in this place."

By the time he was done with his little speech, Jenny was sitting straighter, brow not exactly cleared, but less furrowed than before. She gestured for the cider jug, and he handed it across, then turned to Tegan.

"So, any idea how we do this thing?"

The small Knight exhaled and stream of scented smoke and gave him a wicked, feral grin. "Not a fucking clue. But with enough cider and herb, maybe we'll figure it out."

Or get wasted enough to not care.

CHAPTER 30
ANANDITA

Anandita sat between the long worktable and the window thrown open to the breeze that carried scents from the herb garden into the cottage.

She crushed dried mint and chamomile under the stone pestle. It was a favored tea in Go No More, and despite the fact that people could harvest and dry the common herbs themselves, most preferred her blends. The matching mortar rested in her lap as she worked. It was satisfying to *do* something. Tokki was off at weapons practice. Anandita not only needed to keep busy as her mind worked on the problems the Knights and mages kept bringing forward, but something in her pushed toward action.

Urgency filled the air around her, winging through the town. And her intuition told her she had to make as much tincture and as many unguents and ointments as she could. She just wished she knew which herbs were going to be most needed, but resigned herself to trusting intuition on that, too. She simply grabbed what her fingers gravitated towards, and trusted they were the right things.

Outside, she heard the scuff of boots and a throat clearing. She knew that sound. It was Jenny.

Anandita exhaled, trying to still the fluttering that arose whenever that damn Knight came near.

She wasn't ready. She didn't know if she would ever be ready. Plus, the thought of being with a woman still made her blush like a girl. Which was ridiculous. Anandita was a grown woman, older than Jenny by far, with a dead husband, a thriving practice, and apprentices and a town all looking to her for guidance.

With the sound of the red-haired Knight shuffling up the walkway, clearing her throat with nervousness, Anandita's responsible adultness flew out the window.

The swing of red braids appeared through the window, obscuring the view of the green herbs and other healing plants and flowers. The grassy tang of turmeric leaf lifted by the brush of Jenny's boots, mixed with the scent of dust and the chamomile and mint Anandita ground in the mortar and pestle.

Anandita backed her chair up and divested her lap of the heavy stone tool, setting it with a clunk onto the gleaming wood table.

She dusted off her apron and stopped a hand before it could smooth down her hair. What did it matter what she looked like?

She'd known Jenny since the Knight was a bright and toddling child, and herself a young teen entering apprenticeship. She had known her since Jenny was an awkward apprentice herself, gazing with mooncalf eyes at Anandita, already an established healer and herbalist, and well on her way to getting married to the love of her life. Long.

But Long was gone now, and Jenny was grown, and the age difference between mid-twenties and mid-thirties didn't feel like such a great chasm, such a vast thing.

For one heated flash, Anandita wondered what it would be like to feel Jenny's thin, pale lips pressed against her skin. And then there she was. Tall, broad frame filling Anandita's doorway, red hair a fiery halo, body blocking out the sun. Her hazel eyes peered into the workspace, searching through the relative gloom until they lighted on Anandita's face.

"Knock, knock," the warrior said. "Are you busy?"

"Come in," Anandita said, not answering the question. Of course she was busy. Everyone in Go No More was busy, and right now the council, just like the Knights, was doing double and triple duty. But Jenny knew all that. She was just being polite.

Anandita shook some herbs into a fat brown tea pot. The fragrant blend was made up of licorice root, mint, and red clover, and it smelled of spring. The licorice would do for both of their Ayurvedic types, and mint and clover tasted good. She grabbed the wooden tray that served as her secondary work station, and set it across the arms of her chair. She avoided Jenny's watchful eyes and set the brown ceramic pot and two blue and green glazed mugs onto the tray, then wheeled her way across the smooth floor to the iron kettle resting on the metal hob. The pot rested on a clever contraption, designed to tilt the kettle over the teapot without having to lift the whole heavy thing off the woodstove's hob.

"Can I help?" Jenny asked, moving up behind her.

The big Knight smelled of clean sweat and sunshine, with the slight undercurrent of vegetable oil. She must have been working on her bike.

"I've got it. But you can get the cookie jar down from the shelf up there."

A loose fall of red hair brushed Anandita's shoulder as Jenny leaned over to sniff at the tea.

Anandita inhaled sharply, breathing in the scent of the Jenny's favorite shampoo. The woman's pale, slightly sunburned face was so close. Too close.

Anandita's hands jerked on the chair wheels, backing away from the Knight, splashing hot water onto the tray.

"Shit!" Jenny steadied the tray with one sturdy hand. "Did you get burned?"

Just by you.

"No. I'm fine. It missed me. Sorry about that. Cookies are just up there." She gestured to the shelves along the wall near the stone hearth surrounding the wood stove. Jenny took the two steps required, and then reached, tunic stretched across her muscular back.

Anandita was such a fool.

She wheeled back to the table, toward the clear end closest to the door, setting the pot and mugs down, then lifting the tray away, shoving it toward the tumble of herbs and vessels at the other end.

"Please. Sit."

They were both suddenly acting formal. As if they hadn't known each other for years. As if they were two strangers, circling one another, sniffing the air, wondering...

Jenny set the ceramic cookie jar down on the table and lowered her heavy frame onto one of the sturdy chairs across from Anandita.

"Tegan thinks we need to close the portals."

A finger of ice pierced Anandita's stomach. "Why?"

Jenny's long, broad fingers played around the edges of one of the empty mugs. "Per says it's the only way to stop Silverhair from doing whatever weird magic is stealing people's souls."

"And what do you think?" Anandita poured the fragrant tea, steam rising like a drake's breath through the dust motes that swirled in the sunshine pouring through the window. Jenny slid the other mug across the table. She filled that one, too.

"I don't know. You know I don't know shit—sorry—about magic!" She picked up her mug and blew across the surface. "That's why I came to you. We'll be coming to the council with it soon enough, but I needed to get my head around the idea first."

Jenny's forehead furrowed, and though her face looked young, Anandita also knew the Knight had killed. And once a person had killed another, youth was gone.

"Have a cookie," she said. "They're lemon."

Jenny complied, scraping the lid off the jar and plunging a paw into the vessel, coming up with two cookies in hand, a smile on her broad face. She held one out to Anandita, who took it, and bit down into the crisp, lemony round.

She wished Long was here. He was always Anandita's best sounding board. She glanced at the carved phoenix above the door, then gasped.

"What?" Jenny asked, around a mouthful of cookie.

She looked at the Knight, trying to calm the hope and panic crowding her breast. "The disappearances. Do you think...?"

"Oh. Fracked and cracking earth. Fuck. Fuck. Fuck. Fuck. Fuck. Maura. What if that bitch took Maura?"

The Knight pushed back against the table with scarred hands, shoving the chair with a scrape across the floor. She stood at full height, chest heaving, hands clenching and releasing.

Anandita dropped the cookie and slumped back into her wheelchair, all her fears confirmed. Part of her had always hoped against hope that her own love was still alive, but now? The largest part of her wished him many years dead.

Because if he was alive, and someone else held custody of his soul?

That was a terrible thing.

The worst thing in all the worlds.

CHAPTER 31

SILVERHAIR

Usually the view of the meadow, and the apple and quince trees budding and fruiting in front of her, filled the Queen with a sense of ease and well-being. But today, breathing in the perfect air, and taking in the delicate scents, only increased her fury. The queen paced along the veranda, from the wisteria arbor at one end, back to the once pleasing vista of meadow and trees. Her divided skirts swished and billowed as she walked, frothing like the green rapids of a river about to overflow its banks.

The Queen roared with power, barely contained.

"Stupid. Stupid. Stupid." She bit off the edges of each word as if crunching into perfectly ripe apple.

The harvested souls weren't working. Oh, they were keeping Elzabetta alive, but they weren't making her whole. They were not turning her back into the Elven princess she was meant to be. And that stupid alchemist was worse than useless. Silverhair clenched her fingers, not noticing the green and silver sparks shooting from beneath her sharpened nails.

A mewling idiot, he had taken to complaining about her unreasonableness, when it was his lack of magic that was the problem. Everything around her was the problem.

Including her daughter.

"Ungrateful bitch."

Grief and anger pierced the hollow chambers of the queen's heart.

She was losing her most precious thing. She was losing, not only the realm, not only control of the elven aristocracy.

No, more than all of that, more than everything she lived and worked and strived for....

She was losing her daughter. And not to the wasting disease. She was losing her daughter to contempt. And if she was honest, she was not *losing* her. She was not losing this battle.

She had already well and truly lost.

CHAPTER 32
JENNY

The yard outside the stables and garage was filled with clamor. Knights arriving with gear. Tuning up bikes. Angel and his crew getting the horses ready for the mages, elves, djinn, and others who would follow the Knights.

Council members, flapping around like agitated ducks. She had been trying to ignore them, though one in particular was making that impossible.

"This is out of process!" Rafiq shouted, practically in her ear.

Jenny grimaced, cinching her waxed bedroll more tightly onto the back of her bike behind the small leather pillion. Flex wound around her gear, sniffing, making sure she had packed the right things, she supposed. She was never certain what exactly the faery fox's agenda was, and didn't know what it was trying to tell her unless the small beast flung it directly into Jenny's brain.

"Your process takes too fucking long, Rafiq. We've been discussing strategy and the mages have kept stalling for two weeks now, and how many more people are in danger because of the delay?"

Jenny had been raised to think of consensus process to be almost sacred. It was her family's religion, even more than the vague worship of old Irish Gods that had been passed down through what Jenny's gran had called "psychic hippies," whatever those were. Some more PR shit that Jenny barely understood.

Give her something solid between her thighs—bike, horse, or woman—and either a sword or drink in hand. Give her action. Training townspeople, fighting off warlords, or helping out with projects around town. It didn't matter. What mattered was that it had to be something real.

Not these fucking phantoms stealing souls. Not this spell or that warding. As far as Jenny was concerned, the mages of Go No More couldn't do shit. Not even Aphrodite, whom Jenny liked a lot. They'd never even heard of soul stealing. And though Damson admitted the elves had some stories in the scrolls kept Underhill, she and Peridot didn't seem well versed in how exactly it worked.

Not one person on the council, and not one of the mages, had come up with any plan that seemed feasible. And except for Anandita, her ma, and John, they had all argued with Tegan about the portal-closing plan. Oh, the council wasn't against the idea, but they wanted to study and discuss it for Goddess Brigid knew how long.

But then the elves and trolls stepped in. Abyad, too. They'd sided with Tegan. They had all urged haste.

Since the magical beings were the ones the most at risk if the gates were closed, that was enough for Jenny, consensus be damned. She might not have any magic of her own—though the drake seemed to think otherwise—but that made her trust the ones with the most magic to weigh in on any decisions to be made about it.

She stretched her back and looked at the council member. His usually neat hair was rumpled from the fact that he'd been practically pulling it out by the roots all day.

"Rafiq. Do you really want to go against the beings with the strongest magic of anyone in the township?"

"That isn't what this is about!"

She held up a hand, and raised her voice to carry across the bustling yard. Half the yard was listening, anyway; might as well include them on purpose.

"When the beings most affected by this choice have all come down in favor of it, those of us with less to lose need to listen. The elves and trolls and djinn of Go No More have consensus, while the humans still balk. They even parlayed with the nagas and giant beavers. Sure, they had concerns, *but not one of them opposed the plan.* What does that tell us?"

Her eyes raked the yard. Most of the Knights who were heading out continued to quietly see to their bikes and their gear. The elves and trolls did the same with horses and packs.

The others were still. Waiting. A few shuffled their feet. Some looked angry, still. Others chagrined. But no one spoke, which was all she needed. She raised her voice to carry.

"It tells me that we are thinking out of fear, rather than thinking of what is right. We have lived in relative peace and prosperity for a long time, now. Yes, someone sabotaged our waterworks, and perhaps one day we will figure out exactly who, and believe me, the fist of the Knights will fall. But meanwhile? The engineers and mechanics are fixing the problem, aren't they? And the machinists are figuring out what needs to be re-tooled?"

There were a few nods. Rafiq crossed his arms over his chest and looked away, jaw working.

Danika stepped forward then, graying hair plaited in a heavy braid slung across one shoulder. "Rafiq, you and the others are right. We do not know the long-range consequences of this action. Truth be told, we don't even know whether or not we'll succeed. But Jenny is also right. We're in a crisis, and we need to take a risk. I see that now. This is why we didn't send them off toward Salem. We needed them prepared to face the larger threat. I feel the magic of it, and so do you."

A horse whinnied and was gentled. A breeze whipped some dust into Jenny's face. She paused to wipe it, then tied the kerchief around her neck.

Rafiq's face was still set in a scowl.

Jenny puffed her cheeks out, impatient with the bullshit back and forth. "We all know the stories, and if you need a refresher, Winney there will be happy to sit you down with the rest of the children until you sort it out."

She heard Tegan snort at that. Perhaps it wasn't politic, but at this point? Jenny didn't care. She was pissed off. They could all fuck a pig as far as she was concerned.

"Look. The Founders risked everything to leave the rotting cities. They fought their way here, until one of them said 'Here we stop. We live. We try.' Well, that's what we're going to do now, because whole villages are disappearing, and the magical beings have asked us to. Besides, plenty of the Steel Clan will stay behind. Two thirds of us. That has to be enough."

Rafiq turned his back now, and stalked away, stiff-legged as a furious dog. She would pay for this later. Somehow. But for now at least, a truce had been declared.

She turned to Bocan, who raised a blue fist high into the autumn air.

"We live and serve the township and each other!" His bellow was loud enough to wake Underhill.

"We ride for Go No More!" The Knights and apprentices raised their fists and voices in reply.

And with that, Jenny fastened the metal buckler to her sword hilt on the bike, slapped a helmet on her head, and whistled for Flex. The fox trotted toward her, followed by Tegan's lynx, Starlight, which was a surprise, as that animal rarely showed its face. Serena winged down and perched on Bocan's shoulder. Guess they were all going.

Jenny straddled her hog. Flex leapt up to the pillion.

Fifteen Knights stood on their kick bars, and their bikes roared to life.

CHAPTER 33

ANANDITA

Anandita watched the Knights pull away. Watched Jenny's heavy red braids sweeping down the back of her dusky red leather jacket from beneath the helmet. The Knight kicked the bike in gear with a thrust from her powerful right leg.

Despite the shock of realizing that Long must have been stolen into Elfland by the Queen and her strange magic—despite the knife of anger and missing him so fiercely she thought her heart would hammer from its chest—sitting there as the bikes rolled out of town, Anandita realized something else.

She wanted Jenny.

She had been holding life at bay. She'd thought it was enough, to watch Hypatia grow from what she and Long had thought was a beautiful baby girl, into the beautiful, curious, strong boy he actually was. She got satisfaction from training her apprentices and offering healing to the town.

But part of her was always held back—in reserve—

wondering if Long would return. She had put her own life on hold, banking the fires of her sexuality and passion, and squelching the drive toward anything other than what was in front of her.

Well, one of the things that kept dancing around, *trying* to be in front of her if only Anandita would pay attention, was now on its way out of town. Roaring on a big, old-fashioned motorbike, powered by vegetable oil and banked electricity.

A woman of power. A woman she desired.

Anandita wished she was going with her. Wished she was heading to the portal, trying to figure out how to close the thing that had taken far too much, including her husband's body and, more than likely, his soul.

Usually, she didn't mind her chair. She appreciated its heavy wheels, good for varied terrain. Appreciated its smooth operation. In reality, it was just another part of her body. A handy way to move around. And it wasn't that Anandita never traveled—she did.

But not on a trip like this. Not into possible danger. Too many people counted on her to stay behind.

Staring after the clouds of dust raised by motorbikes and horses, she wondered if she was going to lose Jenny before she even had her. She wondered if she was going to lose Jenny the way she had lost Long.

Rafiq walked towards her, face dark as a winter sky, brow furrowed in frustration and anger. So she had this to deal with now. The Knights and elves, trolls, djinn, and Aphrodite the mage, were off to fight one battle, while she, John, and Charles were left here to fight on the homefront.

Everyone has their work, her father used to say, and Anandita passed that on to her own apprentices. So here she was. She would take up this piece, and fight this battle so the others didn't have to.

She looked around, hoping John was nearby, but the dairy man was already deep in conversation of his own with two other council members.

Brooding time was over. Rafiq was almost at her chair. Anandita shaded her eyes with one hand, took a deep breath, and prayed for strength.

She was going to need it.

"I hope you're happy," Rafiq spat out. "You and those damned Knights."

He plopped onto the ground next to her chair. Even angry, he was still too polite to tower over her for a prolonged conversation. While Anandita appreciated the gesture, internally, she sighed. Rafiq sitting meant this was going to be a long conversation. If he'd intended it to be short, he would have remained standing.

She wished Tokki was around to bring them some tea. She could use some to get through this.

"I'm not happy, Rafiq. I'm never happy when our people head off to possible danger. But I'm even less happy that some high-born elf is stealing people's souls."

And how was that even possible? Anandita could not fathom it.

"But is this really the way?" he asked. "Going off to

do something when we haven't studied the effects? This could prove to be as bad as the Reckoning!"

Anandita saw the fear in his eyes, and sure enough, the compassion she had prayed for welled up inside her breast. She reached out and placed a hand on his shoulder.

"I'm scared, too."

"Then why...?"

"I'm more frightened of what could happen if we don't try, Rafiq. She took Long! And how many others, over the years? Those random disappearances?"

"Yes, but we could be cursing the earth realm and how many others?"

The man was near tears. Anandita wished she had seen it sooner, that his anger was actually made up of terror and grief.

Hand still on his shoulder, she breathed one long cycle of the breath of calm and healing, both for herself and for him.

"We'll get through this, brother, just as our ancestors got through the Reckoning. No matter how much we weigh and measure, we can never know the outcome, but every single time, we have to try. To take a risk."

"I wish I could be so sanguine about it."

Anandita barked out a laugh, causing a few heads to turn their way.

"Sanguine? You think I'm sanguine? Rafiq, I'm as terrified as you!"

He shook his head. "Then how could you send them into danger?"

"First of all, it's the council's job to make the hard decisions for the town."

He leaned forward, starting to object. She raised her hand to stall him.

"Second, it is our charge to listen to those most affected. That would be the elves and trolls. They all *chose* this, Rafiq! Would you gainsay them?"

Wiping his hands across his face, he stood, as slowly as an old man, bowed with the weight of years.

"Okay," he said. "Okay. What's done is done." He held her gaze for a moment. "But this fight isn't over. We still need to deal with the long-term consequences."

She nodded. "We'll talk more tonight, over whiskey in the town hall?"

Raised by Muslim parents, Rafiq drank even less than Anandita, but in a place like Go No More, sometimes even he submitted to call of alcohol.

"A couple of whiskeys," he said, giving her a half smile with no joy in it, then turned to walk away.

"Rafiq!"

He paused and turned back. She saw the whole town arrayed behind him, the Doug fir towering in the center of it all. She caught a glimpse, just for a moment, of the times to come, both hard and good. She felt the future in her bones. Felt the destiny Jenny and the Steel Clan rode toward. A destiny that tugged on them all.

"The Bhagavad Gita says, 'Be intent on action, not on the fruits of action.'"

"And what in Allah's name does that mean?"

"Even though we cannot know the outcome, we still are bound to try."

He said nothing, just waved a hand and walked away.

Anandita hoped whatever the outcome was, Jenny and the Knights would be okay.

CHAPTER 34
TEGAN

The bike rumbled pleasantly and, once they cleared the town, the wind kissed Tegan's cheeks. The Knights were heading back past the cannabis fields toward the white peak of Wy'East. The volcano rose proudly against a clear blue sky. It never failed to fill Tegan with a sense of gratitude and awe, that per could live in such a place, in such a time, under the watchful shadow of such a beautiful mountain.

Bocan and the elves thought that the main portal was beyond Karaktilla's caves, though whether it was the same mountain, per still wasn't sure. The elves insisted it was farther north, toward the rushing Wimal River that ran west to east.

It was good to be back on the road. Being on the bike made Tegan feel powerful. Good. It was better than magic, better than fighting, and almost better than sex. Per laughed beneath the kerchief tied securely around nose and lips.

The endless meetings and arguments in town had grated on Tegan. And per mothers gave Tegan an earful, too, whenever they had the chance. Per father, Angel, at least, agreed the Knights should go. He trusted the trolls and elves. He also knew that Tegan had a job to do and wouldn't be happy not acting when the chance arose.

In the distance, a herd of elk thundered off, running as if chased by spirits. No condor flew overhead, but that didn't mean some other predator hadn't spooked them, including the roar of the bikes carrying across the fields.

The magic that had been pushing at per eased up a bit, as if it knew Tegan had listened and was content to wait for what came next. That was good. Tegan was tired of feeling like fire ants had invaded per leathers.

::*Why are you on this trip?*:: Tegan shot a thought back toward Starlight. The wildcat hadn't told Tegan much, just firmly insisted on an extra blanket over the pillion. It was weird, though. Several animals had decided to come on this trip when they never had before. No one seemed to have any insight into what the plan was. Even Bocan's snowy owl was on board, and she never left the woods surrounding Go No More.

::*The animals have a stake in this.*:: Starlight replied.

Tegan snorted. The lynx wasn't going to talk about it. It was clear the Reckoning had affected the animals. It had affected everything. Water. Soil. Sky. Underhill. The magical people and creatures.

And the humans.

So, Tegan supposed that closing a portal would affect everything, too. But how, exactly, no one knew.

They all just hoped it would stop the theft of souls.

Two thoughts worried the base of per skull, though per hadn't shared them with anyone. What would happen to magic in this realm if the gates were closed? And how would that shift the balance of power?

As seeing the future wasn't one of Tegan's talents, there weren't any answers to either question. So Tegan would do what Tegan did best. Per would show up, protect the town, sharpen per kpingas, fight when necessary, and live life to the hilt.

And maybe someday find a partner or two and not settle down, because to settle down was the surest way to die.

The green fields made way to trees. In the distance, were the weird green hummocks of former a former town, "gone to green" as people said. They were on the outskirts of Karaktilla's mountain, and wasn't that a trip? Drakes were the stuff of legend, and while Tegan knew they existed in theory, just like Peridot and Abyad, seeing and smelling one firsthand was something else. Per intended to pick Recoana's brain about it all once there was a chance.

The plan was that the bikers would scout ahead, following the feel and scent of the magic. They were also charged to find spots to camp where horses could be fed and watered, so as to spare the feed stores the extra horses carried. If they came to a place where the roads and tracks became impassable by bike, they would leave the bikes and all but a few pack horses with a few Knights and apprentices.

Tegan had a sense that the bulk of the trip might need to be done on foot. That was one reason Jenny and Bocan had agreed the bikes would be useful for the first leg, at least. They could be left behind with minimal guards and required far less fuel than horses.

Besides, they were just a fuck of a lot of fun to ride. Tegan grinned under the kerchief bound around per face, opened the throttle and cranked up the speed.

CHAPTER 35
JENNY

The bike purred, happy to be on the open road at full throttle. A red-winged blackbird shot across the road, flashing its shoulders as it flew over the green fields.

She had left Anandita with a wave, having spoken with the healer before the rest of the council descended on the garage yard.

Anandita had raised her arms for a hug. Jenny inhaled, still smelling her honeysuckle laundry soap on her kerchief from where it had crushed against the other woman's chest as Jenny crouched into the hug. She remembered the feel of Anandita's arms, so strong from pushing the chair up and down hills and across the township paths. It took all of her self-control to not sweep the woman onto her bent knees and crush her lips against hers.

But that wouldn't have been right. She had gently released the healer from the embrace as soon as she felt the other woman begin to pull away. She hadn't kissed her neck beneath the dark fall of hair. Had simply given her shoulders a squeeze, and breathed in the scent of her.

To remember. To carry into whatever strange battle was to come.

Jenny felt Flex lean into her back, bracing herself as the bike wound down the curving road, rapidly heading toward the mountains. It was good to have the faery fox on board. Even though Jenny knew the Knights were spooked that so many animals had decided to come, to Jenny, they just added skill and strength, plus an element of chance.

This whole operation was filled with chance. Despite Tegan's surety, not one person or being knew what the fuck they were really doing here. They were following whatever psychic and magical powers shoved at the smaller Knight. The fact that the decision was confirmed by every troll and elf in the township, plus the few First Nations members, and now the animal companions?

There was no way to go against it.

The farther they rode, the more Jenny felt a pressure build inside her. Hard as she tried, she could not get the druke's words about destiny out of her head.

The air rapidly cooled, the farther they rode into the towering trees. She tasted water. One of the network of streams that fed into the Clackamas.

Flex sent a thought into her head. Images of running on narrow trails, dirt soft underfoot, and scents of loam, fir, and blackberries.

"Not yet!" she yelled over her shoulder. "We need

to get as far as we can on machine first. You can run when I walk!"

She felt the faery fox huff behind her, then settle down again, leaning and bracing with the motion of the bike.

Jenny didn't blame Flex for grumbling. She felt grumbly herself. Karaktilla seemed to think Jenny played an important role in what was yet to come. Some destiny crap. As if all the leadership stuff the rest of her clan kept trying to foist off on her wasn't enough. She didn't need some crystal-gazing drake to pile on more.

All Jenny wanted was to swing her sword in service of the town. She was born to ride for Go No More. Born to carry on the legacy of the Founders by keeping all they had built as safe and prosperous as possible. They sought no kings, no rulers. This destiny shit sounded too much like swords in stones, hobbits chasing golden rings, or weird sky battle shit her grandpa used to talk about. And since those sky battles didn't involve drakes or condors, Jenny never knew what he was on about. Motorcycles in the sky or some shit.

The stories were good, though.

But that was all they were, right? Stories.

She'd never met a hobbit, despite elves walking around town, living their lives and going about their business.

Besides, children without magic didn't grow up to be the ones who led important lives. Everyone knew that.

Or they were supposed to.

Jenny scanned the trees for likely camping spots. By the time they got packed up and finished arguing with the council, it was late morning, but they'd all agreed on not waiting one more day to leave.

Besides, a short first day meant both horses and people would be better rested for whatever they needed to push through or face head on. Just because they planned a short trip didn't mean it would end up being one.

She hoped that Tegan and the others would figure out exactly how to shut this portal once they got there, but there was no telling about that, either.

Because closing portals was far outside Jenny's expertise. She was just along to hold a sword while others did the real work.

Yeah. She grinned behind her kerchief. This was a good trip. Despite the huge unknowns—which no one liked—she was on point to do what she did best.

Jenny would provide muscles and her sword.

Everyone else could do the rest.

CHAPTER 36
BOCAN

Bocan finished checking over his big hog and stood. Everything seem to be in good running order. He nodded to Berto and Gladys. The two apprentices were doing well enough to act as backup and take care of whatever the Knights needed on the road.

"Okay so far?"

"Doing fine," Gladys said, then hoisted a battered can of veggie oil and moved on to a clump of the Steel Clan who still tinkered with their machines beneath the canopy of mixed fir and pine.

Bocan glanced over towards a big tarp strung between two spruce and anchored to the ground, forming a wedge sail. A fire was lit just outside the shelter, and a couple of people worked on dinner. He could smell stew and was glad that Psych and Litha were such good trackers. They had easily found some game to add to the vegetables in the pot, along with some herbs, smelled like.

The—looked like five—rabbits would add flavor, stretch the dried fish and meat, and cooked fast enough on a spit over the fire. It didn't do to add fresh meat directly to the pot before it was cooked through. Too chancy. And on the road, the last you wanted was runny bowels.

Tegan stood and cracked per back, then gathered per tools into the roll, tied the whole bundle, and tucked it into a saddlebag on per bike.

Bocan jerked his head towards the tarp.

"We should talk," he said.

Tegan nodded, wiping greasy hands on a rag and throwing that into the saddle bag, too. They wandered over to the tarp, where Aphrodite already sat on a camp stool. Bocan's gut told him they would have need of two mages before this was through, but had stepped aside when it was decided that Charles would remain in Go No More. They simply did not know when another attack would happen, and if the elven bitch's soul-stealing magic came to the township, they needed at least one of the mages there to support the magic of the people.

Bocan caught the eye of Recoana and Feldspar, waved his fingers, then pointed towards the tarp. He knew they would be by as soon as they were done checking the horse's hooves.

He tapped the shoulder of Peridot en route. The elf's sage-green hair swung gracefully over one shoulder as he turned his narrow face Bocan's way, quirking up a sharply defined green eyebrow in question.

His eyes were three shades darker, but in the same color family as his hair.

Fucking elves. The shits would probably look good after a week of hard riding and skirmishes. Considering this was only planned to be a two-day journey, they looked as fresh as if they'd just left the bath house, but not half drowned. Bocan shook off his annoyance. Just because elves and trolls distrusted each other Underhill didn't mean they shouldn't work together in the New Era still being forged by the descendants of all who survived the change.

The elves of Go No More were survivors themselves, having chosen the new world and new ways, just as Bocan's da and Feldspar had.

"We need to confer."

"I'll grab Damson," he said, as Bocan headed off to scare up Abyad from wherever the djinn had gotten to.

Soon enough they were gathered under the tarp, Jenny included, though she didn't look happy about it. Tegan and Bocan practically had to drag her from where she'd settled in, leaning against a saddle, cleaning horse tack and drinking cider.

Well, broody or not, she had to be in on this conversation.

The sounds of the camp continued around them, people getting animals and sleeping spaces ready. Darkness would be upon them soon.

Aphrodite wrapped her blue cloak more firmly around her shoulders and gestured toward Feldspar and Recoana.

"The trolls and I were talking."

"We've been talking for weeks," Feldspar muttered, popping a hazelnut into his mouth and cracking it between his teeth.

Aphrodite shot him a side-eye glare. The troll shrugged and subsided. Not for the first time, Bocan wondered if they were lovers. They acted like it sometimes.

Not that it was anyone's business who Aphrodite shagged.

"As you know, our magic is no match for whatever Silverhair is doing. Like we told the council, soul stealing isn't something Charles and I have even heard of, not from our mentors or the books we have."

Peridot's fingers paused in the middle of plaiting a set of tiny braids in Damson's hair. "We haven't heard tell of anyone actually doing such a thing in living memory. It's part of why I wanted to gather more information before coming to the council. And yes, I recognize my mistake."

Jenny waved his words away and took a swig of cider. "Well, it's happening now, but what the fracked earth are you gonna do about it? I mean, I get that we're going off to 'close the portal,' but I'm fucked if I understand what that means, and none of you magical fuckers seem to be able to explain it clearly."

Bocan didn't blame Jenny for being angry. And he wished he could get drunk, but there was no way to carry enough alcohol to affect his system. Besides, keeping sharp was the name of the game.

"All I know is that I need to get closer," Tegan replied, face pinched with anxiety. The magic had to be crawling all over per. Bocan could practically see it in the flames and shadows bouncing off the tarp.

His stomach growled. The mingled scents of stew and fire, bike oil and leather should have been comforting. Something nice. Something he was used to. But while he couldn't help thinking of dinner, they had to get through this meeting. And whatever this magic was that they were facing was the opposite of comforting and familiar.

It was uncanny, even for a halbtroll, like himself.

"Tegan is right," he spoke. "Portals are strange places. But they are also places you elves know well. You should take the lead."

Damson was already shaking her head, long fingers worrying at a silver bauble dangling from one ear. "It's too dangerous for us. Silverhair..."

"And you think the situation isn't dangerous for the humans?" Jenny snapped out. "Do you think people haven't died in the most gruesome ways, without even retaining their souls?" She smacked her chest with a fist.

Bocan winced. "You think our friends and loved ones haven't just up and disappeared? Danger." Jenny shook her head, red strands glinting in the fire light. She fell silent, grabbed a stray piece of kindling from the ground and pulled out a blade. Curls of wood soon fell beneath the blade.

"Tegan?" Bocan asked. The smaller Knight stared off as if per mind was somewhere else. Tegan turned per head slowly, blinking.

"All I know is the feeling I have. I keep getting

snatches of vision, and this prickling on my skin. Seeing the future isn't my strongest suit, but when it comes..."

Per absentmindedly rubbed hands up and down muscled arms. "I'm there, you're there, and Jenny is there. It's something to do with all three of us. I felt everyone else, too, but right at the gate? It was we three."

"Well, I want to be there, too," Peridot said. "If Silverhair wants my head on a platter for helping you all? It is worth it to break this terrible spell she's trapping the princess in."

"What do you mean?" Tegan said, voice sharp as the edge of per blades.

Peridot shook his head. "I'm not even sure. It's just a sense I get. I think Princess Elzabetta is in danger."

Tegan leveled a dark-eyed gaze at Bocan. He suppressed a shiver.

He really wished he could talk to Da.

TEGAN

Tegan's skin was crawling again. That fracking magic. The afternoon's ride had been a brief reprieve from it all, and seemed a distant memory, here in the overgrown glade.

Peridot's admission that he thought the princess was also in danger made things feel more sinister than before. Tegan couldn't place per finger on it, but the magic inside per responded, filling every crevice with a thrumming sense of urgency.

And what the fuck else was the elf keeping from them? Tegan didn't fully trust that he wasn't leading them all into danger.

Per fingers drummed on leather-clad thighs, but Tegan held perself in the small circle of townsfolk by force of will. Per wanted to do anything but sit here. Tend the dinner fire. Hack up cooked rabbit. Dig a latrine trench.

Go running through the dark woods.

Tegan was a Knight, damn it! Not a mage.

Per had *never* wanted to be a mage. Never wanted to risk being warped by forces that—no matter what parents and mentors taught—did not seem natural. Oh, Tegan appreciated the extra senses, and it was fun to shoot sparks on dark winter nights with the other kids to keep them entertained.

But this shit? It was too earth-fracking, pig-fucking real.

And despite being surrounded by warriors, about to eat stew around the fire, Tegan felt afraid.

Very, very afraid.

CHAPTER 38
JENNY

They skirted Karaktilla's mountain, despite Recoana's protests. The troll wanted to confer with the drake, but the last thing Jenny wanted was more half-cracked talk about "destiny" and "wyrd." She just couldn't deal with it.

That wasn't Jenny. Never had been. Jenny carried steel. Jenny saw the world through non-magical eyes because Jenny was not fucking magical. Destiny and wyrd were for everyone else.

Not her.

The dragoons roared on, full throttle, curving east and then north, toward the Falls. The place both Tegan and Bocan said tingled with gate magic and something more. Maybe steel and muscle would be enough to fuck that magic up.

Flex had finally settled, leaning against Jenny's back and gripping the blanket and pad, only nudging her when it was time for rest breaks. The faery fox seemed content to hunt with the other animals when they stopped, and to half doze on the pillion of her bike the rest of the time.

It was as if the fox knew they were heading in the correct direction now and was saving herself for what was to come. Riding this long while gripping leather with paw, talon, and claw had to be hurting all of the animals, though.

Flex sent her a reassuring thought—a flash of enjoyment at the wind on her face—and she smiled, turning her attention back to the cracked road ahead. She often wondered why these roadways needed to be so broad. Despite what the histories said, and some of the photographic images the PR books showed, seeing the sheer width and length of them in person still baffled.

The bikes roared down the highway, skirting the worst of the cracks and the vegetation that patterned the old dark gray surface like stripes in a huge chunk of jasper. The sleeping volcano of mountain hulked over Jenny's left shoulder, verdant with forest this close to the road. She knew its white peak was there, though. It was always there.

Tall grasses waved, gleaming green and gold, between forest and concrete. It was good to be out on the road. Too bad the trip wasn't for something more pleasant.

A small, dark blur hit Case, who was riding just ahead, jerking his helmeted head to the side. His bike fishtailed in front of her with a squeal. Jenny swerved around him.

Who the *fuck* was attacking?

She steadied her bike, reached down, and unsnapped the sword guard from the sheath. Damn it. They could use backup from the archers on horseback, but the riders —and the two walking trolls—had to be several klicks behind. Bow and arrow were all but useless on a moving bike. Even crossbow required two hands.

There had been zero reports of bandits or warlords up this way. Flex pushed off the bike, the weight change rocking the machine.

"Fuck!" Jenny shouted, struggling to steady the bike again.

The fox raced toward the trees, followed by the gray streak of Tegan's lynx, Starlight. Flex's wild barking cut through the machine roar and raised the hairs on the back of Jenny's neck.

More uncanny shit.

Another small, dark, blur flew through the air, heading for Jenny's head. She ducked, bellowing a warning to the bikers around her as the rock sailed by. There had to be bandits, hiding in the strip of tall grass between roadway and forest. If the animals hadn't shot off into the woods, Jenny might have tried to outrace these fuckers, but Bocan had already pulled his bike to the side of the highway and stood, battle-axe in one big gloved hand, short sword in the other.

And he was right. These pig fuckers needed to be routed out before they got too close to Go No More.

Horses whinnied and two strange riders broke from the woods—hair streaming, makeshift leather armor strapped around their torsos—heading toward them at full speed, the white tip of Flex's tail flashing up through the tall grasses. That must be what Flex and Starlight had gone after. They were flushing the bandits out so the Knights could deal with them.

Jenny scanned the area. She didn't want to leap the ledge that lined the roadway with her bike and didn't trust the ground below, anyway.

She saw more pig fuckers in the grass and scrub, still shooting projectiles through the air. A few others ran toward the roadway.

"Fuck!" she shouted again, then turned, speeding back toward the clump of Knights, some already racing across the grass on foot, others crouched behind the ledge.

Her gears ground as she downshifted, hand on the throttle, foot tapping the brakes. She had to get off this bike.

Jenny pulled up hard next to Bocan's hog, killed the bike, and dropped the kickstand. With one sweep from her right arm, Jenny unsheathed the short sword and leapt off, running at a crouch toward the rest of the dragoons.

"How many?" she asked Psych. His breath was rapid, but his eyes were clear.

The scout shrugged. "Maybe ten?"

"Pretty stupid of them, then," Bocan's voice rumbled. Fifteen of the best Knights were on this trip. "Strategy?"

A horse screamed. Jenny snapped her eyes toward the sound as the rider tumbled and the blond horse collapsed on top of him. Flex's tail shot off toward the other horse.

Fox must've ham-stringed the animal.

"We move," Jenny said, thighs bunching, ready to leap over the cracked gray wall.

"We fight for Go No More!" Tegan screamed, and with a roar, the dragoons cleared the wall, shields and swords and maces up, racing toward the trees.

Metal whirred past Jenny and with a thunk, the second rider was down, one of Tegan's kpinga's in his throat, the horse rearing and bucking before racing off toward the old highway.

Jenny put on a burst of speed, boots digging into the soft earth, trampling the tall grasses. A man popped up in front of her, sword in hand. She took his strike with a clang from her buckler, rolled her sword around and stepped in, closing distance. A hard thrust sent her blade through his leather-covered belly. She didn't stop to think. Thinking was deadly. She just let her body move. As she jerked the sword up and out, his blade nicked her ear beneath her helmet. She pushed, and he fell.

Too easy.

She ran on, breath as loud as the muffled shouts, clangs, and grunts coming from the field around her. Bocan's battle-axe sliced toward another fighter. Looked like a big woman. She parried with a broadsword, metal flashing in the autumn light.

Ahead of Jenny, apprentice Gladys was in trouble. A man half again her size slowly circled the teen, who followed his arc with her halberd, panting. Why the fracking earth was she out here, anyway? Stupid hothead, trying to prove...

Gladys looked about to puke. Always hard, that first fight, when death was on the table for real. No one but the sick wanted to kill.

Heaving in a breath, Jenny bellowed and charged, short sword gripped in her right hand, buckler swishing and twanging as she ran. Gladys bellowed and swung the polearm high, slicing down as the man, one beat behind, blocked with the flat of a broad, curved blade. Steel clanged just as Jenny reached the pair. She dodged low, aiming for the man's groin. He turned. His blade sliced her arm like scorching fire. She pivoted, smashed her buckler into his elbow, and drove her blade home.

His shriek was terrifying. Jenny pulled, and blood fountained from the wound, splashing onto her leathers, sending hot splatters to her cheeks.

"Run!" she called. The girl nodded her bloody face, dark eyes wide with fear, and raced back toward the highway, black braids swinging from beneath her helm. Jenny glanced down. The man was bleeding out, eyes already flickering. No need for a mercy blow.

Jenny took a precious second to scan the field. There were no more bandits running from the woods. Either Psych was right and there had only been ten, or the rest had retreated to safety when they figured out who they were facing.

The question was, why the fracking earth had they attacked? They had to know who they were facing. As skirmishes went, this had barely been worth the time.

Across the field, Bocan stopped Gladys, who nodded and headed toward the shadowed hollows in the grasses, halberd gripped in both hands, looking for downed fighters. If there were any from the Steel Clan, she would shout for help. If not, she would gather weapons, tools, or anything else that looked handy. Too bad the asshole's leathers were for shit. No use in saving those.

Jenny and Bocan headed toward each other, stopping to collect the spoils of battle as they went. Weapons. Amulets. Anything that might be of use. Tegan and Case conferred further down the field.

"Should we send the scouts into the woods?" Jenny asked Bocan once he was within range.

"I don't want to put them into danger, not even to figure out who these pig fuckers were. Psych and Litha can examine the goods and bodies, see if there's any intel that way. Don't see how coming across their hidey hole will give them too much more."

Jenny looked toward the dark pocket of trees.

"Think they sabotaged our waterworks?"

Bocan grunted. "Seems likely. I would've thought that was the assholes from Salem, but could have been this crew."

As they headed toward the bikes, Jenny's mind turned over the facts.

"A crew this small?" she said, "Doesn't seem likely. What would they get from that? They couldn't take the town on their own, no matter how crippled we were. Either they're part of a much larger crew…"

"If they are, we've got more trouble to deal with," Bocan said, never breaking stride.

"Right. But we would've seen signs by now, wouldn't we? Or that fucking drake would've said something."

"Maybe."

No. The Salem warlords were still the most likely saboteurs.

Which still left the lingering question: who was this crew, and why had they attacked? If they were hooked up with Salem, they had doubled back to the other side of town somehow.

But why?

It was almost as if they knew the Knights would be heading this way.

CHAPTER 39
JENNY

The rest of the trip was uneventful. Cuts were tended, and the bandits' gear distributed among the pack horses. The elves, trolls, and mages hadn't been happy when they heard of the attack, but what the fuck were they supposed to do about it? That was how the world worked, and wishing it different was foolhardy at best.

Maybe there was a larger plan at work, or maybe random shit just happened sometimes. The magic fuckers had to face reality.

The djinn had been strangely silent, as if working on a problem all his own. Jenny barely had time to wonder what that was.

So the Knights had forged on, the rest of the cohort following behind, with Tegan growing more antsy with every klick.

But now, here they were, at another racing river, searching for magic.

And Jenny still didn't feel a thing. Oh, she felt

worry, anger, and fear. She felt her own tension, and the tightness that ran through the dragoons like a coiled spring in a machine shop.

The magic was making everyone fractious. They complained of pressure. Or tingling. She and Case had already stopped more than one fight.

So yeah, the mages needed to deal with their shit. Her job was to keep the Steel Clan intact and get as many of them back home safely as she could. But right now?

Tegan was a problem. Day by day, Jenny's comrade had pulled further inside perself, until per was halfway catatonic. Per dark skin was hot to the touch, but Tegan swore there was no fever, and to stop fucking fussing.

Bocan kept shooting Jenny worried looks, and with a nod of understanding, they called the Steel Clan to a halt in a copse of trees Psych had found just off the side of the highway. There were a couple of clearings large enough for the dragoons and all the rest, and fresh water was a short walk away. The horses were happy to get a break, and the mages were bent over maps scribbled in the dirt, arms waving, in discussion with the scouts and the elves. The trolls seemed to be ignoring them, which was strange, and were helping set up camp instead.

Flex came over and butted Jenny's hand. She crouched to stare into the fox's warm eyes.

"What?" she asked.

The faery fox sent the image of a shimmering gate

into her mind. She caught a whiff of orange blossom and honeysuckle.

"You think the gate's nearby?"

Flex dipped his head, and trotted toward Starlight and Tegan. Tegan sat on a log, head in per hands. Starlight stared at the knots of hair that neatly divided Tegan's scalp. Bocan? If an enormous halbtroll could be said to hover, well, that was what he was doing.

Jenny sighed and followed the fox. Tegan had been snapping at her for the past two days. Defensive, but not letting Jenny in.

Suddenly, Jenny knew why. It wasn't just the magic. Tegan was about to pull some heroic shit and thought Jenny would try to talk per out of it.

That wasn't true. Jenny would only talk the Knight out of it if the heroic shit was stupid.

And heroic shit usually was.

"What's happening?" she asked Bocan, giving Tegan and Starlight a sideways glance. He was staring at his snowy owl, Serena, clearly deep in rapport.

The noises in the camp were subdued. The huff of a couple of people practicing fighting with the apprentices, which, after the skirmish with the bandits, was good. Get them back on the horse, and all that. There was quiet voices of the mages and the elves. The creak of leather and the *tink* of tack and knives, getting polished and set aside again. Jenny almost wished for more noise to cover whatever conversation was coming. She liked to talk with the whole Clan only when she was more certain of things.

And things had not been certain for a while. She,

Bocan, and Tegan—with the addition of Case some-times—were the most trusted voices of the Steel Clan. The dragoons looked to them to cut through the horse shit before dragging the rest of the Knights into the decision-making process.

You need to feel in control. That was her mother's voice in her head. *That's why you joined the Knights.*

She couldn't dispute that argument they'd had, going on four years ago now. But she wouldn't have put it that way. Jenny would have said she wanted to feel useful. Of service. Worthy.

And what's the difference? That was her own voice. She told it to shut up.

Bocan blinked and stretched his neck. Jenny wondered if he'd heard her question and was about to repeat it, when the halbtroll finally replied.

"The animals think the gate we're looking for is nearby."

"And?"

"I agree," the halbtroll replied.

"Tegan?" Jenny stared down at her friend, who refused to look up, but cleared per throat, letting Jenny knew the Knight had heard.

"It's...." Per voice was strangled. Low. As if Tegan had to force perself to speak. "Pressure. All over me. All around me. It almost hurts to breathe."

Well, wasn't that great? All the shit the rest of the Knights complained about, but three times worse.

"What does that mean?" she asked Bocan, but it was Aphrodite's voice that answered. When the frack had she wandered over?

"It means that Tegan is right. Person is the one who needs to deal with the magic here."

"No." Jenny's voice was firm. "Why can't you mages, or the elves—or fuck?—the trolls or djinn? Come on! All of you magical fuckers around and you want one of our best Knights to sacrifice perself?"

"You don't know that."

Jenny shook Bocan's heavy hand off her shoulder, ignoring his words. Jenny did know that. This whole situation stank.

"I have to," Tegan said, voice so soft it barely registered. "The magic and visions...I have to do this."

"Fuck that!" Jenny replied. "You still have the freedom to choose! Besides, that stupid drake said I was the one with a destiny here."

She dropped down next to Tegan, who forced a smile to per face. "You think you're the only one who has a purpose in this world? Besides, you don't even believe in this shit."

Tegan patted Starlight's head and rose, dusting off per leather-clad ass.

"So that leaves me, doesn't it?" The scar over Tegan's right eyebrow raised in challenge as per spoke, clearly expecting an answer.

Jenny turned and walked away.

She just couldn't deal with all this shit.

Not with magic, and stolen souls, and elves keeping secrets, disappearing djinn, and one of her best friends about to do something pig-fucking stupid.

CHAPTER 40

ANANDITA

Anandita leaned her whole torso into it, her gloved palms pressed against the steel rims as she fought her chair up the narrow path, half overgrown with blackberries and mugwort, thankful for the fat, stabilizing wheels that kept the chair from tipping backwards. She periodically stopped to hack at vegetation or push things out of the way. Her canvas gloves and the heavy hemp tunic and short trews she'd donned that morning were her saviors, though she'd still sustained a few deep scratches on her face and arms.

The main struggle was keeping her wheels from tangling, which made her wish for her stubbies. Even though navigating with the short prostheses was tiring on such rough terrain, she'd have more mobility than she did in the chair.

She really should have brought Tokki along, or even Hypatia. Both of them had given her pointed looks when she set out an hour before.

Both of them also knew better than to voice what they were thinking. Not when Andandita was in this sort of broody, fractious mood. So Tokki had silently brought Anandita her bow and machete, and Hypatia had filled an extra water skin for her to take.

She tasted bad magic in the air. Metallic and pungent, with the added scent of overripe fruit and decaying flowers, it had entered her dreams these past few weeks, and she caught scent of it off and on at random moments throughout the day. But it wasn't until two days after the Knights had roared off, after she'd let Jenny go without that interrupted kiss, that she realized she needed to see Long's place again.

At this point though, Andandita had to admit she'd been foolish, to come looking for magical traces that had to have been washed away winters ago. Muscling her chair over rough terrain was hard enough, without dealing with a path no one had traveled in what looked like the best part of a year. Her body would pay for this later.

Things grew fast here, with all the rain. Green pulled down and buried PR cities and towns, cracked the old travelways to rubble, and quickly overtook any paths that humans or animals didn't tromp down regularly.

Gone to green was the phrase everyone used for the old, half-swallowed civilization.

She hadn't been up here in years. The last time, it had been a fairly well-maintained path used by hunters and deer. It had been one of Long's favorite mushroom-hunting spots.

And then he had disappeared. After seeing the blood, and feeling his absence, Andandita hadn't been back, not after placing a small marking stone in case Hypatia wanted to visit when he got older. And he was older. He'd been asking about Long lately, and that was part of the resentful glare he'd given her this morning over their aloo paratha when she'd insisted on heading off alone.

So yes, she needed help now, but she also knew she had to face whatever was here, alone.

The Knights heading off to find the big portal farther north had gotten her thinking. More than thinking, actually. The edges of her vision tingled, as if psychic information struggled to come through but was blocked.

Because she was more than certain now that whatever had happened to that village had happened to her husband. He hadn't been set upon by bandits, or stolen by a Sasquatch, though why a gentle, vegetarian creature would want to steal a human, she could not say. Legends were strange things.

At any rate, neither human cruelty nor the indigenous magics of this place had taken her partner away. It was something far worse.

Andandita had no idea what she expected to find up here in this overgrown bit of forest, she just knew she was compelled to push on.

"So, let's do this."

She hacked another vine away from her chair's right wheel and re-sheathed the machete on its spot on the left side of her chair. A drink of water and stretch of her arms and shoulders, and she smacked her hemp-covered palms against the wheels again, leaning into the action, powering the chair over rocks and furrowed earth.

Heading toward the place where Long had died or disappeared.

TEGAN

In the quiet clearing beneath majestic trees, Tegan's flesh felt as if it was being flayed from per bones. Magic pressed inside per head. Tegan wanted to scream, just to release the pressure. But Tegan was surrounded by Knights and trolls and mages. Tegan had two elves, a faery fox, and a djinn staring at per. And then there was Jenny, freaking out and trying not to show it. And Starlight, pressed against per knee.

Tegan sighed, and choked down a mouthful of jerky and forest greens stew. Bocan had insisted on it, shoving the small wooden bowl under Tegan's face repeatedly until per finally grabbed it from his fucking blue hands. Per stomach lurched and tipped as if one thousand of Mugwort's bees had invaded per belly. It was enough to make a Knight wish to have been coshed over the head badly enough to have been left behind in a field off the side of the highway.

Tegan's brain struggled to latch onto the thought.

To figure out why the bandits had been there. But thoughts skittered off as quickly as they came. Tegan could hold onto nothing. Tegan could barely hold perself.

And then Jenny and Bocan were back, crouched at per side, backed up by Aphrodite and the elves. The trolls moved from the shadows to flank them, with Abyad and the black dog just behind. Tegan sensed the camp hush. Waiting. As if every member of the Knights listened. And they likely were.

Even the campfire seemed to snap more quietly, and the nightjars stopped singing for a moment before starting up again. Starlight butted a solid head at per thigh, Flex settled in at Jenny's feet, and the mage ducked as Serena swooped down to land on Bocan's shoulder.

She saw a mouse peek from a collar, and a skink curled up in someone's hand.

"You ready?" Jenny asked.

"It's time?"

No one responded to Tegan's question. Of course it was time. Per rubbed sweaty hands on a kerchief before shoving it back into a pocket.

There was still no concrete plan, just a vague idea that—somehow—Tegan could shut the fracking gate. As if per had ever done such a thing before. As if a Knight could do what mage and elf could not. Peridot flashed her a look she couldn't read, then glanced away. Great. Even the elves were nervous now.

Per inhaled. Found center. Exhaled.

It was now or never.

"Let's go." Tegan stood, forgotten stew bowl dropping with a splash and clatter from per lap. The stew left a pattern like a map on the dirt. Per scuffed it with a boot, kicking dirt over the mess before a fucking mage could stare at it, reading it like entrails for a sign.

"Arm up," Bocan said. Apprentice Gladys handed Tegan per kpingas, helping to strap them on. No one else moved, and that's when Tegan realized they were at the ready, arms and shields and helmets donned. The Clan had been waiting on Tegan. The animals and the forest and all the rest...they'd all been ready for a long time.

Tegan tied another kerchief around per braids and Berto handed over per helmet, painted with the pattern of Tegan's mother's people, so far back their name was barely even memory.

Patterns were important. Patterns remained. Patterns fed the magic Tegan so wished per could set aside.

Tegan paused. Dug boots into the soil. Breathed in forest. The scent of per comrades. Leather, sweat, and determination.

Hand gripping the amulet buzzing at per breastbone, Tegan inhaled again. Held that breath. Breathed out.

"Ancestors!" Tegan spoke the words aloud. They rose up through per body, from the roots deep in the earth. "Be with us all! You who worked magic, and you for whom magic was the stuff of legend! You who survived, no matter how many of your loved ones were ripped from your arms in the dead of night! You who survived war, oppression, and disease. Be with us now! Steady our hearts and minds! Strengthen our arms!"

Tegan paused then, the power of the words and the sense of connection thrumming through per body. Per felt the connection of every being around her, both seen and unseen. Felt as the ranks of the shadow realms stepped forth. Felt the ancestors flanking per shoulders. Felt every ally enter the copse beneath the dark trees.

They moved at night because that was what the magic told Tegan.

They moved at night because that was what the ancestors whispered in per ears.

They moved at night for no reason other than it was right, and Tegan could taste that in the cold air.

"Let the magic ride through me! Let the magic guide me!"

Tegan turned, looking around the circled clumps of per comrades. Jenny. Bocan. Psych. Case.

"We fight for Go No More!"

CHAPTER 42
JENNY

Tegan looked fierce. Powerful. Firelight danced over the narrow planes of per face. Kpinga in each hand, the Knight looked as if per could conquer the world.

But they were also still small.

Still human.

And it was Jenny's job to protect Tegan as best she could.

"Tegan will be fine." Bocan's voice rumbled softly just above and behind Jenny's back.

"We better make sure of that, you big pig fucker."

"Let's go," he replied, letting the nervous jibe slide.

Leaving the bikes and horses with a small crew, they trekked farther into the dark of the woods, following Case, Tegan, Psych, Aphrodite, elves, and djinn. Once again, the trolls seemed to be doing their own thing, bringing up the rear of the small unit.

The creak of pig and deer hide and the soft stomp of booted feet rose the blood in Jenny's breast. They were heading to a battle that she could not comprehend, but was sworn to fight. There was no way out and no way in. All Jenny could do was follow, buckler in one hand, sword in the next, throwing knives in a bandolier across her chest.

And none of her weapons were worth a shit against this.

But they were all that Jenny had.

"It's just up ahead," Bocan said. "Another quarter klick."

"You can feel it?" Jenny touched the knotted amulet with two fingers from her buckler hand. Again, it was slightly warm, but that could mean anything. The hunk of metal didn't offer up anything useful. Jenny just hoped it did its job.

"Makes my skin burn," the halbtroll replied.

A few short minutes later, they were there. Even Jenny could see the otherworldly glow ahead. It glimmered like a riot of candles seen through layers of hemp cloth screen.

"Fuck," she said.

Bocan spoke at the same time. "Fracking earth. It's been a long, fracking time."

His voice sounded strange, half strangled, but Jenny had no time to remark. Aphrodite, looking determined, stood with Abyad and the black dog in formation on one side of the glow. The elves stood on the other. Psych backed away toward the rest of the dragoons.

And Tegan, friend for life. Comrade in arms and laughter.

Tegan stood silhouetted dead center, arms outstretched, helm on, kpinga in each hand, limned in light.

Bocan shouldered past Jenny, heading for the gate.

She followed. It was what her body was trained for.

Move. Act.

Protect your friends at all costs.

IDon'tKnowWhatI'mDoing! Her mind screamed.

Jenny adjusted her sword grip and stepped forward anyway, following Bocan's giant form that blocked out most of the light.

If she could not lead, she would follow. It was what the Steel Clan did.

CHAPTER 43

BOCAN

The gate smelled like springtime and felt like the best fuck Bocan ever had. It called him forward. Pulling. Tugging at his belly. Stroking at the edges of his skin until his dick rose to half mast, shoving at the hard pigskin of his pants.

It was all he could do to hold on to the axe in his right hand. All he could do to not drop his weapon and run headlong through that comforting, lust-filled opening, flanked by two pillars, glowing gold and silver in the forest night.

It was the promise of Elfland. The promise that all things desired would come to be real. The pledge to every person who had one drop of Underhill swimming through their veins, that here, there was order, and a place to belong.

Bocan fought against the lure. He knew the price. Subservience and bullshit.

But the call remained strong. It would be easy. Could be easy.

The blink of an eye. The catch of a breath. One step. One step was all it took. One step toward beauty. One step toward sex. One step toward...

Ma. His mother, beautiful. Laughing. Kissing Da. Shooting a bow. Grinning in the firelight.

Gone.

The closer he stepped to the portal, the stronger the sense of Ma became.

Blind rage blotted out the light.

Ma didn't just disappear. And she might still be alive, trapped Underhill.

The realization washed through him like icy cold Clackamas water. His mother had been taken. Stolen. Bright soul sucked away.

Bocan filled his lungs and roared. He ran toward the smallness of Tegan's shadow, dead center of that poisonous, glowing light.

That pig-fucking silver blood was going to fracking pay.

CHAPTER 44
TEGAN

Sweat poured from Tegan's face, dripping down per body, soaking hemp and leather. It felt as if per had been fighting for half a day, instead of standing in one place for the quarter of an hour.

Tegan rooted deeper, ancestors at per back. Tegan pulled from above. Tegan bridged the worlds.

Tegan was meant to do this.

Tegan never wanted to. Not before, not now, not ever again.

Starlight and Flex pressed against per legs, lending their strength. The mage, djinn, and elves did the same. Arms outstretched, palms wide, Aphrodite and Abyad siphoned off what they could as the elves helped Tegan push. Centimeter by centimeter, the gate ground and screamed. Tegan felt the gate begin to close.

Per energy flared and died, flared and died. Tegan could not hold things steady.

The Steel Clan and its allies were going to lose.

The air was thick as a forest fire. Tegan's breath came in shallow pants. Salt ran in stinging rivulets across per eyes. Fingers in a death grip around kpinga hilts, Tegan pulled again. Drawing. The gateway. Closed. Two centimeters. More.

A flurry of strength and movement buffeted Tegan from behind.

Serena swooped overhead, displacing magic and air. Flapping her broad wings frantically, the huge owl changed course, turning to face Tegan.

Barring the entrance to the gate.

"Yeahhhhaaauuuggghhhh!" Tegan bellowed, the force of per voice flinging Serena backward. With all per might, Tegan pulled on the magic. Pulled from Starlight and Flex. From Aphrodite the mage. From the elves.

Serena shrieked into Tegan's face.

Tegan, hands aching with the effort, drew the two kpingas closer together, using as much force as was left in per body to draw blades and hands together.

They barely moved, but a shout came up from behind. Tingling Elven magic punched Tegan in the chest. The amulet singed per skin, acrid and painful. Torched flesh and rotting flowers stink filled per nose.

CHAPTER 45
BOCAN

Bocan ran, Jenny behind him, shouldering past Knights and apprentices, heading for the glowing gate, propelled by rage and anguish. He hurtled through the forest, fueled by his da's sorrow and the image of his mother's face.

Closing the gate was not enough. Queen Silverhair must pay.

Queen Silverhair must die.

"Out of my fracking way!" His voice felt like thunder booming from his lungs. His feet chewed earth like a PR digging machine. He had one aim.

Tegan's shadow.

He had to get there before his comrade closed the gate.

Bocan had to make it through.

CHAPTER 46
JENNY

Jenny followed Bocan, ready to back him up in whatever way he needed. Body moving as it should. A warrior. A comrade. A friend.

Her lips skinned back, exposing her teeth. She felt wild. Untamed. Filled with a fury not her own.

A fury boiling off Bocan's back, slamming through her, telegraphed in every footfall the halbtroll took, and every swing of the gleaming axe in his right hand.

Serena was shrieking up ahead.

Something was wrong.

Something was very wrong.

Frack! Jenny took on speed, trying to slip past Bocan's left side. There was never a fucking opening.

"Damn it, Bocan! Someone stop him!"

Two large shadows appeared to block her way. Recoana and Feldspar.

"What are you doing? We have to stop him!"

Jenny wasn't sure exactly what Bocan was doing, but she knew it wasn't right.

"He must do this, Knight. You must let him go."

She feinted left, then right again. The trolls tangled with each other and Jenny slipped through, pelting toward the elves and Aphrodite, and the weird gold glow.

What she would do once there, she wasn't sure.

"Stop, Bocan!" she shouted, not stopping to see who heard. Around her, she felt the Knights spring into action.

All of them were running.

Racing toward the shrieking owl. Toward the mages and the elves.

Toward Tegan.

Toward Bocan.

Toward the gate.

CHAPTER 47

BOCAN

"I'm sorry, comrade!" Bocan yelled, then shoved Tegan as hard as he could. It was like shoving a wall. Hitting Tegan, he hit the magic per battled against. Tegan was a force meeting a force, and now the force smacked him like a grizzly paw.

Flesh compressed on bone. Lungs squeezed.

He shoved again.

The little Knight went down, kpingas dropping, face smacking loam.

Serena's eyes caught him, leading him in. He ducked beneath the owl's broad wings and pushed, like rolling a boulder up a mountain. Still fighting.

The magic roared and sparked, pushing him back. He bent, and braced himself, leg muscles screaming, boots digging divots into earth.

"I!" He pushed again.

The power of the gate pressed and shoved.

"Claim!" Dragged one foot a half step forward.

The gate contracted. A giant mouth, poised to spit him out.

"Hearth right!"

The gate opened. Bocan tumbled through.

Behind him, Tegan screamed.

Bocan tripped and smacked the ground. His head bounced; bottom teeth nicked lips. He tasted dirt and blood, and everything went black.

CHAPTER 48

JENNY

The earth trembled. Jenny fought to steady her boots. All around her, Knights shouted and swayed, weapons ready to slice through an enemy that wasn't there. Damson and Aphrodite collapsed into heaps on either side of what she could see now was a natural arch made by wild roses, clambering up the trees. Abyad stood, barely, breath heaving, ghostly white face exhausted. The black dog leaned against the djinn, as if lending him it's strength.

Except for a slender slice of gold, the glowing gate was gone.

Peridot leaned over Tegan, who lay crumpled on the dirt in the middle of that arch.

"Tegan!"

Her comrade moaned. Per kpingas were dropped around per. One had fallen on the tip of one of the three blades. Half buried in the forest floor, it was canted upward, as if the handle waited for the warrior's palm.

But that warrior's hands were both gripping per head. Peridot was doing something, fingers twitching. Jenny shouldered him out of the way, hearing a sizzle as her body connected with his. He yelped, but moved.

Starlight sniffed at Tegan, and gave per cheek a gentle lick. Tegan rolled to per side, eyes screwed tight, knees tight to chest.

Jenny wished Andandita was with them. Or at least one of her apprentices. Wait. Her head whipped around and lighted on a towering shadow.

Recoana cross-trained with Andandita. She should have enough skill to help. Jenny called out.

"Recoana!"

Tegan moaned again.

"Sorry, comrade." Jenny sheathed her short sword. Skinning off a glove, she shoved it in a pocket and lay a palm across Tegan's forehead. Per skin was wet with sweat, but not overly warm. That was good, right?

With great, thumping strides, Feldspar and Recoana both arrived.

Recoana crouched down as Feldspar kept guard. Against what, exactly, Jenny wasn't sure. But it was probably a good idea.

Especially as the gate did not seem fully closed.

"Can you help Tegan?"

Jenny scuffled back to give the troll some room.

Recoana closed her dark eyes and held out a hand that was darker and more blue than Bocan's. She was doing what healers called "scanning." Using psychic senses to assess damage.

Jenny knew about that. It was no different than scanning for enemies in the field.

Letting the troll do her work, Jenny stood and stretched, then tapped Feldspar's arm and craned her neck up to look at his face.

He stopped scanning and met her gaze. His eyes were almost black and Jenny could see tattoos snaking up his dark blue neck.

"Bocan?" she asked.

The dark blue troll just shook his head.

"Gone."

Fuck. Irritation, fear, and anger crawled up her spine, lighting her nerve endings with the will to fight. Her fingers flexed and her right hand jerked toward the sword at her hip before she stilled it.

"What can we do? Can we wrench the thing back open and get him the fuck out?"

He gazed back out into the forest night.

"We cannot. Not without reinforcements. Not without more magic. Unless…"

"Unless what?"

"Unless Bocan is fighting from the inside. But we do not know his plan."

Jenny bit her lip, and turned away, looking out over the clumps of bewildered Knights, Aphrodite, Damson who was just coming to, the forest…

Peridot and Abyad were gone.

Flex trotted over to her, bumping her leg with one shoulder. She looked down at the patterned fur of the faery fox. There was something there. Something in the whorls of red oak, black moss, and white.

She crouched back down, to look into the fox's face. "What do you know?"

The fox showed her. A flickering of images, none of them good.

Jenny's stomach fluttered with a rush of fear before the warrior in her took over.

Bocan was her comrade. Bocan was her family.

Somehow, the fucking pattern laid out by the queen, by magic, by the Reckoning, by whatever Gods had taken a sick interest...they would figure out how to break it. How to scuff the lines. Shift the course.

Trace out something new.

"We're going to get him out," she said. "I have a plan."

Or she would, by the time the night was through.

CHAPTER 49

TEGAN

Pale sunbeams slanted through the forest, dust motes dancing like sprites in the air. Birds called, squirrels chucked, and the sounds of breakfast cleanup filtered through it all. Tegan sat cross-legged on per bedroll, periodically sucking in nasty tea from a waxed wooden mug, trying to get per shit together.

Per mouth still felt as if Tegan had eaten unripe pears, and every bone hurt. Recoana had been fussing around Tegan, which had only made per feel worse. Luckily, she had been called into a conclave with the elves.

Tegan groaned softly and took another sip of tea. It was supposed to help per head and stomach, but so far, it just made Tegan want to bite something, curl up, and die.

Peridot and Damson's voices carried softly across the makeshift camp.

"We need more magic, clearly, to get the gate open

again. Either that, or we sacrifice the fool halbtroll to his own fate. It's going to be hard enough to close it all the way. We almost had it until that fool pushed his way through." That was Peridot. Arrogant ass.

"We do not abandon our own." Jenny's voice was rough with anger.

"And why should we trust elves, when it is elves who have caused such strife?" Abyad was pissed. The black dog growled low in its throat.

"Stop that." Case's voice was raised. "We don't need dissension when a comrade may be in danger!"

Tegan glanced over to where the meeting was happening. Case and Jenny sat with the elves, Aphrodite, and the trolls, as the djinn paced just outside their rough circle. All of them had wooden mugs in hand. Jenny looked determined. As if she had a plan. Aphrodite looked slightly ill. The elves looked as pissed off as the djinn.

The trolls? They were the inscrutable ones this trip, and Tegan wondered why.

Tegan had no idea how the elves thought that more magic was going to work to close the gate, after what they'd pumped through the air the night before, but was also in no shape to argue.

Besides, Tegan had no say in the matter. Despite Peridot blaming things on Bocan, it was Tegan who had failed.

Tegan sipped at more tea, wishing per head was clear enough to parse out what the fracking earth had actually happened.

Why the fuck had Bocan and Serena gone inside?

Starlight padded over, along with Flex.

::Halbtroll is okay.:: the lynx said.

Huh. That was interesting.

::How do you know?::

Flex threw an image of the great snowy owl into her head. The animals must have a way to communicate with one another, even through the portals.

Tegan took another sip of tea, and scratched behind Starlight's ears.

"Thanks."

Starlight huffed with impatience and shoved at per hand hard enough to rock Tegan's mug of tea.

And then per got it.

Rising painfully, per headed toward the fracking tension of the meeting. The animals padded alongside, ready to share the news.

CHAPTER 50

KARAKTILLA

It was a pleasant day for flying, but Karaktilla and her sometime-mate Daraktal sat perched high up toward the peak of the volcano. The snow crisped the air and no haze filled the valley down below.

In that valley, two impressive condors and a few smaller turkey vultures circled over black dots of screeching, unrelenting crows. Karaktilla's keen eyes picked out gray shapes moving among the birds. Wolves. Later, the smaller creatures would emerge to claim their portion, too. The spoils of human battles fed the land.

It was the proper way of things. Unlike the way things had gone before.

In the days before the Change, human battles had killed too many and too much. Karaktilla could not mourn those days, and did not comprehend why so many Underhill still did.

::Will this affect us?:: The smaller drake's clattering

voice bounced off the rock and snow. His sunset-tinted scales looked like fire among the white and brown. *::This gate closing your warriors attempt?::*

::If I thought it would not, would I have called you here?::

He flicked his tail toward hers and huffed out a laugh. *::Sometimes you call me here for very different reasons.::*

Karaktilla turned toward Daraktal and hissed in annoyance. Well, annoyance and maybe something else. He was a handsome drake, after all, especially with his scarlet and orange scales shining in the sun.

Then she sighed. *::I wish I had called you here for flying and other pleasures. But these actions of Silverhair are of concern to me. They bode ill. And if the humans succeed in closing off this portal, the realms may become trapped apart again, at least in this part of the world. There's no telling the effects, really.::*

::And?::

::And we do not know what that portends, my friend. But everything I see in the crystal orb tells me that it will be no good. Not for Silverhair. Nor for the humans. Nor for us.::

::This current age suits me, I admit. I am loathe for it to change again so quickly,:: Daraktal replied. *::I will ponder the problem, though so far I see no more answers than you do.::*

Karaktilla grunted, and they both returned to gazing out over the land. The river shone like a drake's long tail. The human fields were green.

::It is a good day for flying,:: Karaktilla said.

::*Shall we, then?*:: he said, pushing his strong legs into position, ready to push off.

::*Catch me,*:: she said.

Opening her brown and purple wings, Karaktilla shoved off with her haunches, and soared into the sky.

Being a drake in these times was a magnificent thing. Clean air, plenty of space to roam without interference and no fires raining down from the tin bellies of growling, unnatural beasts. Now, if only they could keep it that way.

Karaktilla caught a warm draft of air and soared. She thought of the Knight, Jenny, and the destiny foretold. The woman was part of this, but seemed reluctant to step forth and do her part. There were others, too, that Karaktilla had seen inside the orb. The small, dark Knight. Recoana the troll, and the pale blue halb-troll, too.

And a djinn and elf who had agendas she could not yet discern.

There was another human, too, though the drake had not been able to puzzle how she fit. A dark-haired beauty of a woman. A healer, who taught Recoana what she knew about the mountain herbs and other things. Sun glinted off Daraktal's neck and shot a piercing ray into her eye. Her nictating lid closed, and then the fleshy eyelid, closing off the glare.

The humans were wrong. The elves, too. They thought that magic would fight magic here, but Karaktilla wondered if that was not so. She could not read the web of wyrd clearly enough, but she knew one thing, flying high above the sleeping volcano: the dark-haired woman was tied to the red-haired Knight somehow.

Their destinies were written in the same ink.

Karaktilla tilted her wings, and pointed her long and graceful neck toward the ribbon of river south and west.

Daraktal roared a question. She roared back.

Wings displacing air, Karaktilla led the way toward the green, green fields that lay like patchwork beyond her mountain home.

CHAPTER 51
ANANDITA

The council had been arguing for days now, ever since the party had rolled off to investigate the portal gate.

The Steel Clan and the others rode toward what they hoped was a solution to the terror of death, disappearance, and worse. Far, far worse. Even the thought of soul stealing filled Anandita's mouth with bile, and made her want to prostrate herself at her shrine.

She had tried that, actually, though there was little comfort in it. So, like everyone else in the township, she poured herself and her healing magic into work because there was always work to be done.

Her journey into the woods had not been without fruit. Sure enough, half buried in loam, at the base of a small, rounded boulder near where the searchers had found Long's brooch, was a carving of the sundered leaves and triangle shape. It helped, somehow, to know where he had gone, though the thought of his soul being stolen and used was too great to bear.

But other than prayer, there was not much she could do about it. Not now. So, as the Steel Clan rode, she sat with the council once again.

"We've been going around and around about this, and so far, you haven't said one damn useful thing." John's hands gripped his cider mug, his pale skin flushed with anger. The dairy man resented being kept from work. They all did.

"We need the Knights here, to ferret out whoever it was that sabotaged the waterworks. Not off on some foolhardy magical quest." Arcady ran a hand across his tightly coiled dark hair. Anandita sympathized with the engineer, but couldn't agree. However, she'd said that half a dozen times in several different ways.

Give me strength.

Anandita had done extra puja the past few days. And she'd prayed for Long's soul, wherever it was.

She had to believe he had returned to Source somehow because any other possibility was far too great to bear. That his soul might be used to someone else's ends? Her mind balked at the thought of it.

Fragments of dreams slipped through her head as she half prayed, half listened to the ongoing debate.

Images of deep forest. Rushing river. Golden light. Yaksha trembling beneath the roots of trees.

A picture of Tegan, crumpled on the ground. Two drakes flying against blue sky.

Jenny. Tall and powerful, short sword raised, shouting.

"We need to move on. What's done is done. The usual contingent of Knights stayed behind for protection, the whole town is trained, and Charles stayed to continue to ferret out the magic." Rafiq's words surprised her, though they shouldn't have. He was a good man, and despite what he felt, was willing to compromise if he decided it was in the township's best interests.

As Anandita stared at the steam rising from the pottery mug, another image flickered through her mind. It was herself, sitting in the forest next to the standing Jenny, both facing a sliver of a golden glow. And Charles was beside them.

Everything clicked into place. The sense of rightness returned to Anandita's body.

"Charles won't be here for long. They need him at the portal."

"What?" Arcady practically jumped out of his seat, spilling tea. It slid in a slow-moving river across the broad wood table, until Porrac came around from the bar, rag in hand, to stop the flow.

Something had to stop the flow. Something... Anandita wasn't yet sure what, she just knew the feeling that matched the image of herself and Charles. Her intuition didn't tell her exactly what needed to happen, but it was clear that somehow, she and Charles needed to head around the mountain and try to find the Knights.

While her mind railed against the impracticality of it, and the pain in the ass it was going to be to get herself and her chair all the way out there, her heart beat like Porrac's Irish drum at the thought of it. This was what had been missing since Long disappeared. More than companionship and love, it was the way he always made her feel brave.

As if she could do anything. Anything at all.

"I need to go, too," she said.

The room erupted into shouting. Anandita didn't care.

"You can't go!" Rafiq was on his feet, face flushed dark, leaning over her chair.

"You're going to back down." Anandita stared up at the current council head, forcing herself to speak clearly and calmly, though him leaning over her chair made her angry. "Now."

Rafiq came to himself, flushed even deeper if that was possible, and stepped back, bumping into his own chair and stumbling before righting himself.

He swallowed, clearly about to say something.

Anandita cut him off with a raised hand.

"First of all, as most of us have been taught since childhood, no one rules over another in this township." Her voice cut through the side conversations, carrying through the meeting hall. "Secondly, whether by horseback or cart, I'm very well capable of traveling any length of land that I please. And we have enough Knights here to spare an escort for myself and Charles. Thirdly..."

One of the big front doors slammed open and Hypatia ran in, dark hair tumbled, brown tunic torn at the sleeve. He panted, out of breath as was too typical these days. She and her son were going to have a talk once this was through, about what he really wanted to do with his life.

"There are two drakes flying overhead!"

Chairs scraped across the floors. Porrac shouted for his partner. The kitchen door swung open to the bar, and Jamie and two apprentices came barreling through.

"Drakes!" Hypatia shouted again, then ran back outside.

Anandita felt as if the breath had been knocked out from her lungs. Drakes? She knew they lived nearby, and had seen black dots flying in the distance, around the snow-capped peak of Wy'east, but had never seen one up close.

Drakes never traveled this far west that she knew of.

Despite the warmth of the town hall, Anandita shivered, and tucked her bright shawl around her shoulders. Then, the rest of the council having already run outside, she wheeled her chair through the now-propped-open town hall doors.

As she crested the threshold and pushed across the wide-planked porch to the ramp, she saw that the whole town was gathered around the central circle that formed the hub of Go No More.

Every face was turned up toward the sky, from toddlers in arm to the oldest members of the township.

And everyone—child, woman, person, and man—was silent.

Anandita cleared the porch and rolled down the wooden ramp. Then she looked up.

Two drakes flew, colossal wings outstretched, shadowing the town. One purple, one red, scales shimmering in the late September sun.

She raised a hand to her face in wonder, and realized her cheeks were wet with tears.

CHAPTER 52
JENNY

Tegan looked like shit, but Jenny was amazed her comrade was up at all. She'd kept a loose eye on per all morning, and noticed when per finally rolled up to a sitting position. Tegan had staggered off to the latrines with Recoana's help, then gone right back to sleep.

But Tegan shambled over now, going very slowly, paced by Flex and Starlight. All three clearly had something on their minds.

Jenny started to rise, but Feldspar touched her arm. Right. Tegan wouldn't want the help, would per?

Aphrodite rose and gave Tegan her blanket-covered log to sit on. It was a testimony to just how crappy Tegan felt that the Knight did not refuse.

"The animals are in communication." Tegan's voice was scratchy and barely audible. Every person in the circle leaned forward to catch per words.

Jenny's heart pounded in her chest. "What?"

Tegan cleared per throat and winced. "Serena. Starlight and Flex can communicate with Serena."

"Astounding," Aphrodite said, shifting her focus from Tegan to the elves and back again. "They can communicate across the realms?"

"That is excellent news," Feldspar rumbled. "Now, how can we use it?"

Everyone waited for the elves to speak. Damson pursed her pale lips in thought and looked toward Peridot. It was clear the silver bloods were communicating psychically, which Jenny had no patience with.

"Say that shit out loud," she said. "We've got no time for secrets."

Flex snapped his jaws and the black dog's chest rumbled as if holding back a growl.

Peridot's pale skin flushed with anger, clashing with his pale green hair. He still looked beautiful, the pig fucker.

"We don't know," Damson quickly replied. "We've heard of such things, of course, but never had cause to test them before. I was asking Peridot if he thought we could commune with anyone Underhill from this position."

"And?" Jenny asked.

The male elf glared at her. Jenny didn't care. These Underhill fuckers knew that to deal with the Knights meant to deal honestly, and to not stand on ceremony. Oh, they said they repudiated Underhill ways, and were good with the way things worked in Go No More, but scratch the surface or piss one of them off? They were still aristos, through and through.

"And we're going to try," he said, pointedly aiming his words toward the trolls and Aphrodite, freezing out the Knights.

Fine with Jenny. As long as they knew what was what.

"Do you have a close contact there?" Aphrodite asked, wrapping her hair in a kerchief, as if readying for battle. As if she'd finally realized that they would have to fight for whatever came next.

"We intend to try the queen's daughter. Elzabetta."

In a breath, Jenny was on her feet. She shoved the elf from his log and ground his slim shoulders into the dirt with the palms of her hands. Fucker was lucky she'd left off the buckler for this meeting, or he'd have a chin full of steel, too.

"What the fuck?" she snarled. "You're going to contact the one who is feeding off our souls?"

Off the souls of those poor people in the village. Off of the soul of her childhood friend, Maura, and how many others?

"Jenny!" Tegan's voice was harsh as a crow's. "Stand down."

Jenny relaxed her grip on Peridot's finely woven shirt. He tensed beneath her, ready to strike the second her weight shifted.

"Tell the elf to stand down as well, and I will."

"Oh for Brigid's sake! Both of you, grow the fuck up. We don't have time for this!" That was Case, voice loud and close enough to hurt, hand on Jenny's shoulder, tugging her back.

She relented. They were right. As soon as she

rocked backward to her heels, Peridot shoved her onto her ass. He didn't follow through, just brushed himself off and stood, and Case's hand once again gripped her shoulder. Jenny let the insult go, but her skin was tight with the heat of anger and the morning's porridge sat heavy in her gut.

"Explain yourself," she said, once she'd calmed enough to speak. She held Peridot's green-eyed gaze. The elf looked as if he wanted to bite her face.

"Keep a civil tongue in your fucking mouth, clod-head," he replied, voice tinged with venom.

She growled. Case grabbed her arm and forced her to back away.

"Fuck you, elf." She knew the elves talked about her behind her back. About her lack of magic. About her size and strength. Damson was polite enough, but with Peridot? The lack of respect was mutual.

Catching sight of Tegan's pinched face, Jenny forced herself to calm down. The other Knight looked actively in pain. That made Jenny even more angry, but as a strategist, she knew that right now, her anger was only making things worse for Tegan, not better.

"Get your shit together, comrade," Case said in her ear. Jenny jerked away and stalked to stand behind Tegan, arms crossed over her chest.

"What do you mean, you'll communicate with the princess?" Recoana's deep voice was calm, as though nothing had just happened. The troll wore a puzzled expression. "How will you do that, and why might that be good?"

"Peridot cared for Elzabetta when she was a babe

in arms. He was one of her...friendly guardians. So they have a bond. We hope that he can reach her through that." Damson sounded uncertain.

"Why the frack didn't you tell us this before?" Case sounded ready to spit. "Before we dragged our asses out here? Didn't you think the mages could have done something with this information?"

Case stalked off a few yards and beat his fist against a tree. Unease flickered at the base of Jenny's skull, but she had no time to trace the thought to its conclusion.

"And that's good why? Contacting the princess? I still need that explained," Jenny said, fighting to control her breathing and keep her own voice calm.

"She's right, Damson," Case said, stalking back. He looked mostly back in control of his temper. "If Silver-hair is stealing souls to help Elzabetta, how does contacting the princess help us at all? Why don't we focus on contacting Bocan?"

Jenny cursed her limited psychic range and lack of magic. She cursed sitting around in this forest, arguing with elves. She wanted to bust through that fucking sliver of a portal and rescue her friend.

It was Peridot who answered. He stopped smacking the dirt from his dark brown tunic and leather trews and looked at Case, though it was clear his words were aimed at Jenny. "The Queen is a piece of gilded shit, and we all know it. But Elzabetta? She's still a child. Barely into her teens. None of this is her fault. We cannot lay the Queen's actions at Elzabetta's feet."

"Just as we do not blame you for the Reckoning," Damson said. "We blame those who came before you. If we are to give this new world a chance, we have to stop assigning blame and build. Is that not what your forebears taught?"

Well, fuck, Jenny thought. The fury drained from her limbs and she moved back into the loose circle, sitting down onto bare earth.

"So what do we do?" Feldspar asked again. "And how can the animals help us?"

It was going to be a long fucking meeting. And Jenny really wished Bocan were here.

She also couldn't help but think of Anandita. If the healer were here, Jenny would feel better. That was part of her magic. Making everyone feel better. Even clod heads like Jenny. But Jenny was also glad she was safe in Go No More.

At least she hoped so. The attack en route still weighed heavy on Jenny's mind, but there had been no time to strategize, and no way to get word to the town. Unless...

"Can Flex or Starlight send word to Go No More about the bandit attack? Tell them to post an extra watch?"

"That's a good idea," Tegan rasped out, then closed per eyes, communing with Starlight and Flex; then blinked and shook per head. "Too far away. There's something about it being the wrong atmosphere in this realm or something. Easier to communicate across the gate to Elfland."

Jenny straightened, thoughts pinging through her head.

"It was worth asking. But given that, I want to know if Recoana, Feldspar, or someone else, I don't give a fuck who, can contact Bocan."

She turned her head back to where Peridot and Damson stood together, heads already bent in confer-ence. "You elves do what you want to, but if it screws over any of our comrades, you're as good as dead."

Then Jenny turned, not waiting for response, and stalked off through the makeshift camp, heading toward the gate.

CHAPTER 53

ANANDITA

The drakes landed with a mighty press of wind and air that tugged at Anandita's shawl and caused her hair to fly around her head. As soon as the winds died down, she shoved at the smooth metal knobs protruding from the wheels, and headed toward the paddock as quickly as her arms would push the chair. Everyone else had the same idea and crowded her way. Hypatia noticed the trouble, grabbed Tokki, and the two of them helped clear a path for her chair.

When she got to the edge of the field, what she saw took Anandita's breath away. Sunlight shimmered on colossal flanks, flashing variegated shades of purple, brown, and red so bright, they caused her to squint and shade her eyes with one hand. Her first thought was to wish that Long could have witnessed such a sight.

Her second thought was to wonder how Jenny had spoken to a drake at all, let alone spent the night in its cave. Strange magic emanated from both of the mountainous creatures. If she didn't know better, she would think the drakes were made of magic themselves. But no. That was foolishness. They were clearly flesh and muscle, tooth and bone. The shimmering scales simply refracted light, like glass or metal did.

The drakes had magic like the elves and djinn and the others did. And the humans, too, though in a much lesser degree. It was funny to think this world had once been all but bereft of this sort of magic. How foreign that seemed.

But the magic of the drakes was as foreign to her magic as the old world was to the new. It was a heavy, powerful, fragrant and frightening thing.

It smelled old, like crumbling PR paper, sprinkled with stardust and crackling in the sun. It smelled like change.

She took in one shuddering breath.

Remember who you are. That was something her mother always admonished, especially after the accident that crushed her limbs. In those days, Anandita had sunk into deep depression. It was only her parents, aunties, and the constant badgering of Doc Warren that had gotten her through.

And Jenny, too. Jenny had been there for Anandita through it all. Anandita just hadn't noticed—hadn't remembered—until now.

Then there was Long. And apprenticing to learn the ways of the healing herbs. And the cycles of life that had led her to this field. To face this magic.

To exist in the presence of barely fathomable magnificence.

Another deep breath, and one more moment of simply looking, tasting, and sensing...

"Ma, hurry!" Hypatia practically danced in place by now. The crowd circling the drakes had grown thick, but no one had ventured closer than that shadow's edge where her son and apprentice stood.

Okay. It's going to be okay. Her hands returned to wheel rims, and Anandita rolled across the soft grasses and flowers toward the two young people and the shimmering behemoths.

Inaya already stood near the larger, purplish drake, head raised, clearly speaking, though Anandita couldn't make out the words. The only one who had dared to venture so close, the grower had tucked her hands, hand to wrist. She leaned toward the towering body as if the two were old friends.

The reddish drake spied Anandita coming with one black, nictating eye. She had never felt more like a slip of a strange plant laid out on a table for closer inspection. She wheeled on, determined, though she noticed Hypatia and Tokki were now just behind her, instead of ahead. They'd turned her chair into a buffer, as if it would offer any protection from the magic surrounding the drakes, or from their claws, each of which was larger than one of her hands.

She did not know why the drakes had come, but the fact of it was so unusual that, taken with her visions and everything else, she knew it was a key to the mystery somehow.

"This is stunning."

Charles's voice was less than a meter from her head. Startled, she stopped the chair again. She'd been so captivated by the drakes, she hadn't noticed his approach. The mage squinted toward the drakes, one hand raised to shade his eyes. His long, pale hemp tunic was edged with simple patterns today. The man must embroider well into the night to have as many embroidery-edged tunics as he did. But everyone had their own way to work their magics, and a trained mage more than most. Sewing was clearly one of his magical focii.

"I wonder what caused the drakes to venture here?" he asked.

"That's what I aim to find out," Anandita replied, forging ahead again. Tokki and Hypatia had continued and looked back at her now, standing at the edge of the drake's shadows, faces uncertain, but still glowing with excitement to be this near to the strange creatures.

Strange and beautiful. For such ungainly beings, they were almost regal, though Anandita supposed a member of Go No More shouldn't use that language. But they had a grace about them, especially in the air, with the leathery, muscular wings somehow holding their long, meaty bodies aloft.

For the first time in her life, Anandita wondered what it would be like to fly.

::Come forth, wheeled human.:: The purple drake's mouth made strange, varied clicking and clacking noises. A rumble in its chest shook the earth beneath

her chair as its telepathic voice shook Anandita's mind. *::It is you we have come to seek.::*

"Holy shit," Tokki said. Anandita looked at her apprentice, startled. It seemed that the drake's mind speech carried to several minds at once. She had heard of such things, but never experienced them.

And she had never seen a beast as magnificent as the scaled creature who waited in front of her.

Holy shit, Anandita thought, then rolled toward whatever life held in store.

CHAPTER 54

BOCAN

Bocan lifted his head and groaned. His whole body ached and his upper mouth felt like chewed pig meat.

The gate was a shimmering sliver behind him, but he was not sure how to get back through. His head pounded and his belly churned.

And he was in the strangest place he'd ever seen.

His mother was not here, was she? She had to be long dead, as he and his father had always thought she was, and Bocan was a fool. Or had Da known, somehow?

"Gone," Da had said, that day when Bocan, still a child, had come upon him weeping. "She is gone."

Gone could mean any number of things, couldn't it?

He shook the memory from his aching head and looked around, trying to get his bearings.

Apple trees were in both fruit and flower, as were plum trees. White and pink blossoms drifted on a slight breeze, falling on Serena's head like snow. The owl blinked at him, waiting patiently for the moment.

A brook sang nearby, not simply the slip of water over stone, but as if it had a human voice. Or a faery one. The air was fragrant with a flowery scent he did not recognize. Gone were the dark, towering, ragged winged Douglas firs and the balsam-scented hemlock spruce. Here was watery sunshine as though the world were one big orchard or meadow.

He pushed himself to his feet, limbs heavy, straining with the effort. He patted his hands around his person, making sure every weapon was in place. They were, including the battle-axe strapped to his back and the knife and short sword at his belt.

Unlike the choked off byways of the realm he had just left, here, the path ahead was clear. A winding, pale brown ribbon among verdant green and delicate lavenders and yellows.

Bocan longed for the dark forest and his comrades with all his heart.

Yet something drew him forward, heavy boots striking the earth, as out of place as Angel's stud horse at a Mayday dance. Bocan moved down the pathway as if tugged on by a silver chain, lured by the promise of his heart's desire.

But his heart's desire was not here, the brain inside his thick, muzzy skull protested. His heart's desire was with a feisty animal healer near Salem. His heart's desire was with Jenny and the Knights.

His heart's desire was with his da, living half

broken in the caves between Underhill and Go No More.

A need for vengeance, and the memory of Ma's face and laughter had drawn him here, but all he saw were fracking beautiful trees and a peaceful, sterile sense of order. Order he wanted to smash with his fists until it shattered into shards of dropped glass.

Tears flowed down his face and sobs wracked Bocan's body, but his feet moved on, as if they had their own will.

Or as if he was under a spell.

"Who are you, sorrowing halbtroll? And what brings you here?"

The voice was light as a rainbow-shot bubble, and as pleasant as spring. He turned to find a young, slim elf maid gazing at him with serious, moss-green eyes set on either side of a tilted nose, and hair as pale as the barely green tinged underleaves of Anandita's sage. She looked...insubstantial. Sickly, if such a thing was possible. Too thin even for an elf. Her long dress was blue as the hydrangeas his mother had loved so well, and her silvery-green hair was plaited in a crown around her head.

"Who are you?" he asked, his voice too loud, too sudden. He heard the whir of wings behind him, as if he had startled some small birds. Serena swooped overhead, then disappeared from his vision.

"I might ask the same of you, as you are a stranger here, and your friends are massed outside our gate."

His head jerked up at that, but he said nothing. Her face knew too much.

"My name is Elzabetta," the bright creature replied. "Daughter of Silverhair…"

"The one who killed my mother," Bocan replied, sprinting toward her, hands outstretched as if to strike her down.

She raised her small, pale hands in return, as if she could ward off his blow.

"Halt!" The voice was stentorian, coming somewhere from his right. Bocan heard the sound of bowstrings being pulled and arrows nocked. He slowed his boots, falling to his knees, hands raised above his head. Small creatures fluttered and buzzed around his face. His fingers twitched to bat them away.

"It is fine, Jacques," the elven maid spoke again. "I'm sure he means no harm. Sprites! Leave him be."

The small winged menaces retreated. The princess was a fool.

He did mean harm. He meant to harm this girl. And the queen. And anyone in this forsaken place who had slaughtered a village of innocents as if they had been slavers, cannibals, warlords, or thieves.

Bocan held his tongue. Best to stay alive as long as he could.

He spared a thought for Serena, wondering where she was.

::*I am above you, and fine, thank you. The Queen's mage is the one you wish to speak to. I think he can help us, and I think he's being used.*::

He had long ago learned to trust the snowy owl, and throttled down his anger, banking it until the embers glowed in his belly but did not enflame his head and hands. He was a warrior who could control himself. He was a Knight of the Steel Clan.

And he was inside the enemy's camp.

"Take me to your mage," he said.

"Lower your bows!" Elzabetta said. Her voice was weak, and barely carried, yet the lower-ranked elves obeyed. "You claimed hearth right upon entering. That makes you our guest."

In the old tales, guests murdered their hosts after sharing salt and bread. Hearth right didn't mean shit if both parties did not agree to keep the peace.

The princess had made her first mistake, but Bocan would play along until he found what he was looking for.

His mother.

And the mage.

CHAPTER 55
ANANDITA

It all happened so quickly. Not only were Anandita and Charles following the Knights and the others, they were doing so on drake-back.

Once the announcement was made, the field burst into uproar and Anandita sank back in her chair, the breath knocked from her chest as others figured out logistics, packing food, and gathering other supplies. She should be checking over her arrows and blades, but couldn't get herself together. Not while the drake spoke. Listening took all of her attention. Her mind wanted to race away.

.::I saw you at the shining waterfall gate. You are needed to support the destined Knight.:: Karaktilla's mind voice had grown as soft as the clicks emerging from the back of her throat. Perhaps this meant the speech was private? Anandita tucked the thought away and attended to the words.

The "destined Knight" would be Jenny, which would likely surprise no one except the red-haired

Knight herself. That woman was always trying to avoid who she was. She had a big dead zone around that, which was funny, because everyone else saw her plain as day.

Jenny was a leader, through and through. In a place where everyone had their own dreams and talents, Jenny still stood out. Special.

Regardless, the drake's confirmation of Anandita's dreams and visions meant the remaining council members had to stand aside. They weren't about to block consensus on something like this, which was good, because the drakes might have just carried off Anandita and Mage Wong without the council's leave if it came to that. And that would've been bad for the township.

You didn't want to break consensus, ever. Agree, or block, or stand aside, but don't go outside protocol or the fabric of the township—and all of their agreements —would slowly begin to fray.

So it was decided, and both drakes were being fitted with special harnesses being adapted as quickly as Angel's horse trainers and grooms could figure out. The Wasco leather workers made long straps for horse girdles and Angel's crew had belted together several lengths of the leather and were flinging them over the drakes, two people on each side. They were also affixing soft hemp ropes which looked as if they would loop around herself and Charles, holding them to the drakes. The groom's activity reminded her of one of those circus tales she had enjoyed as a child. The schoolhouse had a picture book of giant tents, ringed with people, trying to lift them with poles.

In the midst of it all, Anandita sat in her chair, looking into the black eyes of Karaktilla and Daraktal. She was going with them. Just as she had dreamed. Just as she had told the council.

But she had never dreamed she would be heading to the portal riding on the back of a drake.

So while the township buzzed around like Mugwort's bees, Anandita tried to remain calm. It was not easy. Karaktilla kept speaking of visions and portents and a bunch of other things that Anandita felt in her gut but had a hard time following with her head, and Angel's crew kept stepping around her chair, trying to secure the leather bands.

As the drake paused in its speech to lift one impressive leg for a groom, Angel took the opportunity to confer with Anandita, gesturing to the unfathomably long system of belts and straps.

"This hemp rope, here," he pointed, "should bind you well enough to the neck. We'll fit another strap of leather for you to hold onto further up, but you'll need to use your thighs, too. That still okay?"

Angel's brown face looked concerned. Years ago, the horse trainer had worked with the Wasco on gear that would allow Anandita to ride horses. They had tested and trained off and on for a year or so, until Anandita finally admitted she just didn't much enjoy riding horseback, and stopped.

She had planned to head toward the gate in a cart,

but figured she'd agree to horseback if Charles's intuition said they needed more speed. And now, this.

"My muscles are strong," she replied. "If you strap me securely, I should be fine." She'd gotten into the exercise habit during her recovery, and Long and Jenny had taken over badgering her when Dr. Warren left off. Muscle training was now as much a part of her routine as puja and yoga in the morning and evening.

But traveling on drake back? She was both terrified and intrigued. Finally, there was something she could *do*. Even if she had no idea why, when the compulsion was this strong, Anandita knew to follow.

"What about my chair?"

Angel stopped in the middle of hoisting a ladder against the purple drake, ready to secure the straps. He looked startled.

"What about it?"

She huffed in annoyance. Sometimes people were so dense. "I'm going to need it once we land. What? Did you think I was going to crawl through the forest or something?"

He had the good grace to look ashamed. "Lo siento, Anandita. I'm having a little trouble thinking past"— he waved a hand at the giant drake who looked down at both of them, amused—"all of this."

Crossing her arms over her chest, Anandita shook her head. "Apology accepted." She couldn't really blame the man. The situation was probably the most unusual thing that had ever happened in Go No More since its founding. But she still wished more people thought beyond themselves all the same.

"The chair is heavy, but it can fold..." she began.

::Affix the chair to my back, along with the healer's weapons. Daraktal can carry the mage and whatever food supplies the humans need.:: Karaktilla clicked and rumbled, louder again. Broadcasting. *::We can carry much heavier weights than these two humans, if we must.::*

The drake then fixed an eye on Anandita, as if thinking. *::It is cold for humans so high up.::*

"My apprentice is fetching my warm tunic and short trews as well as my winter wrap and some blankets."

Karaktilla nodded and went back to her monologue as if Angel and his crew had not interrupted things. Anandita breathed deeply, trying to settle back into herself. Attending to the drake, she needed to listen with far more than just her ears, and it took up the bulk of her attention. As the buzz of activity around her faded to the background, one thing became clear: the magic surrounding the shimmering purple drake had purpose, and Anandita's own smaller magics were quickly tuning themselves to the larger force, like grasses bent to wind.

Then something the drake had just said penetrated her skull. "Wait. What? What do you mean there's a field of dead people near Wy'east?" Her skin iced over. It couldn't be Jenny, because Jenny was still part of the visions, but... "Was the Steel Clan attacked en route?"

And if that was the case, so close to home, why wouldn't they have turned back to tend to their wounds or take care of their dead?

Steam puffed from the drake's nostrils. Its teeth clacked together.

::We do believe the Knights were attacked but were able to vanquish their foes. The carrion eaters were taking care of things when we passed. None of the dead wore the red favored by the Knights.::

Anandita called to Hypatia, who had been alternately clinging to her and hopping around with excitement.

"Beta! Tell Arcady and Rafiq I need to see them right away!" She couldn't see the council members through the throng. Hypatia raced off to find them, weaving through townsfolk with ease.

If the Steel Clan was attacked, it meant Go No More might be in greater danger than they thought, perhaps from the saboteurs, perhaps from some other source. Either way, that wasn't good.

She hoped the Knights had taken care of whatever the threat was, but the council and the Knights that had remained behind needed to hear about it.

Karaktilla raised her triangular head, and sniffed the air. *::We'd best hurry. The magic has changed.::*

"What do you mean?" Charles walked over from where he'd been fussing with a pack, wrapping amulets and vials of who knew what in soft furs and cloth.

The drake looked toward the white point of Wy'east, as if it could see through the volcano to what lay beyond.

::It is simply a thing I can feel. Something has shifted and we'd best be on our way.::

Anandita turned her chair and looked back toward the town. Tokki rushed from the cottage, a stuffed leather pack filling her arms, Anandita's bow and quiver slung onto her back. Good thinking. She might need the bow.

Hypatia hurried from the other direction, his arms filled with dull metal that looked like... Yes! Her stubbies! The mechanics must have fixed the plate hinges, despite the extra workload they'd had these past weeks. Several meters behind her son were Arcady, Rafiq, and Danika, plus a small contingent of Knights.

Good.

Anandita shaded her eyes with a hand and looked up at the drake. "As soon as I confer with the council, I'm ready to go."

Though how anyone could ever be ready to be hoisted on a drake's back and carried higher in the sky than any human had a right to go, she wasn't sure.

But telling herself she was ready was the surest way to become ready. Right?

She exhaled and reached for the winter-weight tunic Tokki hustled into her arms. Slipping into the warm blue wool, she sent up a quick prayer to whoever might be listening.

"I brought your stubbies, Ma!"

"Thank you, beta. Would you stand in front of me, and hold out my cloak?"

Nudity was not frowned upon in Go No More, but fitting prosthetics to her thighs was an intimate process that she didn't need the township to witness.

As she wrestled her short trews down her thighs, she spoke to her apprentice.

"Secure the bow and arrows to the pack, please." Tokki nodded.

The council members and Knights arrived as she finished securing the soft-lined metal thigh caps with their sturdy, square metal and rubber feet. The feet would help her grip the drake, she hoped, and would certainly help in case parts of where they were headed were impassable by chair.

She pulled the trews up over the metal and fastened the ties, then touched Hypatia's shoulder. He dropped the cloak cover, handing it to her. She wrapped the golden wool around her shoulders, securing it firmly with Long's brooch. The cool metal felt comforting beneath her fingertips.

"Karaktilla says there are dead bodies at the base of Wy'east, past the cannabis and barley fields." She directed her words at the council members and approaching Knights.

"Are they ours?" asked Jerrod, his dark face serious, even as he ruffled Tokki's hair affectionately. His daughter squirmed away, but Anandita caught a pleased look on the teen's face all the same.

"No," Anandita replied. "The drake says none wore the sumac leathers. And the fact that the Knights didn't return suggests they got them all, but..."

"But, still, we'll send a crew to check it out." Jerrod swore softly. The Steel Clan was already stretched thin with half of their comrades gone, but they had to be used to it, Anandita supposed. That was just the way things worked.

"Are you sure you still want to do this?" Rafiq asked. His brow was creased with worry. She knew it had been hard for him to step aside and allow Charles and her to go.

"I am."

That got her a curt nod in return.

"Tell that daughter of mine to stay safe, or I'll kick her ass," Danika said, bending down to shake Anandita's hand. Then she eyed the drakes. "And you stay safe, too. No falling off."

"We'll get them both strapped in tight!" Angel called down from the ladder propped up against the drake's side.

And then it was time to go.

She hugged Tokki, then drew Hypatia into a long embrace, smelling her son's sun-warmed hair.

"I love you, beta," she said into his sweet neck. "Stay safe."

"You, too, Ma."

Then Hypatia and Tokki backed away.

"I'm ready," she said to Angel. "How in the world are you going to get me up there?"

In answer, Karaktilla and Daraktal crouched all the way down on their bellies, flattening themselves as much as their mountainous frames could. Charles and Anandita prepared to be lifted up by Angel and his crew, with Jerrod and a couple of other Knights stepping forward to help. Too bad the trolls weren't here. They could've used their height.

I'm coming, Jenny, she thought, and hoped with all her heart that the big, red-haired Knight was okay.

CHAPTER 56

SILVERHAIR

Queen Silverhair walked the paved portico, gazing out upon the green. The slate beneath her slippers was cool and refreshing. Her unbound hair swirled and moved as if it had a mind of its own. The skirts of her gown were perfectly pressed. Her nails sharpened to talons. Her eyebrows arched just so.

She was perfect. She looked perfect. But inside her was a perfect storm. She was never so careful, never rode her maids so hard, as when something was awry.

Her pale, slender fingers clutched the smooth glass of an alembic. Held in with a silver stopper was the pale, smoky remnant of a human soul, quickly fading. Elzabetta had refused it. Was refusing to take in any more.

Stupid child. The princess sought to be brave, like a hero in some stupid human tale. She did not know what was at stake.

The Realm was disturbed, though you'd barely

know it. The courtiers still swished about, drinking apple wine and jostling one another for attention. The stream still flowed and sang. The sun shone in its pleasant not-too-warm, not-too-cold way.

But one of the three primary portals to the human realm had been forced almost closed. Silverhair had felt it, juddering in her bones. By the time her best magic workers were in place, the deed had been done.

And a halbtroll roamed her grounds. Useless to her, and perhaps dangerous to the realm.

She could not use his soul to heal her daughter. Blood and essence from any magical being was forbidden. This halbtroll had just enough of it to matter.

His mother, however, had an essence so sweet and strong the queen could almost taste it still.

But she had faded like all the rest, once her soul had given Carondel all that it was possible to give. What little of it remained lay trapped in an alembic like this one, resting on a shelf in the alchemist's laboratory. Unlike some, her body lingered still, and she walked like a wraith on the cool broad floors, pausing only to eat and drink, falling heavily into a sleep the alchemists and mages said was dreamless.

Silverhair wondered what it was like to dream. Most elves could not. The few who did were considered seers.

Dreaming was a form of magic, but a magic elves did not have.

And now the undreaming human's son was here. Was he looking for answers, or looking for war?

Regardless, the creature must be expelled.

Whatever he brought into the realm? It could not be anything good.

The stars of Elfland were askew. The realms had been tilted since the human Reckoning, and everything the queen had done to fix things only proved to make things worse. As the outside realms healed and flourished once again, no elven children had been born in years.

Underhill languished, and if Elzabetta's soul could not be mended, she would die. And if she died? The realm itself would start to fade.

Only strong royal blood could keep the realm alive. That was the teaching. That was the decree.

That was the order of things.

The way things had always been.

CHAPTER 57

ANANDITA

Anandita felt Karaktilla's purple and brown wings began to move, displacing air, causing the grasses of the field to tremble, and lifting the hair and clothing of the people of Go No More.

Sitting above the drake's shoulders was like having a view from a hill that breathed and moved. She tucked her fingers more firmly around the forward strap and was grateful for the soft hemp rope that secured her thighs and wrapped around her hips. Angel was right, she would need to use her muscles once aloft in order to keep from slipping around, but he and his crew had done a pretty good job of securing her at the glimmering tree-trunk base of the drake's neck.

She was glad for the metal and rubber squares that formed the base of her stubbies. Pressing them against the dragon scales gave her better purchase.

With a bunching of their powerful legs, the astounding beasts pushed off. Anandita had no doubt that their claws had left large divots in the field. Her body jerked against the restraints and she gripped her muscles as tightly as possible and pressed rubber and steel more tightly to the scales to keep from slipping backward. Luckily her arms and thighs were strong.

And then they were aloft, flying past the tops of the trees, winging toward the blue. Anandita was thankful for the scarf Tokki had brought her, which she'd bound around her hair and wrapped over her nose and mouth to keep her breath warm. Her eyes watered from the sudden rush of wind. As she blinked, the drakes both banked, and Wy'east appeared, in all its awe-inspiring glory. The volcano was a thing of beauty even from the ground, but from this vantage? If her breath had not already been stolen by the flight, and she wasn't so busy shifting her weight every time the drake moved, Anandita would have gasped from the beauty of it.

Flying was like nothing else in the world. To experience it thus, in her fragile human form, was such a gift. Anandita choked up.

Thank you, she thought, though she was not sure to whom she directed her prayer.

CHAPTER 58
JENNY

Crashing and scrabbling sounds came from the trees, as if something was moving fast. Right toward the encampment.

In an instant, Jenny and Tegan were on their feet, blades out, scanning the trees. With a clatter of dropped tools, cups, or plates, so was every other Knight.

"Formation!" Jenny called out. The Knights closest to their grouping clumped in a wedge behind Jenny, Tegan, and the elves. The trolls split to the flank. Glancing right, then left, Jenny saw two other wedges form on either side. Everyone faced the direction of the noise.

She deepened her stance and shifted her buckler further from her body, increasing the range of protection.

And Psych burst through the bushes near the latrine trench, face red beneath his blue tattoos.

"The drakes are here! Bringing riders!"

Riders? Jenny had never heard of such a…

Her head snapped toward Tegan who, now that the adrenaline burst was wearing off, looked ready to drop.

"Want to come with me? Check things out? Or stay here with half of the dragoons?"

"Here." Tegan looked grateful, which showed Jenny just how badly off the Knight still was.

"Recoana, Feldspar, come with me if you please. And the rest of this wedge." If she was heading into battle, she wanted a couple of skilled blunt weapons backing her up. Since that pig fucker Bocan had run off through the gate, the two trolls would have to do.

She turned to Peridot and Damson who waited, weapons drawn, the djinn Abyad at their side. "If you don't mind helping to guard the encampment with Tegan, I'd appreciate it. But do as you will."

Damson gave a sharp nod and no one else voiced any disagreement, so Jenny walked to the scout, who was busy downing water from a skin.

"Lead us there, please."

Psych wiped his face with a stained hemp kerchief and nodded. "Looked like they were heading toward the clearing just east of here."

Jenny followed, short sword in hand. Everyone kept their weapons out. Just because she'd had contact with the drakes didn't mean she fully trusted them. And who knew what riders they had brought to the waterfall at the portal's edge?

CHAPTER 59
KARAKTILLA

She landed in the green clearing as carefully as possible in an attempt to not jar the human too much. Daraktal was less graceful and his rider slid, gripping the straps with all his might.

The straps. Karaktilla could not wait for the bands of leather and rope to be off her body. There was a reason that drakes flew alone. They were not meant to be beasts of burden. But then, no creature probably enjoyed it. More likely they were just resigned to their fate.

A drake's job was to see far, and in Karaktilla's case, to see far into the future. Her sight had shown her that they must do this thing. It was her fate then, to bear such indignity.

But the humans had best not think it was their due to ride on drake back in the future.

As if her thoughts had called them, a small band of humans boiled from the trees like ants in a summer storm. Karaktilla recognized the red-haired Knight of destiny. The reason she and Daraktal were here, and had brought the other two humans. They were linked somehow. And Jenny was required to fully close this portal.

Karaktilla wondered if she would be required to close all the portals, in time. The drake hoped not. That would be a sorry day indeed. The realms did best in contact with each other.

The first sundering of the realms, more than ten thousand years in the past, had begun the long, damaging slide that led to war, devastation, and eventually to the cataclysm the humans called the Reckoning. And the magic realms grew stranger and more brittle over time, establishing hierarchies that were unnecessary and cruel.

The opening of the portal gates would have likely happened anyway, but Karaktilla and her people had nudged the process forward. It had been a short time, and the realms were only now regaining their equilibrium. Or they would have, hadn't Silverhair's anguish caused such an imbalance that she had resorted to mass murder.

For that was the only thing to call what she had done.

She had a sickness in her emotions that had been overlooked, as long as she was only a danger to herself and to those who served her. But now? It was clear she must be stopped, or things could explode again.

Outright war between the human realms and Underhill? The would be a worse disaster than the fiery Reckoning, or the original sundering itself.

"How am I supposed to get down? Same way I got up?" The healer's voice brought Karaktilla back into the present moment. The warriors were almost upon them.

::I will lay as flat as I can upon the earth and your Knight will help you down, with the help of the trolls.::

"She's not my Knight."

Karaktilla huffed a laugh and scooted as flat as her bulk would go.

"Anandita!" The Knight's voice rang across the clearing as she broke into a run, followed quickly by the rest of her comrades.

What was foretold was falling into place. The ancient days would return. Harmony would reign in all the realms.

If the cohort of the red-haired Knight succeeded.

CHAPTER 60
JENNY

Seeing Anandita astride the huge purple drake was like seeing a myth come to life. Her wind-burned cheeks glowed warm and beautiful beneath the blue scarf that bound her hair and wrapped her lower face. Swaddled in a golden-yellow cloak, she looked powerful. Dangerous. Brave.

And Jenny wanted nothing more than to sweep her off the drake's back and carry her off into the woods where she would...

Do nothing.

Because clearly Anandita needed help getting off the drake and so did Charles, whom Jenny only now noticed on the smaller, red-scaled drake's back.

Anandita and Charles coming had never been part of the plan. Something had changed. And some force or vision must have brought the drakes here, and had them consent to allow humans to ride. Something urgent.

Feldspar and Recoana were at Jenny's side. "How can we help?"

"Can you help reach Charles and Anandita? With my help and one other's?"

"Of course," Recoana said. "Karaktilla, well met! We're going to help get your riders down and then loose those heavy bands from around your flesh."

::*Thank all the ancient Gods of rock and stone.*:: Karaktilla clacked and grumbled, long snout practically buried in the grasses, flowers, and dirt.

Recoana got into place, and Jenny, with a quick apology to both troll and drake, stepped on Recoana's knee, then up the drake's foreleg. Once she was as high as she could get, Recoana hoisted her further and braced her against muscle and scale. The papery lizard scent was strong, and the scales rasped where one of Jenny's jacket sleeves and gloves had gapped, leaving bare skin.

Anandita had already unbuckled what she could, and waited for her, licking moisture at her plum lips grown dry from the flight.

"You look so beautiful," Jenny blurted, then blushed what she was sure was a violent shade of red. "I mean..."

Anandita's eyebrows raised and her eyes widened in surprise, but she also smiled, which made Jenny slip and grab onto the harness.

"Just help get me down, would you? We can talk about how beautiful I am later."

"Right," Jenny replied.

Later. She said later. Later was good.

Jenny wrapped her hands around Anandita's waist, feeling muscle beneath a soft and lovely layer of fat.

Steady on, asshole. Pay the fuck attention.

Anandita gave a small gasp and began to slide toward Jenny's chest.

"I've got you," Jenny said, "and Recoana is here to catch us if we fall."

"Thank you, Recoana!" Anandita called past Jenny's shoulders. A groan fell from her lips. "My muscles feel as if I've been in battle."

Suddenly, her breasts were pressed against Jenny's own bound chest, and Jenny's arms were around her body. Anandita wrapped strong thighs around Jenny's waist.

Jenny stifled a groan of her own.

"We're coming down," she said to the troll, then began to ease their way down the drake's body, muscles working to counterbalance Anandita's weight, braced by the troll below.

She tried mightily to ignore the combination of herbs and Anandita's own particular scent that cut through the strong smell of drake and Jenny's own oil and sweat.

She tried mightily and failed.

Soon enough, they were back on solid earth where two Knights waited with Anandita's chair.

Jenny placed the healer carefully into the cushion-padded seat.

She couldn't resist dropping a surreptitious kiss onto Anandita's cheek, hoping against hope the action was hidden by her own broad shoulders and the troll's girth.

If not, well, she would take whatever teasing her comrades dished out around the fire. The unguarded look in Anandita's dark eyes, for just one moment, was enough.

Jenny pulled away, gloved hands lingering for a moment on that golden-yellow cloak.

"We bring news," the healer said. "Where is the rest of the Steel Clan, and what in all the realms happened at the base of Wy'east that left a score of humans dead?"

CHAPTER 61
BOCAN

As they walked up the smooth path, anger boiled in Bocan's belly, but had been joined by a sense of curiosity.

He sensed intrigue afoot, though he could not yet pin it down. The soft boots of the princess's guard shushed softly around him. He was surrounded, but clearly not considered too much of a threat. He still had steel to hand.

Which was foolish of the guard.

But Princess Elzabetta wanted him unharmed, and clearly she still had enough power that her word held sway. They quickly arrived at a small pavilion made of living wood and hung with flowing cream and green draperies. The gardeners and builders of Elfland were clever to have created such a comfortable and inviting-looking space, all without killing a single tree.

They could keep plants and trees alive and bend them to their will, but human beings? They slaughtered them as if they were nothing. He tasted copper and bile, but swallowed it down.

The princess's pale silvery-green hair shone ahead, flashing through shifting bodies of her guard as they walked along. She looked young. Bocan searched his memory for the stories about her. Elzabetta was born in recent years—within the last fifteen or so—the first child born to Elfland since the Reckoning.

And things had not gone well with either the pregnancy or the birth. Her souls were said to wander freely, all nine pieces separated from each other. It was said she could only keep three working in harmony at any one time, and that three were enough for her to live, but not enough for her to rule. Bocan didn't know much about elven dynasty, but surely the only child of a queen had to be able to rule, or the royal house was fucked.

He didn't know what effect that would have upon Elfland itself, but it couldn't be good. Bocan grinned at the thought, though that was quickly swallowed back into a grimace. There was nothing good about this situation, at all.

It was said that the deaths were part of the princess's healing. Somehow, the vitality of a human soul helped mend the rifts inside of the princess.

All of this was strange. Certainly she was thin and pale, but was she any thinner or paler than any other silver blood? Her voice had seemed weak and she did look ill. Off. Not quite right. The shadows beneath those moss-green eyes were deep, marring the paleness of her skin.

Princess Elzabetta walked gracefully up some steps he could not see and entered the pavilion.

His guard stopped. One, a skinny bald man who still managed to look beautiful despite his scars, looked Bocan up and down. Considering.

"Touch nothing if not instructed to," he said. "Sit when you are told. Respect the princess, or your head shall be served to the Queen."

Bocan's hands clenched into fists but he held his tongue. With a brief bow, he allowed himself to be ushered up the stairs into the shaded outdoor room. He blinked at the shift in light and paused to let his eyes adjust.

"Your axe." The head guard had finally figured it out.

"Take it," Bocan said, reaching back to unsnap the leather bands that held the mighty bearded axe in place. He hated to lose it, but he had a knife and short sword at his belt, and another blade inside one boot.

The haft felt good inside his palm. He looked at it, and then at the guard, who blanched, but trapped the wooden haft with two hands and tugged. Bocan released his favored weapon.

He would have it back in hand soon enough. And if not? He would either be dead, or able to have another one made upon his return home.

The princess sat on a carved and polished wooden throne that looked as if a dryad had deigned to freeze itself in order to hold her light frame. A low table, inlaid with amber and jet designs, held cakes and a white pot filled with fragrant tea. An elf stood at her side, a scowl fixed on his face. She shooed him to a chair with one sweep of her hand.

"Come forth, halbtroll. Please, sit. Eat cake and drink tea. Tell me why you have come here."

Bocan moved forward as instructed, but glanced at the offered chair with trepidation.

"It's stronger than it looks," the elf guard said, speaking low behind him.

Bocan hoped so. He sat, gingerly at first, then grew more relaxed as the wood, groaning a small amount, held his bulk.

He took the offered tea. Declined a piece of cake, though he was hungry.

"Your heart is broken, isn't it?" the princess said, eyes quizzical and sad. "I recognize that look."

Bocan forced himself to hold the cup lightly, though his fingers twitched in surprise.

"Why do you say such a thing to me?"

"Because..." She sighed. "My heart is broken, too, and likely for the same reasons."

"Your friends and family have disappeared and been killed in horrific sacrifice so another may heal?" The words flew out like darts.

She barely flinched, eyes turned to steel, holding steady on his face.

Formidable.

"My mother has slaughtered and sacrificed beings in an attempt to mend my soul. And what is worse? It has not even worked. I carry this burden each day."

"Princess..." the seated elf protested, but she lifted one finger and brought his tongue to silence.

"I am no better off than I was, and your mother is a wraith."

Bocan flashed hot and cold with fury, rage, and an anguish so raw it threatened to consume him whole.

"How do you know that my mother is a wraith?" he rasped, scrambling to his feet.

"Because the alchemist has been watching since your cohort arrived outside our gates. Carondel recognized the arch of her brows in yours, and knew why you had come. I am heartily sorry, though I know those must feel like empty words."

Carondel. The mage. The elf sitting there, cool as you please, teacup poised near his fucking handsome face. At least he had the good grace to look terrified at Bocan's sudden stillness towering over him.

And he was still. Still as a stone. He stood there, in front of these two frackingly beautiful creatures who were telling him they had ruined his mother's life. His father's. And his own.

Bocan stood there, stunned and staring, caught between the desires to weep, to break the pavilion to splinters, to wring the elven princess's slender white neck, or beat the elven mage's face into an unrecognizable pulp.

Elzabetta flashed him a sad yet luminous smile, as if she understood, though he could not see how that was possible.

"We have been waiting for you. You and the red-haired Knight. I am hoping you can help me, and that I, in turn, can offer you what aid I can."

"Take me to my mother. Now."

CHAPTER 62
TEGAN

The last thing Tegan expected to see was Anandita, bumping her chair over the uneven forest ground.

"Charles!" Aphrodite called from behind per, then stepped up to Tegan's side, and spoke only for Tegan's ears. "What in the nine worlds is going on?"

Tegan gave a quick head shake. Frack if per knew. But the sense of magic in the glade had changed ever since the drakes arrived, rolling like a wave through the forest, announcing their landing. The only person not vibrating with it was Jenny, who walked solidly, calm as you please, though Tegan noticed the looks per comrade kept glancing toward the healer in her chair.

Poor pig fucker had it bad. Made Tegan almost happy to be solo. Less entanglement meant a clearer mind. Tegan needed all the advantage per could take right now. Per mind and body still felt like a wet rag wrung out by a giant.

Tegan and the rest held position as the others

moved toward the camp. They would wait until there was news, and then there was either a long meeting or a battle ahead. No use relaxing in either case.

Tegan just wished per was in better condition to face whatever it was that had brought Anandita and Charles here, and had compelled two drakes to allow humans to ride. Per struggled to sense what was going on, but per magic was sporadic. Even per psychic and emotional senses were muted.

What a fracking time to be magically spent and half useless, with the job half done and more trouble likely on the way.

Finally, Jenny, Anandita, Charles, and the rest of the Knights were near enough for easy conversation.

"Anandita and Charles have brought news." Jenny pitched her voice so everyone in the encampment could hear. "Gather so we all can easily hear."

Good move. Tegan would have preferred to consult in a smaller cell, but with everyone's nerves on edge this way? It was likely better to tell everyone at once.

Per friend walked toward Tegan, and clapped a hand on per shoulder, before leaning in.

"This does not feel good to me. What does your magic say?"

Tegan considered, trying hard to sense. The perception was muddied, as if Tegan was pushing for information through layer after layer of wavering, apprentice-made glass. But what sense there was, was not good.

"I hate to say it, comrade, but it tastes like the shit

the drake was on about. The shit you've been trying to avoid."

Destiny.

Jenny took a step away.

"Fuck you, comrade." There was no heat in the words. Only worry and sorrow.

"Fuck you, too." Tegan blew Jenny a kiss. That got a wry smile that was gone as quickly as it came.

"Let's call this meeting to order!" Case said. Tegan saw that the dragoons and all the others stood or sat in clumps, arrayed in a rough crescent moon, Anandita and Charles in the gap.

Per tapped Psych on the shoulder. The scout leapt up and offered per his space on the moss-covered log. Tegan was going to have to start packing a fracking camp chair in the future, like the mages and fracking elves.

Anandita spoke, clear voice carrying across the glade, but her eyes darted between Jenny and Tegan, even though they were on opposite sides of the crescent.

"First, the drakes alerted us to the dead bodies at Wy'east, and we saw the carnage as we flew. What was that about?"

Tegan let Jenny take the lead.

The red-haired Knight stood tall. "We were ambushed, but took care of them in short order. We don't know who they are or why they attacked."

"And we've had a few things to deal with since." That was Berto. Tegan winced at the impatience in the young apprentice's voice. Case smacked the younger man's arm and gestured for him to shut the fuck up. Berto looked away, light brown skin flushing with anger and shame.

Anandita pressed her lips in a tight line. Tegan didn't often see the healer angry, but when it happened...

Tegan didn't blame Berto, but Knights had to learn when to strike and when to hold, and that included tongues.

Jenny held up a hand to forestall any response to Berto's outburst.

"Bocan is gone," she said. "Tegan almost managed to close the portal gate, but something went wrong. We don't know if the magic ran out, there was other interference, or Bocan broke things somehow."

Charles exhaled, and rubbed a hand over his face. "Well, shit. Guess your vision about us being needed here was right."

Anandita just nodded, but Tegan noticed that her eyes never left Jenny's face.

"So along with closing the portal, we need to get Bocan out," Anandita said. "That's what you're telling us?"

No one answered. A jay scolded from above.

Finally, Tegan cleared per throat, and fuck if that didn't hurt, too. Fuck if everything didn't hurt.

"That's the size of it," per said. "But what I don't understand, Anandita, with all respect due to your station and all, is why you're here. Charles? I can get that. But please don't tell me you've had hideous visions where we're going to need someone with your expertise."

Because frankly, if things got that bad, Anandita alone wasn't going to help any more than the patchwork healing jobs the Knights themselves could do. If things got that bad, it was more than likely a lot of them would end up dead.

"Though it did not feel like a massacre, the dreams told me to come. Something is going to happen on the other side of the portal and I must to be ready to face it."

Anandita gave a slight shake to her head.

"My magic is healing. And there is sickness here, of body, mind, and soul. And no matter what happens, there will be those who need tending to."

CHAPTER 63

BOCAN

Still surrounded by guards, the princess and the elven mage led him down a long corridor of gleaming wood, finally stopping outside a curved door that stood open to a light-filled room.

Any other features of the room were lost on him, because there she was. His ma. The woman he thought gone forever. The one he had not set eyes upon in far too many years.

She was barely there, like a wraith, just as the elven princess had said.

No older than when she had left them, Bocan's ma was thin. Too thin for a woman as tall as she. Blond hair straggled, loose around her face. It used to shine like the sun, but now was dull and dry as straw. Her cheekbones were too sharp, and blue shadows ringed her once-bright eyes that gazed at him as if he was not there.

But she raised a hand, as if about to stroke his face. He touched her wrist, so gently, and cupped her small, pale hand inside his much larger, blue-tinged one. Tears and snot ran down his face, but he didn't care.

"Ma? It's me. Bocan."

She mewled, like one of Go No More's barn cats' kittens, and took a step toward him. Then two. Finally, she was cradled in his arms, face pressed between his sternum and his belly. She did not shake or cry. She just stood, completely still, inside the circle of his softly creaking leathers.

Her breath was soft, but he heard it anyway. It felt strange to hold his mother in this way. The last time he had seen her, she had still been taller than he was, though not by much.

"I missed you," he said. They breathed together for another moment, before she pulled away from his embrace. Then she just turned and walked away, settling onto a plump green cushion against one silver-patterned wall, gazing out the open windows at nothing.

He rubbed at his face with a kerchief pulled from the rear pocket of his leather trousers, cleaning the tears and snot away. The princess and mage said nothing, just waited on the other side of the room as he blew his nose, then carefully folded the damp hemp square and slid it back into his pocket. He heard the guards shifting just outside the door.

They had not entered the room, which could work to his advantage. Bocan quickly scanned the space, with a flick of his eyes. Were the windows large enough to let him through?

"Why is she alive?"

He rested his gaze on the mage, who had the good grace to flick his topaz eyes away, as if ashamed.

"She was one of the early ones."

"An experiment." Bocan's voice was flat. The only thing keeping him from killing the elf right now was the need for information, and the fact that he needed to get his mother out of this place with minimal interference from the guards.

The mage swallowed and nodded, mumbling something.

"What did you say?"

The princess came toward him then, one hand out as if she was going to touch him. Bocan turned his left foot in a half pivot so she was no longer on course with his arm. She dropped her hand but slightly shifted course, stepping softly until she stood an arm's length away.

When she spoke, her voice was like a ringing bell, and he had never hated a sound so much in his life.

"He said they are all experiments, and he is right. Which is why I want this travesty of magic to cease." She coughed then, holding a lacy kerchief to her fine-boned face, covering her pale mouth.

He looked down at her, a small shining, creature, with barely a flicker of a thought at how strange the situation was. He, a halbtroll Knight, sworn to serve no kings, standing in front of elven princess, who seemed to be apologizing for the state of his human mother.

Then what she said finally penetrated the thickness of his grief and his hard skull.

"What does that mean? Won't you die?"

She shrugged one elegant shoulder, as if he had just asked if a jaunt in the woods wouldn't ruin her tapestry slippers.

Then she trained those moss-green eyes on him.

"Better to die than to live on other being's pain. The souls have made me strong enough to know that now. I am only sorry that I had no strength to fight the Queen before."

CHAPTER 64
JENNY

"No!" Jenny shouted, dodging roots and bushes, pacing through the trees. She didn't care if the whole encampment heard her. Didn't care if Anandita couldn't keep up on the path. Didn't care...

She stopped just short of a long shaft of sunlight, breaking through the thick canopy of green and brown. The scents of the forest usually calmed her, but not today. Not after what the drakes and the woman she loved had told her.

The drakes were back in the big clearing. Jenny had stormed off, leaving Tegan, Case, and the others behind. Peridot had tried to stop her, but Damson stayed his hand. Abyad had looked upon it all as if suspicious, but Jenny had always found it hard to get a proper read on the djinn.

Anandita came doggedly toward her, though Jenny knew pushing the chair through this mess of forest must have taxed her arms.

The woman she loved. A thought she'd not allowed before, except in weak moments, half-asleep in the middle of the night. Never during the day.

She turned to see Anandita pushing the right wheel of her chair against a root ball, then backing up to maneuver around it. Jenny knew better than to offer help. There was no more certain way to get a knife thrown at her throat.

"It's what the drake foretold, Jenny." Kind patience filled the healer's eyes. Jenny wanted to crumple up inside her arms.

"I don't care," she said, the words tasting of defeat.

Anandita rolled toward her. Jenny knew she should be the one to move, but her feet had grown roots. She was breathing too fast, but couldn't stop it, and sweat poured beneath her leathers despite the cool air beneath the trees. There was rustling in the bushes to her right. Some small animal. She noticed Flex had not followed her. The faery fox either had business of his own, or was letting her work out her own shit.

Likely the latter.

"I have no magic, Dita. How in Brigid's name am I supposed to go up against this? And with Bocan gone, and Tegan spent and staggering on per feet..."

She hadn't realized just how much she relied on her comrades. Not that the rest of the Steel Clan weren't comrades. They were. But Bocan and Tegan were closer. They *knew* her.

"You have to do this, Jenny."

"Do what? What exactly am I supposed to do? The drakes are so fracking cryptic! All this talk of destiny and bullshit with no strategy. No tactics. No plan! I need a fracking plan!"

Anandita bumped her chair closer, stopped. Reached out a hand from beneath her golden-yellow cloak. Long's brooch winked in the patchy sunlight.

Long. The man Anandita loved still. The partner she had lost.

Jenny was a fool.

But she took the offered hand anyway. She couldn't resist it. Couldn't resist the lavender scent. The ripe plum lips. The deep-set eyes. And right now? Jenny needed a friend.

"You have been training for this your whole life, Jenny." Anandita's palm was cool in Jenny's own. Jenny crouched down, so Anandita didn't have to keep looking up, but kept her head bowed. She couldn't bear to look at Anandita's face. Couldn't bear to have her raw fear, indecision, and need exposed.

"I've watched you for years," Anandita continued. "Go No More is filled with talented, skilled, dedicated people, and you are one of them. But there's also always been something about you that stood out just a little bit, even though you tried to hide it."

"I'm nothing special." The forest floor was littered with fir needles and small seed cones. A century's worth of layer upon composting layer, working together to make new soil.

"We're all special, Jenny. It's part of what makes the township work. Everyone has a different take on their craft and the way they learn, practice, and teach. There is no one among us stamped from a mold or shoved into a box they don't belong in...." Anandita's voice tapered off. A fly buzzed near Jenny's ear. Her feet and calves stabilized her thighs. Her hand that had so recently killed a man held the healer's as if it were a tiny bird. A finch or sparrow that could be crushed in an instant. But that was ridiculous. Anandita's hands were strong.

"Except sometimes I think you shove yourself into a box, Jenny. Because you think there is a mold that everyone fits but you. And that is not true." Her voice grew stronger. Harsher. "Fostering that belief has led you to wallow in self-pity, to diminish yourself. And now? You're letting yourself off the hook because of it. Abdicating your responsibility to your clan, to the town, and frankly, to all the realms."

It took all of Jenny's strength to not wrench her hand from Anandita's, but then she looked up. She saw the strength and determination in the other woman's eyes. She saw a complete lack of pity.

There was understanding there.

They breathed together there, beneath the towering trees, amidst the calling birds and rustling animals.

And then Anandita licked her lips, and leaned. Jenny leaned forward until their noses almost touched, and she could feel Anandita's breath on her cheeks. She closed her eyes, and leaned a little more.

Were they really doing this?

And those lush lips were against hers. They were warm, and tasted of peppermint.

Jenny reached her left hand through the dark,

smooth sheet of Anandita's hair, and slid to cup her neck just as Anandita's tongue teased a path between Jenny's lips.

Jenny moaned. The kiss deepened. Anandita's hands fisted Jenny's braids. A wave of lust crashed through Jenny, filling her body with heat and desire. She felt herself grow damp inside her leathers, the friction of the seam rubbing at suddenly swollen flesh.

She broke the kiss, forehead pressed against Anandita's. "I want you. Goddess, I want you so badly. I've wanted you for years."

"I want you, too," Anandita replied, and caught Jenny's left wrist, leading her hand down to brush against a lush breast. Jenny moaned again.

"Gods. You're so gorgeous. I want this so badly. And I'm so scared...."

Scared of everything. Of the unknown battle to come. Of what was required of her. And of giving in to the power of this desire she'd held banked for so long.

"Shhhh. Make love to me, Jenny. I'm ready."

Anandita undid the circular brooch, carefully repinning it into the golden-yellow fabric so there was one less barrier between her body and Jenny's hands.

"But this isn't how I wanted to..."

"I know." Anandita laughed. "You have a sweet, romantic heart. You wanted a soft bed or a flower-strewn patch of green. But this is what we have. Right now. And I want this."

She lifted the bottom of her tunic, exposing the metal and hard rubber platforms at the base of her steel thigh caps, covered in short, loose wool and hemp trews. She untied the drawstring holding the fabric up.

"I want your mouth on me."

The words hung in the air for one, crystal clear moment. And then Jenny was in motion. Metal clanking. Buckles snapping open. Shield and heavy leather dropping to the forest floor.

She grabbed Anandita's face in her bare hands.

She kissed Anandita's lips again, tongues sparring as if they were fighting to the death. And then Jenny's knees were on the forest floor, the toes of her boots digging into soft loam. Her mouth made its way down the wool of Anandita's tunic. Her hands tugged at the cloth trousers that covered everything she wanted in the world. Slid them toward the metal prosthetics.

Anandita gasped as the cool air hit her.

Jenny froze. "Is this all right?"

Anandita nodded yes and pushed the fabric further down.

The scent of arousal mingled with the smell of forest and mint. Jenny inhaled. She wanted to remember this forever.

And she wasn't sure how long forever would last.

CHAPTER 65
ANANDITA

Anandita shoved aside the self-consciousness that came from being so exposed. So vulnerable to another person.

Breathing deeply, she gloried in the feel of Jenny's hands and lips. She bathed in the sounds of the forest, the scent of the cool air, and the warrior on her knees in front of her spread thighs, red braids coiled across broad shoulders and that impossibly muscular back.

Long was gone. She would love him always, but Jenny was here. Now. And the world might or might not be ending, but for certain they were on a cusp and things were about to change. That realization had broken down the final fence around Anandita's heart, exposing the strength of her desire.

Even if it was only this one time, this single moment, Jenny was what she needed. Jenny was what she wanted. Jenny was what she desired.

Strong hands spread her thighs even more, until

they were pressed up against the bent metal and elk hide sides of the chair.

"This still okay?" Jenny asked. "You're sure?" Looking at her with those whiskey-colored eyes. Awaiting her answer.

"Yes."

Cool air and hot breath pebbled the skin on her thighs and stirred the hairs over her mound. She was swollen and soaking and hadn't felt this wild and beautiful in a long time.

With one swipe of her tongue, Jenny opened Anandita's wet slit, startling a gasp from her lips as every nerve ending shot to attention.

Lips and tongue and teeth worked at her swollen flesh. Anandita wove the fingers of her right hand through Jenny's braids, and her left hand gripped her chair. She held on. As tension built inside her body, she threw her head back, gasping and panting, eyes opening and shutting, storing images. The canopy of ragged fir and hemlock. A goldfinch darting overhead.

And the sounds. Jenny, moaning and licking. Growling into her cunt.

A finger filled her. Anandita shouted, the sound too loud. Too open. She muffled her sounds, moaning and screaming in the back of her throat as a second finger joined the first and the mouth continued, relentless, tonguing fire and water and earth into one triangle of pleasure and desire.

The cushion beneath her already soaked, Anandita freed her right hand from the red tangle of braids. Clutching both sides of the chair, she pushed into the backrest, angling her hips toward Jenny's mouth. Jenny's strong hands slid beneath her ass, tugging her closer. Anandita felt herself sliding and didn't care.

Jenny would catch her. Jenny was there.

"Jenny!" Her voice rasped, blending with the forest sounds.

The Knight lifted her mouth just long enough to say her name.

"Anandita."

And then hands and fingers and tongue and hips... Anandita held her breath and screwed her eyes shut.

Shudder and after shudder rocked her frame. Her clit exploded in an arc of warm, liquid fire and she sucked in a huge breath, belly trembling. Jenny's tongue and fingers didn't stop.

"Oh!" Anandita bore down against Jenny. Sparks lit up behind her closed eyes. Pleasure rolled through. Her whole body contracted and she shouted to the sky. Her body jerked. Her eyes snapped open.

She relaxed, trembling like an aspen leaf.

Jenny crawled up to embrace her. To kiss Anandita's lips, wet with the taste of her. Strong arms held her. Crushed her close.

Anandita shuddered and sighed, inhaling the scent of leather, forest, Jenny, and sex.

She turned her head and rested her cheek against the strong, hard slope of Jenny's chest and arm.

Blinking, she saw that the world was still there. Green. Brown. The flash of orange from a flicker's wing. The pale gold of filtered sun.

She turned to kiss Jenny again. One more time.

The Knight tasted her sweetly. Gently. As if they had all the time in the world. As if they were the only two humans in this vast forest near the rushing Wimal River and the distant, thundering waterfall.

If only that were true.

CHAPTER 66

BOCAN

The windows were far too small. That meant he had to get through the guards somehow. And where was Serena?

::Outside the window. Half your guards left to report back to the Queen. You have only four left outside the door. And there is a door to the gardens down the hallway to your right.::

::How do you know this?::

::The swallows. They swoop in and out of the pavilions. The courtiers find them amusing.::

The owl's voice was dry with contempt.

::Okay. Get ready to move soon. I may need you to distract.::

She sent a clear image of diving, talons extended, toward the shining heads of the elven guards.

Bocan grinned inside, but made certain to keep his face schooled into a stern mask. It wasn't hard. He could kill these gold-asshole prigs. He didn't care how contrite or sickly the princess was. She was still responsible for the fact that his mother was curled in a heap on a too-soft cushion instead of working at Da's side.

She was still responsible for his da sinking into his own soul, drowning in the oblivion brought on by pain.

He turned from the princess and the mage and walked toward his ma, who sat, arms around her knees, rocking gently.

"Ma?" He kept his voice soft and low. She kept rocking. He felt as if his heart would crack in two. He place a hand on her arm. It felt large. Ungainly. But large and ungainly might be what was needed to get them out of here.

"I want to take you out of here. You want to come?"

She looked up then, and consciousness flickered in her eyes. She gave one slight nod. That was enough for him.

Bocan scooped her into his arms and stood. She weighed no more than one of the wildflower bouquets he'd brought her when he was a child.

"Where are you going?" The mage's voice was sharp.

The princess moved in front of the mage, holding out a placating hand.

"I thought you were going to help us," she said.

Bocan sneered. "You think I would help you? When you have done this? Step aside, please. And tell your guards I need my fracking axe."

"You'll need your mother's soul if you are to leave with her." The alchemist's voice was wary, his tongue darting out to wet his lips as he glanced from Bocan to the princess.

Bocan froze, staring from one to the other. He shifted his mother and reached for his sword.

"Get it," Elzabetta replied. "But be quick."

"And my axe?"

"You shall have that, as well, and as much time as I can buy."

He saw no calculation in those moss-green eyes, only weariness, as if she was sick to death of it all. As if she was heart sick as well as soul and body sick.

Bocan understood that sickness, though where it enervated Princess Elzabetta, it filled him with a strange and holy fire, straight from the bowels of the earth.

CHAPTER 67
JENNY

"Thank you." She whispered the words into Anandita's dark hair.

Jenny's clit still throbbed with arousal, but her body's need for sex was satisfied. For now. She'd gotten what she had wanted for so long, which was to feel Anandita gasping and shuddering as she worshipped at the altar between her thighs.

Buzzing with the power of sex, Jenny felt whole. Solid. Complete.

Ready for whatever was yet to come.

Anandita turned her head and captured Jenny's mouth in a deep kiss. After a sweet moment, Jenny broke her lips away.

"We've got to get back to camp."

"But I didn't...you didn't..."

Jenny grinned, and smoothed a finger down the furrow between Anandita's beautiful thick brows, smoothing it away.

"I got everything I needed," she said, giving Anandita a soft kiss. Then she grinned again, and rocked back onto her heels. "Though if you want a rematch when all of this is done, I'm more than happy to let you have your way with me."

"I'll hold you to that," Anandita replied, then set about adjusting herself back to rights. "Would you help me with these damn trousers? They're all tangled in my foot plates."

Jenny straightened out the cloth over the short prosthetics and tugged the fabric over the dusky curve of hips as Anandita braced and lifted with her back and arms. The drawstring was tied, the dark tunic slid back down.

"Ugh. I'm sitting on a damp cushion now."

"Would you like me to reverse it?"

Anandita nodded. "If you could slide it out while I lift myself again."

That was quickly done. Too quickly, and not quickly enough. Goddess, this woman made her want to stop time.

Jenny heard the sounds of boots walking up the path, and caught the white tip of Flex's tail heading their way. The tiny bubble of bliss had definitely popped.

Coming toward them, following the faery fox, were Tegan, Case, and Starlight the lynx. Tegan still moved slowly, and per skin was tinged with gray, but the Knight looked better than even a few hours before.

"We've got company," Jenny said.

"Shit." Anandita tugged and tucked everything back into place as Jenny grabbed her leather coat from the forest floor and slipped it on. Then she reached for her buckler.

Damn.

Both Knights were grinning ear-to-ear, and Tegan's scarred eyebrow was quirked up even higher than usual. Jenny scowled at them before busting back into a grin herself. She'd take all the shit they wanted to dish out because she had just had sex with the most beautiful woman in the world in the middle of the forest, and they hadn't.

And both Knights knew better than to rib her in front of Anandita if they wanted to avoid a major smackdown.

Flex trotted up, delicate looking paws sending up puffs of dust. Five paces from Anandita's chair, he stopped and stared at Jenny, sending a clear image of the drakes into her head.

Anandita managed to turn her chair around just as Case and Tegan arrived to stand behind the fox and lynx.

"Flex is trying to tell me something about the drakes?"

Case nodded. "Karaktilla says you are needed at the gate within the hour. Some shit's about to go down."

Fuck.

"She bother to say what kind of shit?"

Flex sent an image of the shimmering gate, and one of Bocan's face, wet with tears.

Case just shrugged.

"Okay," Jenny said. "We got a plan?"

Both Knights just gave her the look that meant they

thought Jenny was being dense. Flex just turned, skirted the Knights, and cut across the forest on a direct route back to camp.

And the damn portal.

"Well?"

"You're the plan, comrade," Case replied. "Charles and Aphrodite have set things up with the help of the elves and trolls, but the drakes were clear...."

"Clear about what?" Jenny snapped. The warmth of Anandita's skin and the sweet taste of her was fading far too fast. Damn it.

Anandita touched her arm. Jenny jerked as if she'd caught a spark from a campfire.

"Clear that you're the one who has to do this, Jenny. It's what brought me here, too. I'm supposed to help you."

Help her? Help her when she was drowning in helplessness? There was no army to fight. No bandits to kill. There was only this...magic. What good was Jenny against all that?

"Help me how?" Her words were directed at Anandita, but she looked at Tegan. Her comrade and friend quirked an eyebrow and crossed per arms.

"I don't know yet," Anandita said. "But we need to be at the gate together. My visions told me that much. And we need to get Bocan back."

Bocan.

Jenny whirled and stalked ten paces away, then back again. Nothing in the forest told her what to do. The flickers and crows told her nothing. The wolves did not come near with news. Flex had already made his opinion clear by wandering away.

And her comrades just waited. Waited the way they always did. Waited for Jenny to make a decision.

The only decision was to act. Jenny knew that. But how? What kind of action?

Her buckler felt heavy in her hand, and the short sword bumped her thigh.

She was a Knight. The only actions she knew were to fuck and ride, or protect and attack.

She had ridden. She had fucked.

And out here, leagues from home, under the canopy of Douglas fir and hemlock, she was damn well done protecting.

She looked at Anandita. At Tegan and Case. She felt Flex waiting for her at the shimmering sliver of elven magic floating in the forest, in a space between here and there.

"All right," she said. "Let's go attack some fucking high-born elves and get our fucking half-crazed comrade back."

CHAPTER 68
TEGAN

The area outside the portal gate was controlled chaos.

Apprentices ran back and forth, working with a few Knights to try to get fires doused and covered, and the rest of the encampment shut down. Looked like they were hauling things back toward the clearing where the drakes had landed.

Though camp wasn't right against the gate, there was no telling what would happen, or whether they would all need a clear field on this side.

Closer to the shimmering gold sliver—all that was left of the gate—the elves and trolls conferred with mages. Charles Wong's hands gesticulated wildly, likely trying to explain a complex set of sigils. Tegan didn't want to know. His style of magic never made sense to per and weirded per out a little. Aphrodite looked worn out, as if she might fall over at any moment. It was a good thing Charles had come, then, though Tegan still didn't know how in the world the mages and elves planned to revert what they'd already done, let alone get the damn gate closed again.

Abyad paced the edges of the meeting, clearly troubled. Well, who wouldn't be? Though the djinn had been acting strangely this whole trip, and Tegan wasn't even certain why he'd decided to come. Usually Abyad was a bit of a loner, but all the magical beings had their own agendas and it wasn't Tegan's job to figure it out.

It was Tegan's job to help per comrades, even the most stupid and pigheaded of them all.

"Fucking halbtroll," Tegan muttered, then walked over toward Jenny and Anandita, Starlight padding softly at per side. The two were in the center of a hub of Knights, including that tasty morsel, Case. Tegan barely registered his succulent thighs under their leathers. Too tired. Too spent. Tegan took a deep belly breath and tried to drag per mind back into focus. There was still a battle to fight here, and Jenny needed backup.

With Bocan gone, Tegan had to try per best.

::*You could sit this out. No one would fault you.*:: Starlight sent an image of a cozy cave and a nest of blankets.

Tegan groaned. "Don't do that to me."

::*You know I can't*:: per replied mind-to-mind to the lynx. ::*I've got a job to do.*::

Jenny caught sight of Tegan and gave a sharp nod, then bent her head back to Anandita, who was speaking rapidly.

Jenny straightened. "Okay!" she shouted. "It's time to get this fucker back open!"

Broad-shouldered in her leathers, red braids gleaming in the filtered sun, Jenny looked like a hero from one of Winney's books. The Knight turned toward Charles and the others.

"You ready?"

"No. We aren't." Charles strode toward Jenny just as Tegan arrived at the Steel Clan cluster.

"Well get ready," Jenny said. "The animals say we're running out of time."

::*She's right*:: Starlight sent. ::*Serena is half in a panic but I can't tell why.*::

::*Fuck.*::

Tegan stood beside per comrade, kpinga in hand, and squared per own shoulders.

"Jenny is right. We need to get this done. We're never going to be more ready than we are right now."

"What do you know about it?" Peridot sneered.

"I know that if you don't get this fracking gate back open, things are going to get even worse."

And just like that, a trickle of Tegan's magic was back. Not enough to matter, but enough to tell per that the words per'd just spoken were correct.

Ready or not, shit was about to go down.

CHAPTER 69
BOCAN

His mother was draped across Bocan's broad shoulders. He gripped one wrist and one ankle in his left hand and ran, battle-axe firmly in his right. The fat-bellied vial the alchemist had handed over was strapped to one of his belts. He hoped it didn't break.

It contained what was left of Ma's soul.

She bounced with small gasps and grunts, but at least she hadn't started up mewling again. He'd explained himself to her as best he could, but wasn't so sure she understood half of it.

For some reason, the princess had ordered her guards to let him go, but as soon as he cleared the manicured grounds surrounding the pavilion buildings, another faction of warrior elves in different livery rounded the corner in pursuit.

Serena dodged and dived over their heads, getting as close as she could without being grabbed. Her interference and his ground-eating stride were the only things keeping them all safe right now. If he had to stop and fight... Bocan grimaced and dug his boot soles deeper into the dirt, pushing off from the earth, helped by his allies, the rocks beneath the soil.

Da's face flashed in his mind. The troll taught him to love the metals of the earth and the earth itself. Bocan was grateful for the power of it now.

Serena's increased panic penetrated the thought. That was new. A master predator, the snowy owl was always focused. Calm.

Not now.

Putting on a burst of speed, Bocan tried to outrun the guards. He could hear them gaining now. Could hear the thump of boots and clank of metal, and Serena screeching overhead. His mother groaned in his ear.

"Sorry, Ma." Sweat ran, stinging, into his eyes, but his body did not tire.

A tung and whoosh sounded behind him. Seconds later, he felt a stripe of fire across his skull. Another tung and whoosh. He dodged left, but not quickly enough to avoid a slight prick as an arrow tip penetrated his leather.

Fuck. There were trees up ahead. He was almost at the gate. He had to get his mother to cover before he turned to make a stand.

With a bellowing breath, Bocan dug harder, sprinting faster than he had in his life, his mother gasping, his axe handle slick with sweat. He was built for fighting, not racing through strange landscapes at top speed. But for his ma, Bocan would do whatever he had to.

The arrows came faster, thicker. His mother screamed. Hit.

Serena shrieked. Circled. Dove.

Bocan roared.

CHAPTER 70
JENNY

Sword in hand, Jenny knelt in the soft loam just outside the portal gate, roar of the distant waterfall mixing with the sound of warriors readying for a battle for which they could not truly prepare.

She stole a moment to close her eyes and pray. "Holy Brigid, Mighty Lugh, kindle my heart and strengthen my arm...." The ground rumbled beneath her. "Let me get through this one alive."

She rose to her feet, looking toward the portal. The rumbling came from the trolls, working magic to destabilize the earth beneath the gate as the elves did something to shift the air above. Not Jenny's job to understand it. It was Jenny's job to stand with Case, and Tegan, and Jerrod, and the others, and defend this ground and get Bocan out of there.

Psych and Litha stood on either side of the gate area, ready to run in in case they needed to track Bocan. They weren't leaving him in there without a fight. No matter how foolish a pig fucker he was, Bocan was a comrade. One of the best comrades Jenny ever had.

The trolls shouted in a language Jenny did not understand, as the rumbling vibration increased. The elves sang higher, in counterpoint, as Charles waved his arms in arcane patterns. The djinn crouched to one side, eyes trained on the elves. Jenny shrugged. Must be feeding them magic somehow. Helping with the wind that tossed the branches overhead.

Settling more firmly in her boots, she rode the waves of shifting earth and stood unbothered by the changing currents of the forest air. This was the strangest magic she had ever encountered, and strong enough to be palpable even to her, but if it would take care of whatever had decimated that village and stolen her childhood friend? She could put up with it.

Tegan stood to Jenny's right, and Anandita sat at her left. That was the only thing Jenny did not like about this whole situation. Anandita should not be here. The healer insisted, no matter how long and hard Jenny and Case had argued against it. She was a liability. A distraction.

But Anandita had insisted that her dreams had shown her here. And the cursed drakes had agreed.

Above the songs of the trolls and elves, Charles began to keen. All the hairs on Jenny's arms stood at attention beneath the heavy leather of her coat.

"Fucking magic shit," she whispered, then took in a shuddering breath.

"Jenny!" Anandita's voice sliced through it all. "Your greatest gift is who you are. Don't forget!"

"What the fuck are you talking about?"

With a sky-splitting crack, the portal gate opened in front of them, and Anandita pushed herself through.

"Nooooo!" Jenny shouted at her back.

She pushed off and ran toward the swirling golds and silvers of the rapidly expanding gate, just as Anandita disappeared.

CHAPTER 71
ANANDITA

The portal swirled and pressed, tingling against her exposed skin and making her teeth feel as if she'd been chewing silver. The magic was foreign. Strange. She pushed harder at the chair rims, just trying to get through.

With a pop, she was through, sides heaving, arms aching, sweat on her brow.

And Bocan was barreling toward her, axe out, with a body on his back as Serena shrieked and dove behind him.

A troop of a dozen elves were close behind, some periodically pausing to nock and shoot the arrows currently flying toward her.

"Anandita!" Bocan's eyes were huge as pies and black as a pool of night.

"Give her to me!" She didn't know who jounced and juddered on his back, but it had to be his long-lost mother. Clearly, she needed help, and just as clearly, Bocan needed to hold off the fast-approaching elves.

If his ma was alive? Anandita didn't have time to think about it. She braced herself as Bocan slowed just long enough to swing the woman's body onto Anandita's lap. The woman bounced, jarring her. She hissed at the sharp pain where her right leg met the prosthesis.

"Fuck!" As Bocan stood, his large bulk planted in front of her chair, Anandita struggled to adjust the woman's body and get them both firmly settled in her chair. The last thing she needed was for the woman to tumble to the ground.

Anandita heard a grinding, popping noise behind her, and then Tegan and Jenny were at her side.

"Take this!" Bocan thrust a glass alembic at her, then turned to face the rapidly approaching elves.

Tegan bent to help her arrange the half-conscious woman so her head tucked into Anandita's shoulder and her legs dangled over one side. Jenny spared her one glance, shouted "Take care of her!" then raced to Bocan's side, buckler up, sword in hand. Case took up position on the other side.

"Do you need me to push you out of here?" Tegan shouted in her ear.

Anandita felt the other Knights surround them. The elves had arrived and the sound of clashing metal rang through the soft air.

"No! Just put this damn alembic into my bag, and clear a path to the trees!"

Tegan turned and began to push perself through the Knights still struggling into formation.

"Make way!" the small Knight called. Anandita pushed the chair behind per, struggling to keep the woman from shifting. Her arms screamed in protest. She grit her teeth and followed Tegan's sumac-red back to what she hoped was shelter.

She didn't want to take this woman back through the gate until she figured out whether or not it would kill her.

Because if his ma died, so quickly after he had found her? That would kill Bocan, for sure.

CHAPTER 72
JENNY

Jenny barely made it through the gate. If it weren't for a mass of Steel Clan pushing from behind, and Tegan gripping her left hand in a wiry vice, she was certain the roiling, stomach-churning magic, so strong even she could feel it, would have spat her right back out.

She stumbled, blinking and bewildered, smack into a skirmish, and Anandita, draped in what looked like a dead body in the center of her field of vision.

"Take care of her," she shouted to Tegan, who was already at Anandita's side, then ran to Bocan.

Jenny had no time to stop. She had to trust that Tegan would take care of Anandita and that whatever happened, both of them would be okay.

Neither the Knight nor the healer should be on this side of the damn gate, but neither was the type to acquiesce to sense and reason when the fire burned inside.

An elf ran straight for Jenny, silver sword arcing through blue sky, green braids flicking like poisoned darts around her finely chiseled face.

Jenny raised her buckler, and the sword connected with a bone-shaking clang. Jenny pivoted her right foot and swung her torso, pushing toward the elf who stumbled backwards from the blow. Jenny swept her short sword toward where the elf's neck met her shoulder. The elf blocked. Jenny disengaged around her opponent's blade.

The sound of steel meeting elf metal ringing in her ears, Jenny closed in.

She struck the elf with her buckler while her sword sought an opening. Jenny danced in and out, away from the elf's knife and sword. The elf's sword was longer, which was a disadvantage close up, but that didn't mean her knife wasn't just as deadly.

A slice of heat scored the gap between Jenny's gloves and coat. She shoved again, then backed off half a pace before diving in, covering her hand with her buckler. Spit flooded her mouth. She thrust her point toward the elf's face, forcing her to parry or be stabbed in the eye. As the elf brought her blade up to oppose Jenny's, Jenny rolled her buckler, pushed the elf's sword across her body, trapping the knife hand and lowering her blade, then cut through the gap below the chest armor.

"Fy!" the elf gasped as Jenny felt the soft pressure of flesh meeting steel. She swept the pommel back toward her own torso, deepening the slice as she went. The elf fell, clutching her side.

Jenny stepped away and whirled, ears ringing, seeking her next target.

CHAPTER 73

BOCAN

He had downed three elves already, and acrid sweat streamed in a river beneath his leathers. The axe felt good in his hands. A slash across this cheek joined the furrow on his skull, but the stinging only goaded him.

Two elven warriors rushed him, swords out. He slammed the head of his axe at one and stepped through, trapping the sword and crushing the pale, slender throat. The second stabbed at Bocan's face, which was stupid. It was the only uncovered part of the halbtroll, true, but at two-and-a-half meters tall, he was still much larger than the tallest elf. A quick thrust to the left and the axe head sliced off the top of the warrior's head in a spray of pink brains and silver-tinged blood. Bocan stepped to the right as the body fell left. His foot crunched down on the first elf's shin. The elf let out a garbled yelp.

Bocan swung his axe down, going for the exposed neck.

The elf raised both arms in defense. "Peace! Peace!" he shrieked from his crushed throat.

Bocan paused, curved axe a hair's breadth from the two trembling arms. The elf looked up at him, face contorted in fear and pain.

"Peace?" Bocan growled. "Is that what you gave my mother? Peace?"

"It wasn't me! It was the Queen...."

"And you work at the Queen's behest, you sniveling asswipe. You bow, and scrape, and then lord it over folks like me."

He slowly pressed the axe blade down, bending the elf's arms toward the ground.

"Please," the elf panted.

Bocan was focused on the feel of the blade against elven armor. He was focused on the topaz eyes, darting frantically back and forth between his own. He barely noticed the sounds of the skirmish had stopped and that someone was bellowing.

Bellowing his name.

"Bocan! You pig fucker! Get out!"

Jenny.

That was Jenny.

He stood, releasing the pressure. A roaring filled his ears. Bocan swiped his axe blade down, severing head from spine.

"That's for my ma," he said, then turned and, sobs wrenched from his aching chest, ran toward his red-haired comrade, axe in hand.

CHAPTER 74
JENNY

Tegan and the mages were half frantic. Something was happening with the portal and Jenny didn't know what. She just knew she had to get her comrades out. Adrenaline thudded through her chest and her whole body felt alive. She was muscle and heat, spit and fury. Case and two other Knights helped Tegan and Anandita exit the field as Recoana followed, carrying the ailing woman.

The Underhill elves were down or had run away. Peridot and Damson flanked the gates, along with Feldspar, Aphrodite, Charles, Abyad, the black dog, and the two scouts.

The retreat wasn't moving fast enough for Jenny.

And here came Bocan, running toward her, full tilt. It was all Jenny could do to hold her ground and not flinch out of his way.

A voice shouted behind her. "Bocan!"

And then a streak, running toward the big halb-troll. Psych.

What the...?

"Psych! Halt!"

The scout ran a direct trajectory toward Bocan. The halbtroll bellowed and swerved.

A low *tuuunnngg* came from a tree.

And with a cry, Psych was down, Bocan turned, and Jenny burst into a run.

An arrow swished over her head, then another, coming from behind. She spared a glance backward as Anandita nocked another arrow into her compound bow.

Putting on a burst of speed, Jenny ran toward her comrades. Bocan straddled the fallen Psych, and used his axe to parry the arrow strikes. Unbelievable.

She dove to the ground and crawled to Psych's head. Beneath the blue whorls of his tattoos, he was white as milk, and his eyes were fading. The arrow shaft protruded from his neck.

"Oh fuck. Psych. Why the fuck did you do that?"

Above them, Bocan moved and creaked, slicing at the air, deflecting arrowheads with sharp pings and clangs. Damn the archer. Weren't they getting tired?

"My hero," Psych muttered. His eyes were closed now, fluttering as if he was dreaming.

"What?" Jenny sobbed and swore. There was nothing to do for him. No one to call on. Not even Brigid the Healer could be petitioned.

She looked up, eyes watery with unshed tears. Arrows flew in both directions, in unsteady cadence.

A cry came from the tree, and then crashing and the sickly thud of a body hitting hard ground.

Anandita—or someone from their cohort—had finally gotten her shot.

Psych sighed. A gentle puff of breath touched Jenny's cheek.

And he was gone.

The elves were gone. The scout she had trained since his boyhood was gone. Bocan was crouched at her side.

"Ah, shit, lass."

His hands gripped her shoulders then, trying to move her to stand.

"This isn't over yet, Jenny," he rumbled. "The mages are shouting that something bad is happening to the gate."

"Fuck the gate," she said. "Fuck this fucking magic."

But she stood, nonetheless, as Bocan snapped the arrow shaft and gently lifted Psych into his arms.

"Go," she said. "I'll cover you."

Bocan didn't argue, just loped toward the swirling gate, as Jenny backed herself, buckler and short sword raised. She slid her booted feet along the fragrant grass, feeling for bodies. When she bumped one, she slid to the left or right until clear, glancing down to see: elf or Knight?

Most often it was the body of an Underhill elf her foot bumped into, but so far, Jenny had looked down into the waxen faces of three comrades of the Steel Clan. Gone, like Psych, their souls winging free.

There would be mourning in the Steel Clan, and in

Go No More, but thank Brigid, at least they weren't caged by the thrice-damned Queen.

She heard the magicians shouting behind her, and swore that down the ribbon of manicured pathway, beneath the gently shining sun, she saw a long, sweeping flash of silver hair.

CHAPTER 75

TEGAN

"Ancestors help me," Tegan gasped.

They'd finally gotten Anandita the fuck out of there, but not until the healer had taken out the elven archer. Per and Case had to practically force Anandita to turn her chair toward the gate and head through. She'd been ready to push her way through the fallen warriors to get to Jenny and Psych.

"He's dead, Anandita!" Tegan had shouted, as Case grabbed her chair, forcing it into a turn. Anandita might never forgive him for that, but Tegan didn't think the Knight would care. In the middle of battle, you did what you had to, and sometimes that meant crossing boundaries you shouldn't. Your comrades knew what was necessary and might fight you over it later, but only to let off steam.

Anandita wasn't a Knight. She might not understand.

Right now, Anandita was out of her chair, standing on her short steel limbs. She and Recoana bent over the woman, passing their hands lightly around her, checking out the energy bodies that sheathed her flesh. Litha looked on, face stricken, body trembling. Tegan could see the woman's souls were mostly missing. Humans only had three, along with the body, and this woman seemed to be missing one entirely, and half of another.

"Taking her through the portal shocked her souls further," Anandita said. "But she's alive. For now."

Tegan shook per head.

And then the gate exploded, flinging the mages and the township elves out, barreling into the Knights on the other side. Feldspar's giant body crashed into a tree, cracking the broad trunk and showering needles and dead branches onto Tegan's head.

Tegan whirled to see Case and Jerrod running toward the gate, which pulsed with light and sound. The air felt as if it were on fire, and pressed on Tegan's skin.

Jenny was in the center of it all, sword and shield arms out, feet braced, and mouth set in a sick rictus.

"Fuck a pig," Tegan said, and ran, head pounding, back toward the gate.

CHAPTER 76
JENNY

Everything was on fire. Jenny didn't know how she could feel it, but she could. The gate had thrown the magic workers out, but had left Jenny untouched.

The back of her mind screamed at her to get out, as did Flex's distant, panicked barking. But her gut told her to stay.

So stay she did, one foot in Elfland, one foot in the forest beyond, as the pressure built around her.

Jenny had no idea what was happening, but one thing she knew about being a Knight was to trust her gut.

But if this was what magic felt like all the time, she didn't know how people bore it. It felt as if her body was trying to separate into all of its component parts.

She trembled and shook. If she held position another minute, she just might shake apart.

Gritting her teeth, Jenny pressed her feet more

firmly into the loam, tightened her belly, and straightened her spine.

She was a Steel Clan Knight and she would fracking well do her job.

From the back of her throat, a keening started, and Jenny could not make it stop.

Her right leg raised itself as if of its own accord, bringing her booted foot hurtling down toward Elfland soil.

Stomp!

And then her left leg, in the river forest.

Stomp!

Breath huffing, the keening in her throat like some strange song, Jenny stomped and stomped and stomped.

Her sword and buckler joined the rhythm.

Stomp! Clang! Stomp! Clang!

Stompstompstompstomp! Clangclangclangclang!

The rhythm took over her body. Her whole being. Jenny became one with the rhythm. Stomping out a pattern to counteract the pressing that threatened to squeeze her lungs to empty and compress her flesh until she was no more.

Jenny moved. Jenny growled and keened. Jenny stomped and shook and crashed buckler and sword together.

Pressing. Pressing. Pressing. Pressing. As if her flesh was crushed by a giant hand.

Jenny screamed and stomped and clanged.

Pressing. Pressing. Pressing. Pressing. As if her breath was being squeezed from her lungs.

A high whining began, sounding like one thousand insects. Louder and louder. Threatening to burst her ears.

Stomping. Clanging. Stomping. Her body couldn't stop.

And, as if everything around her took in one roaring breath, the air around her vanished. She was choking. Gasping. Stomping. Sweating.

With a grinding sound, the gate pulled together. Closer. Closer. Jenny screamed.

The gate shattered.

Jenny was hurled into the forest.

Her body slammed into the hard, dark soil, jarring teeth and bones.

She stared up at the familiar canopy of trees. She heard shouts. Running.

Painfully, she lifted her head.

The shimmering line of gold that even her broken senses had been able to see?

It was gone.

The earth smelled of earth again. The goodness of a late autumn forest, thick with trees.

With a whisper of wind and a rumble from beyond the high canopy of trees, it began to rain.

CHAPTER 77

ANANDITA

She looked up to see the woman who would be her lover flung backwards, laughing. Felt her strike the ground. A crush of Knights raced toward Jenny, but Anandita was right behind them, running as fast as she could. Stepping past obstacles, bumping over the uneven earth, barely looking to see that Recoana stayed with Bocan's injured mother.

"Let me through!" she called out to whoever could hear. Litha pushed past her and started shoving Knights out of the way.

She pushed through the opening between stinking warrior bodies and saw her beloved, still laughing as if crazed, face turned up to catch the softly falling rain.

"Jenny."

Those whiskey eyes looked her way. "Anandita," she said, then held out her arms.

Anandita walked toward those outstretched, leather-covered arms, toward that face that looked illuminated by some otherworldly light. She reached, trusting, as Jenny's arms grasped her own. Jenny tugged until those strong arms were around her, pulling her off her steel and rubber feet and into Jenny's broad lap.

"You made it," she said.

She felt Jenny nod against her head. "I did."

"You closed the portal."

"I did."

"But how?"

And then warm lips met warm lips, and Anandita kissed Jenny with all her might.

The rain continued to fall.

CHAPTER 78

TEGAN

Tegan helped Jenny, Case, and Litha wrap Psych into a blanket and lay him out in a hollow against a stone where his body would be protected. Flex and Starlight sat nearby, faces attentive, making sure their human companions were okay, it felt like to Tegan.

"Stupid fucker," Jenny said, looking down at the tightly wrapped, slender body, eyes brimming with tears.

"He knew Bocan had to get out," Litha said, white lips thin and tight, face drawn with grief and exhaustion. "To be with his ma."

Tegan slipped an arm around per comrade. Jenny leaned against Tegan's smaller frame. They tripoded against each other, holding one another up. That's what comrades did for each other.

"We want to make a pallet, or carry him horseback?" Case asked.

::The red drake will carry him down.:: Starlight said.

"Starlight says the drakes have offered to take his body." She listened for a moment. "And Bocan and his mother, too."

Jenny huffed out a sigh. She'd looked more powerful than Tegan had ever seen her, standing in that gate, but now, she looked completely worn down, as if there was nothing left.

Luckily, it smelled as though someone had given a thought to feeding everyone, because the smell of stew filtered through the air. It would just be dried meat and dried herbs and broth, but at least the meat would be somewhat softened. Tegan didn't think anyone had the energy to chew on bison jerky just now.

They all bowed toward Psych. Tegan made the crossed arms sign toward his shrouded form. Then they turned back toward the slow-moving camp and wound their way toward the crackling fire in the center.

"What do you need, comrade?" The question was soft, aimed toward Jenny, though everyone in their small circle could hear.

"For our comrades to be alive." Jenny rubbed at her face and sighed. Tegan felt that like a weight upon per own body. That sense of grief and of being bone tired. Per said nothing in response, because what was there to say?

Jenny continued. "To go home. And to figure out what in Brigid's name happened here."

"You don't know?" Litha's voice was filled with wonder.

Jenny's head jerked toward the sorrowing apprentice. "What?"

"You broke the magic," the girl said.

Tegan laughed, the sound harsh to per own ears. Jenny shoved at per and scowled. "Don't laugh. You ass."

"Bocan is going to birth a rock," Tegan said.

"What the fuck?" Jenny looked wounded, now.

More laughter bubbled up. Tegan couldn't contain it, despite per comrade's injured look.

"You've been so fracking convinced you were useless because you had no magic. But that's the thing that closed the gate!"

Tegan shoved at Jenny's shoulder.

"Jenny Magic Breaker! Oh, the songs that will be sung over Porrac's beer!"

"I hate you," Jenny growled, and stomped off toward the fire.

"I hate you, too," Tegan called.

It felt so fucking good to laugh, however tinged with pain. So fracking good to think of dinner, and maybe some cider or a spliff passed among friends.

Despite the effort. Despite per own failure. Despite the wounded, and the dead whose bodies were still trapped behind the now-closed portal gate. The Steel Clan had made it through this one.

Case glanced back at her, quirked a lip, and smiled.

Fuck, he was a handsome asshole.

Tegan quirked an eyebrow back, then followed per comrades toward the crackling fire, heart filled with tears.

CHAPTER 79

KARAKTILLA

It was good to be home in her cavern, with a bowl of fragrant tea and a weighted scroll on a stone table in front of her.

But Karaktilla could not concentrate upon the words. The markings swum like fish upon the crackling vellum. Her stomach grumbled, in need of food she was too weary to prepare.

Tomorrow, she would hunt. Take down a bison or some elk. She would skin the animals and roast their bodies in a roaring fire. Tonight, she would drink tea, and fast, and ponder what was to come.

The portal to Underhill was closed for now. There were other portals, true, but closing the one nearest to her territory should slow the mad queen down. The closed portal was only a temporary fix, but it should slow the spread of tainted magic until the magical beings and the humans could find a better solution.

But Karaktilla trusted that they would. Somehow. She did not yet know what her part in the unfolding would be, but would do her best to give this fledgling world a chance to become...something better than had been seen in æons. A world out of legend. A place where magic rode the wind and helped things flourish, rather than destroyed.

A place a drake could happily live, for another five hundred years.

The story was not over. The red-haired Knight and her comrades had more tales to call to life.

But for a breath or two, there would be peace.

Yes. Karaktilla took a sip of soothing tea.

Yes.

CHAPTER 80

JENNY

Anandita's breasts lay warm and heavy against her own, her face pressed against Jenny's neck. Despite the fact that Jenny practically trembled with exhaustion, she was sorely tempted to have another go.

As it was, she wanted to lie in bed forever. The mattress felt amazing. The pillows were firm. The sheets and blankets soft. And Anandita smelled delicious.

If only Psych were still alive, and the others…. The cost of being a member of the Steel Clan was high. They all knew it from the first day of their apprenticeships.

That didn't take away the hurt. Or the responsibility. It didn't take away the keening wails of their friends and families, still echoing inside Jenny's skull.

"It wasn't your fault, you know. He died bravely, protecting a comrade. The way I'm sure you all intend to go."

Jenny grunted. She wasn't ready to talk about it. Not yet. Not until they laid Psych's body into the ground beneath his favorite maple tree, and they'd made prayers for the others left behind. She and the Clan would get drunk after that, and maybe then she'd talk about it. To Bocan and Tegan.

She wasn't close enough with Anandita to discuss such things, though if they stayed together the way her whole body, heart, and mind wanted, they'd get there someday, too.

For now, she stretched, then drew Anandita's luscious body more tightly against her own.

"Goddess, woman. You practically killed me. You're the sexiest woman alive. Did you know that?"

She felt Anandita smile. Luckily, she didn't call Jenny out about the change in subject. "I didn't know that, but you can tell me anytime you like."

Jenny stared up at the wooden ceiling joists, and ran a calloused hand across the soft, fleshy roll of Anandita's stomach, then up to stroke her hip.

Being with this woman, she had to admit, went a long way toward easing the pain.

It had taken them two days to ride home. The bikes had stopped frequently so the horses and walkers could catch up. There were enough injuries among the Knights that no one complained about the slow pace. Oh, they could have pushed and ridden through the night, but folks seemed content to take it slowly. The drakes had flown on ahead, carrying their precious cargo.

Bocan's ma was now under the watch of Doc

Warren and Anandita's apprentice, Tokki. They still hadn't figured out what to do with the alembic, but Doc Warren had insisted a few more days would not change the woman's state too much. Doc Warren had ordered both Recoana and Anandita to bed, and lucky for Jenny, after making certain Hypatia was okay, she'd left him happily ensconced with Gears the engineer, and decided Jenny's bed would do.

The sex had been just as glorious as that first taste in the woods. Anandita, despite her protests at having never been with a woman, had done more than fine. Jenny's limbs were loose with just how fine the sex had been.

"You know, you said you had no experience, but my body tells me otherwise."

Anandita pushed herself up, dark hair falling around her gorgeous face. "I have no experience with women other than myself," she corrected with a wicked grin, before capturing Jenny's mouth in another kiss. "But now this woman's body is hungry. What do you have by way of food? Or shall we head to the town hall and see what Jamie and Porrac have cooking?"

Jenny groaned. "I've likely got nothing but stale bread and moldy cheese, considering I haven't exactly been home to replenish my stores. But damned if I feel like getting dressed."

Anandita lay back down. "I don't blame you."

She settled back into the crook of Jenny's right arm and shoulder, her soft hair tickling Jenny's unbound chest.

"Can I ask you something?" Jenny said.

"Anything."

"Did you think you would find Long there?"

Anandita was silent. Her body went still, and she held her breath for a moment, before letting it out in a long, sustained, exhalation.

"Part of me hoped, of course…but truth be told? I knew he was gone. And I'm grateful. Grateful he wasn't left to suffer the way Bocan's mother has. Grateful that his soul—or what was left of it—was able to move on."

Jenny traced a seam in one of the beams above. "That makes sense."

Anandita planted a soft kiss on Jenny's collarbone, and wiggled closer.

Jenny's stomach growled.

"We really should get dressed and see about food," Anandita said.

"Let me see what I have." Jenny kissed Anandita on the top of her dark, shining hair, and slipped from between the sheets, swinging her legs to the floor. She stood and groaned. "Gods. I need to soak in the bathhouse for around ten years."

She padded across the cool wood floors, pausing to bow to the small altar on top of a chest of drawers. The altar held a woven hemp cross, a cup, a candle, and a spear tip. Brigid and Lugh, the Goddess and God she swore fealty to, who kept her whole, and well, and protected. They had been with her in the forest, she was sure.

That done, she headed to the small kitchen area and threw open a cupboard before opening the hatch to the cold box set into the floor. Crouched on her haunches, she looked back at the bed, where Anandita smiled a lazy smile, lust in her eyes.

Jenny's heart fluttered.

"I've got some dried apples and the aforementioned stale bread and moldy cheese. And some wine."

Jenny ran some water over a soft cloth and rung it out.

"I like watching you pad around your house naked, but you know what moldy cheese means."

"But I don't want to go to the town hall."

"Why not?"

Jenny closed the hatch and the cupboard and walked back to bed, damp cloth in hand. She leaned on the firm mattress and gave Anandita a slow kiss before handing her the cloth to clean up with.

"First of all, I have a gorgeous woman in my bed and I don't really want to leave."

"And second?"

Jenny scowled. Caught again. "I can't face more of the fracking 'Magic Breaker' shit." There'd been talk of little else in the bath house. Not that Jenny could blame anyone. Ribbing your comrade was easier than thinking about your dead.

And the fact that, though the portal was closed, the fight was by no means over.

"I hate to tell you, this...."

"What?" Jenny's stomach dropped.

"They've already changed it."

She just stood and stared, not sure if she wanted to know.

Anandita smirked. "To Jenny Magic's Bane. Hypatia told me."

"Oh! Fuck a pig-fucking pig-fucker ass!"

Anandita laughed, head thrown back, teeth white against her dusky skin and sweet plum lips. That laugh rang loud and clear through Jenny's cozy home.

It was a beautiful sound.

"Okay," Jenny grumbled, smiling despite herself. "Come on, lover, let's get dressed."

She leaned in for one more kiss and took the damp cloth back before tossing Anandita her clothes.

Truth be told, Jenny would take as much joking shit as her comrades wanted to dish out. The gate was closed. Bocan's ma was back. And she'd made love with Anandita.

Twice.

And from the look in the healer's eyes, as soon as they had eaten, there would be more.

Hopefully a lot more.

It wouldn't wipe away the loss, but it would mend the hole in Jenny's heart and soul that she'd barely even known was there.

A warm bed with a willing partner in it, some food and drink and smoke. These were a Knight's rewards. Go No More was safe for now, and that was all the Steel Clan could hope for.

CHAPTER 81
SILVERHAIR

Silver glinted from the mirror frames, and light from the open windows limned the deep blue green upholstery of the sofa, and the carved wood chairs. All of this, and the scent of apple blossom and honeysuckle, went barely noticed, except as irritations. Distractions.

Silverhair would take no comfort in beauty. Not today. Today, her world was filled with red-tinged rage.

The guard stood trembling in front of the queen, slender face marred with dirt and sweat, dark green armor dinged and scratched.

"How did you allow this to happen?" Anger boiled in her veins, heating her skin.

"There were more of them than we expected. And their magic is stronger, too."

She grabbed his sharp chin and pulled his face closer, hissing.

"No human magic is stronger than the magic Underhill."

"But they had trolls. And two elves. And a human who somehow..." Sick sweat ran down his face, touching her fingers. Silverhair tightened her grip. Small, animal noises came from the back of his throat.

"Who. Somehow. What?"

"She was the most powerful human I've ever seen. She...she broke the magic. She broke the magic, and everything holding the gate together just shattered."

The red-haired Knight. Silverhair stared at squirming elf, unseeing. Then she reached her other hand around behind his skull. With a sharp twist, she snapped his neck.

"Bring me the alchemist." Inside the spacious, light filled room, no one stirred.

"Now!"

Behind her, feet scurried off to do her bidding. When she felt the room was empty, Silverhair turned and smiled.

The situation could have been much, much worse. The halbtroll was gone. The humans were gone. And her daughter was still in Elfland. Safe.

The realm would continue, as it always had.

There were other gates. Stronger elven magics.

And that magic-breaking human?

Whoever she was, she would get her due.

And if it took the soul of an elf to save Elzabetta? Rules be damned.

A queen must do what a queen must do.

THE SAGA CONTINUES...

Gods of earth and stone, it was good to be back on the road, beneath the steel gray sky. At forty-five klicks an hour, deep green trees whipped past, and the air smelled fresh, with the barest hint of winter on its way. A squad of his comrades rode with him, all rumbling metal and deep red, sumac-dyed leather.

The world was wet, fragrant, and wild.

After all the grief and anguish of the past month, Bocan needed this. He needed to remember what it was to feel fully alive.

Thorn has more books plus a weekly newsletter at thorncoyle.com if you want to keep in touch.

ACKNOWLEDGMENTS

I give thanks to all readers, everywhere. I'm grateful also for the long line of anarchist and visionary storytellers for being wells of inspiration.

Thanks to Leslie Claire Walker, my intrepid first reader, to Dayle Dermatis, editor extraordinaire, and to expert readers Mala, Sara P., and Mushtaq ali Al Ansari. Any mistakes are my own. Thanks to Shawn and Stefon for further encouragement.

Valerie Herron did the amazing artwork for the series, bringing Jenny, Bocan, Tegan, and their bonded animals, to life. Check out her work at valerieherron.com.

Big, grateful shout out to the members of the Sorcery Collective for spreading the word and to Jack for typo catching.

And thanks as always to Robert and Jonathan, my family, for consistent encouragement and support.

And last...

Thanks to everyone who believes in magic. This series is for you.

ALSO BY T. THORN COYLE

FICTION

The Bookshop Witch Paranormal Cozy Mysteries

Bookshop Witch

Haunted Witch

Tarot Witch

Running Witch

Hallows Witch

Solstice Witch

The Pride Street Paranormal Cozy Mysteries

Sushi Scandal

Flower Frenzy

Muffin Murder

Hairspray Horror

Dandy Distress

The Mouse Thief

Mouse's Folly

Mouse's Fight

The Witches of Portland

By Earth

By Flame

By Wind

By Sea

By Moon

By Sun

By Dusk

By Dark

By Witch's Mark

The Panther Chronicles

To Raise a Clenched Fist to the Sky

To Wrest Our Bodies From the Fire

To Drown This Fury in the Sea

To Stand With Power on This Ground

The Steel Clan Saga

We Seek No Kings

We Heed No Laws

We Ride at Night

Short Story Collections

A Hint of Faery

A Touch of Faery

A Spark of Magic

A Flame for Yuletide

A Hope for Winter

A Time for Magic

A Speculation of Stars

A Speculation of Hope

A Speculation of Time

Risk It All: Queer Stories of Love, Suspense, And Daring

Thresholds: Queer Stories of Love, Suspense, And Daring

Ghost Talker

Cats and Other Creatures

NON-FICTION

You are the Spell

Sigil Magic for Writers, Artists, & Other Creatives

Crafting a Daily Practice

Resistance Matters

Evolutionary Witchcraft

Kissing the Limitless

Make Magic of Your Life

ABOUT THE AUTHOR

T. Thorn Coyle worked in many strange and diverse occupations before settling in to write books full time.

Author of the *Bookshop Witch Paranormal Cozy Mystery* series, the *Pride Street Paranormal Cozy Mysteries, The Steel Clan Saga, The Witches of Portland,* and *The Panther Chronicles,* Thorn's multiple non-fiction books include *Sigil Magic for Writers, Artists & Other Creatives, Kissing the Limitless, Make Magic of Your Life,* and *Evolutionary Witchcraft.* Thorn's work also appears in many anthologies, magazines, and collections.

An interloper to the Pacific Northwest U.S., Thorn drinks a lot of tea, pays proper tribute to the neighborhood cats, and talks to crows, squirrels, and trees.

Connect with Thorn:
www.thorncoyle.com